THE JOURNEY OF THREE

STEPHEN PAUL
WILLIAMS

Kindle Direct Publishing

ISBN-10: 0692579923
ISBN-13: 978-0692579923

Library of Congress Control Number: 2015920427

2026 edition
with additional content added

Printed in the United States of America

Dedicated to all whose names are found etched on the Wall.

ACKNOWLEDGMENTS

I wish to give my sincere thanks to my son Zachary Williams for designing and formatting the cover art, and to my younger son, author Zane Williams, for his good advice. I also want to thank my wife, Nancy, for her initial proofreading of the story and for her support and encouragement.

CONTENTS

***

PROLOGUE

He leaned over the Sharp Park pier and stared south across the long stretch of the gray sand beach toward a bluff known as Mori's Point. The air had a chill, and a lingering fog forced him to strain his eyes to see the point, with its jagged rocks that sloped one after the other into the Pacific Ocean. It was shortly after sunrise, but you'd never know it because of the overcast sky and the drifting fog that partially obscured his view. As the fog began to lift, he could see the waves smashing against the three largest rocks off the point. The force of the waves sent a spray of water over them, then retreated only to repeat the assault. It was a beautiful sight to see, even with the overcast sky. Ah, but the view was not why he looked toward the point.

It was hard to believe that long ago, three young boys ventured out onto those jetting rocks. Two of the three boys stood on the rock just for the thrill of it, but the other was fulfilling a dream. He wanted to live the adventure, to feel like a Viking sailing on his prized vessel.

The man was there to find and visualize a memory that was not his own, to see where it all began, and to search for what was missing.

"This is where I'll complete the story of their journey and what they found, or perhaps I should say, what found them," said the man, speaking into the voice recorder in his hand. "More people need to hear the story of these three friends."

The man began walking along the high berm walkway separating the ocean from the community of Sharp Park. It would be a long walk from the pier to the point, but as the sun broke through the overcast sky, the rays of light seemed to calm the sea. As he passed the last group of homes, a golf course came into view.

The man knew the boys had a special spot near the edge of the course. He looked over a small fence and down the slope on the other side. There was a flat spot, just under a group of cypress trees. *Where's the rock?* He thought. The man continued looking, but the ice plant had overgrown the downward side of the slope, making it difficult to see much of anything. *I followed exactly what was written, and the ground underneath these trees is flat, as the journal described. The rock is gone, or maybe it's just covered by the ice plant. This must be the spot. I'm sure of it,* he thought.

He then crossed over to the ocean side of the berm, where he rested before continuing his walk to the point. The man sat on a group of rocks overlooking the sea. He leaned back and gazed at the sky. It was so clear now. He could see the boys in his mind's eye as if it were yesterday. *Yes, I know them all so well…*

CHAPTER 1

THE THREE

It was the year 1953, and in those days, children were free to roam just about anywhere they chose. In the coastal community of Sharp Park, California, every child was expected to follow just a few simple rules—stay off the beach, don't go too far, be home on time, and never leave the house without telling your mother where you were going. Break them, and you probably wouldn't see the light of day for a week.

Lenny and Joey ran down Carmel Avenue toward the ocean, turned left, and followed the sand dunes that separated the beach from the homes and a golf course that ran along the shoreline. The two boys had known each other since kindergarten. Lenny lived just down the gravel road from Joey.

Following well behind them was a third boy who was unusually tall, especially for his age. It gave him an older look. He labored as he ran. *Where are they going?* he thought. *Are they trying to ditch me?* Eddie called out to the two boys who ran ahead of him, but they didn't respond. He ran as fast as he could while tightly clutching a bag of marbles in his hand, but soon they were out of sight.

Lenny and Joey ran to get away from Big Eddie Davis, the new kid in town. They hardly knew him; he had just moved across the street from Joey three weeks before. He told them he was starting fifth grade, the same as them, but they didn't believe him. In their eyes, he looked much older and stood well above Lenny, who himself was a tall, thin boy. He must have been held back a grade or two, they reasoned.

The two boys were heading for their secret spot to play marbles. They didn't know Eddie well enough to share their secret meeting place, located just below a large rock and a group of trees at the edge of the golf course. He was just too big and loud for their liking. Besides, they had already played marbles with him twice before, and he nearly cleaned them out each time.

***

Lenny's mom, Sofia, and his dad, Benjamin, or Benny as most people knew him, had moved from New York to California a year after Lenny was born. It seemed that a Jewish man and an Italian Catholic woman were not welcome in either of their parents' homes. Both sides of the family viewed the marriage as a betrayal of their respective faiths.

After Lenny was born and baptized, it became very apparent that he would be raised as a Roman Catholic and not a Jew, and that all but ended Benny's relationship with his parents. Sofia's momma and papa despised all Jews and would not accept Benny as part of the family.

Try as they might to reconcile with their parents, it was a hopeless cause. Leaving New York City was difficult, but something they believed they had to do. Moving as far away as possible from the family bitterness seemed the best option at the time.

Lenny's father, Benjamin Leibowitz, was a skilled jeweler, and he easily obtained a job at one of the finer jewelry stores just ten miles north of Sharp Park, in the big city of San Francisco. He was an expert at fixing clocks and watches and designing fine jewelry. Lenny's mother, Sofia, was a homemaker and took care of Lenny and his precocious six-year-old sister, Lidia.

***

Joey was an only child whose parents had grown up in the Bay Area. His dad lost half of his left arm during the early part of World War II. His mother, Ruth, learned to drive their 1940 Studebaker when Joey's dad, Roth Gunderson, went off to war. Once Roth came back with a good portion of one arm missing, and since the car had a stick shift on the steering column, Ruth did nearly all of the driving from then on.

Prior to the war, Roth worked as a sheet-metal worker near the Hunter's Point shipyard in the big city. Roth was once a heavy smoker, but after losing his left hand, he quit cold turkey. Smoking was considered manly, even vogue back then, but Roth already knew he was a man and couldn't care less about being vogue.

Before the war, Roth Gunderson loved to play his guitar and sing sweet songs to his wife every Sunday afternoon. It had become a loving tradition. After losing his left hand, the Sunday guitar-playing and singing tradition ended. Now he worked at a shoe shop just south of San Francisco. He did the best he could with what he had and always had a kind word for those he knew.

Joey's parents couldn't afford to buy a home, so they rented the downstairs portion of a house from a widow named Maria

Morales—or Mama, as she was most often called. Mama Morales was a lifelong resident of Salada, which was what she preferred to call the small community of Sharp Park. For a reduced rental fee, Joey's mom cooked, cleaned, and cared for the kind elderly widow.

Although the poverty was quite evident to everyone else, Joey didn't see his family as poor. To him, his parents were the greatest in the world, and life was good. He never saw his father as one-armed. He only saw him as his hero. Every Sunday, Joey would dress up in his best shirt, patched-up blue jeans with high cuffs, and a bow tie. Then he would walk with his parents to the Salada Beach Presbyterian Church—a little brown church that sat on a small hill overlooking Highway 1. They never missed a Sunday service.

Back in 1953, all the stores in town were closed on Sunday. Only the auto service station and the golf course remained open. Even in the big city of San Francisco, many shops shut down on that one day of the week. Back then, it was common for the big city folks to spend a sunny Sunday afternoon driving down the beautiful coastal Highway 1. Most city men wore a suit and fedora hat as they slowly cruised along with their girlfriend or family, all the while enjoying music or the baseball game on their automobile's AM radio station. Windows down, cigarette in hand, radio playing, there was no need to hurry; it was Sunday after all.

"Damn Sunday drivers!" was a common phrase spoken by the locals whenever the rare warm weather clogged the two-lane coastal highway with a seemingly endless line of cars.

***

Lenny and Joey rounded the first set of trees on the golf course, and then they jumped down and hid behind a large rock. When Lenny ducked, the helmet he was wearing fell off his head. He quickly picked it up and set it beside him. Both boys watched as Big Eddie scurried by, following the sand mounds toward what was known as Mori's Point.

As Big Eddie passed them by, guilt overtook Joey, and he called out, "We're over here!"

Big Eddie turned around and headed down the sandbank toward the big rock. Lenny looked at Joey and whispered, "Are you nuts? He's such a loudmouth! I can't stand him, and he'll just clean us out again."

Joey shrugged his shoulders in response.

Oh gosh, they weren't trying to ditch me, Eddie thought as he approached. The disappointment he had begun to feel while chasing them faded away. He now looked at Lenny and Joey as trustworthy friends.

Both boys sat below the rock, smoothing out and packing down the ground below them, leaving a thin layer of sand on top. It was a perfect surface for playing marbles. Eddie sat down on a large piece of driftwood next to Joey as Lenny drew a nearly perfect three-foot circle in the sand with his finger. The boys each placed thirteen of their marbles within the circle. The object of the game was to shoot the most marbles outside the ring. The first shot would be from outside the circle, and the remaining shots from within the circle. Each player would continue shooting until he missed. Then the next player would begin his turn. The game, which was called ringer, would end when no marbles remained in the ring. Normally, most boys played for keeps or keepsie, meaning they would keep all the marbles that they knocked out of the circle. When it was just between Lenny and Joey, they played for fun, meaning they would return the marbles they won after the game.

Lenny drew two lines in the hard-packed sand about three feet apart, at the top and bottom of the circle. They would each lag to see who would go first. Closest to the far line would start the game, next closest would go second, and so on. With a larger-than-normal marble (a shooter or boulder, as they were called) tucked against his thumb, each boy took a turn flicking his shooter to the far line.

Lenny referred to his shooter as Thor, after the famous Viking god. While every other kid wore cowboy hats and holsters with cap guns, Lenny often wore his homemade Viking headdress, which was what he was wearing that day.

"I'm surprised your name isn't Odin," Eddie quipped.

"Oh, that's the name of my dog," Lenny shyly replied. "Enough talk, let's get started."

Eddie won the lag and would go first, followed by Joey, and then Lenny.

As Eddie was about to begin the game, Joey placed his hand in front of Eddie's shooting thumb.

"Wait. Before we begin, just so you know, Eddie, we're not playing for keeps. We're playing for fair, for saves. After the game, each of us gets our own marbles back. Understood?"

"Why?" Eddie asked.

"These are the last of my marbles. I won't have hardly any left if I lose them," Joey replied.

"God! All you have left is cheap clay, commies. They're not even made of glass, and your shooter looks like crap. Half its paint has worn off. You should be glad to lose them. Besides, you already believe you're going to lose, so you might as well just give them to me now," Big Eddie blurted out. Lenny stared at him disapprovingly. "Just joking. I really only want to win

Lenny's marbles anyway. At least he has glass cat's-eyes and swirl marbles. Your marbles are nothing to me. I already won all your good marbles last week. Don't worry. I'll give the commies back to you after I wipe you out. Lenny, what do you say? You and I will play for keeps, and Joey can play for fair."

"No, we all play the same way. We return the marbles to each other after the game," Lenny retorted.

Lenny knew why Joey didn't want to lose the last of his marbles. They were a gift from his mom and dad for his last birthday. Typically, Joey only received new socks with Life Savers candies or Tootsie Rolls tucked inside as gifts. For Christmas, it was new shoes with candies. It was that way every year. It was obvious to Joey that receiving the same gifts each year had a lot to do with his dad working at a shoe store. This year, though, along with the usual Tootsie Rolls, his socks had also contained a bag of marbles. The marbles, however inexpensive, were among the few toys he had ever received from his parents and were thus special to him. Joey never complained. He was happy with what he received. That was just his nature and one of the reasons why Lenny considered Joey his best friend.

For a relative beginner, Joey was a fast learner and a pretty good shooter. With a heavier boulder, he might be able to hold his own, but the only shooter he had was made of hard clay with a painted surface. Eddie, on the other hand, had an assortment of different types of glass marbles, and he used a highly polished ball bearing as his shooter. He had large hands and could flick the large steel ball at nearly twice the speed of anyone else.

"OK, we all return the marbles we win after the game, but the biggest loser has to buy the winner a Snickers candy bar at the Anderson store right afterward. Agreed?" Eddie proposed.

Before Joey could say no, Lenny agreed to the deal. Lenny saw the worried look on Joey's face and said, "Don't worry."

They played the game, and just as before, Big Eddie was the overwhelming winner. Lenny came in last. Joey was suspicious because Lenny had never played so poorly before.

Did Lenny purposely come in last because he knew I only had two cents on me? Joey wondered.

Lenny had enough change in his pocket, and true to the agreement, the three boys walked to the small nearby Anderson store, and Lenny paid for Big Eddie's favorite candy bar.

***

The following Monday marked the beginning of a new school year. The three boys walked together to Sharp Park School, just up the road. Following close behind them were Lenny's talkative little sister, Lidia, with her dark hair fashioned in pigtails, her friend Bridgette Dubois, and another neighborhood girl, the cute fifth grader Beth Ann Codington. Beth Ann, as she preferred to be called, was one of the most popular girls in school. She had her long blond hair wrapped in a ponytail and always wore nice dresses. Her eyes were a pure light blue, and she always seemed to be in a cheerful mood.

***

In those days, girls typically wore dresses to school. It was considered the proper attire. Boys wore blue jeans with cuffs that were easily adjusted as they grew taller. Joey's mom always purchased his jeans one size larger, so he could wear the same pair for two or three years. Joey would simply loosen his belt and adjust the cuffs accordingly to compensate for his growth each year. If his knees became too worn, his mom would patch them. He was one of the few boys in school who wore patched-up jeans. Joey didn't like patches, so he was very careful to stay off his knees as much as possible.

***

Big Eddie looked behind him as he heard the girls giggle. "Lenny, who's that older girl with your little sister?"

"Beth Ann Codington," replied Lenny. "Some people call her Bethie. She just came back from vacation in Yosemite last Friday."

"Wow" was all that Big Eddie could say.

A few steps ahead of the three boys were Beth Ann's older brother, Brian, an eighth-grader, and her younger sister, Colleen, who would be starting third grade. Brian looked back, overhearing Eddie's *wow* remark. Colleen looked up at Brian and smiled. She'd be sure to tell her older sister about it. Brian knew Bethie was popular, but if anyone got too fresh or ever insulted her, they would have to deal with him.

On the first day of class, Mrs. Burk, their teacher for the whole school year, assigned each student to their desk in alphabetical order. To his delight, Big Eddie sat directly behind Beth Ann. As the weeks passed, it was clear that Bethie was not only beautiful but also very smart. She aced nearly all of her homework assignments and tests. Big Eddie could easily see over her shoulder and knew she had some difficulty on her math tests. She still received high marks on her homework assignments, where she had plenty of time to figure out the problems, but on a timed test, her math grades suffered. To everyone else in class, Beth Ann was a top student in everything, including math. Eddie was one of the few who knew Beth Ann could do better. After all, looking over her shoulder had its benefits.

Beth Ann was nice to Eddie, but she was that way with most everyone. Rumor had it that she had a particular liking for Ken Hawkins, a popular seventh-grader. Ken secretly liked Beth Ann, but having a crush on a ten-year-old girl would ruin his reputation, and besides, he didn't want to deal with her protective brother, Brian, so he kept his distance.

One day, after a difficult math test, Eddie realized an opportunity, so he summoned the courage to offer to tutor Beth Ann in math each day after school. At least that's what he told Lenny and Joey. Eddie went on to say that while Beth Ann was eager to improve her math grade, she felt that tutoring her every day was a bit too much. She agreed to one hour, two days a week, in the living room of her parents' house, only if her father and mother agreed.

"Great, huh?" Eddie exclaimed with a big smile on his face. Lenny and Joey looked at each other in disbelief and just nodded their heads in agreement.

It was obvious to Lenny and Joey that the whole tutoring idea had more to do with Eddie really liking Beth Ann than anything else.

To Eddie's delight, Beth Ann's parents agreed, but having an after-school study partner would only continue if her test scores began to match those in her other subjects. If her scores didn't improve, his help would end, and they would find someone else. He began what he called "tutoring" that same week and continued meeting with her for the next two months. Beth Ann's test scores improved noticeably, and her parents were impressed.

Just after the Christmas break, Beth Ann informed Eddie that she no longer needed him as her study partner. Eddie hid his disappointment, but inside, he was heartbroken. His special private time with her was over.

***

After the holidays, at the start of English class, Mrs. Burk handed each student a blank booklet with spaced lines. She explained that when her father was a young boy, he began to keep a journal. In it, he had written about his life's journey and memorable events, and about his friends, including a young woman who would one day become his wife and her mother. She briefly paused for a moment, turned, and looked out of the classroom windows. It was clear she was deep in thought and no longer looked at her fifth-grade class. She continued, still gazing outside.

"My father, the man I admired most in life, passed away when I was ten years old." She paused once more before going on. "Sadly, I could only remember things going back to about three years of age. The only memories I had of my father encompassed those years of my childhood. My mother tried to keep his memory alive in me by sharing stories about their life together before I was born. The day I turned sixteen, she gave me my father's journal. He had written over 360 entries, filled with both the good and bad in his life. His words came alive. It was as if he were there, reading to me himself. I had thought I knew him before, but after reading about his life and times, I realized how little I really knew him at all. Still to this day, I sometimes go back to relive his words once again."

Mrs. Burk turned her attention back to her students. "It's now January 1954, a perfect time for each of you to begin your own personal journal, your record, happy, sad, good, or bad. Be honest but mindful of how you tell your story, for someday it may be shared with others. I encourage you to use correct spelling, proper English, and good sentence construction. Don't feel you need to write every day or even every week. A few lines of important thoughts or personal history each month or quarter is fine, and don't worry. I won't be reading or even collecting your personal journal. It belongs to you and no one else. You don't even need to bring the journal back to class. At the end of the school year, you just need to let me know you made a good effort. I'll rely solely on your honor and integrity, which will be good enough for me. You will receive a 100 percent score as you would for turning in a perfect homework assignment. Now, does anyone have any questions?"

For the next ten minutes, she answered various questions, and then it was off to other topics. Most of her class made an honest effort to complete their journal for the remainder of the school year. A couple just doodled or left the pages blank altogether. Her story about her father inspired a few to write in their journals for years. Eddie updated his journal periodically, but sometimes skipped a year or two. Joey, on the other hand, would continue his journal for life.

***

Throughout the course of the year, Joey and Lenny observed Eddie and could easily see what he was doing in class. They had become very suspicious of the praise Big Eddie always received from Mrs. Burk. He must be cheating, they thought. Mrs. Burk would always smile and congratulate him every time she handed back his homework and test scores. This occurred in almost every subject, and it was especially apparent in math. It was obvious to them that Eddie was copying off of Beth Ann on every test. He was always looking over her shoulder. Then he'd smile and look down at his paper. To Joey and Lenny, Eddie just couldn't be that smart.

One day during recess, they purposely avoided Eddie and hid in one of the restrooms.

"You know, Joey," said Lenny, "maybe he did lie to us about his age. Maybe he is actually twelve years old, not ten. That might explain some things. He's probably taken these subjects before at his prior school. After all, he looks a lot older, and he's taller than the seventh graders. Heck, he's taller than most eighth graders, too."

"Yeah," responded Joey. "Not only that, he's blind if he thinks that Bethie will ever think of him as more than just a classmate. Everyone knows she still has a crush on Hawkins. Jeff Baker told me he saw Ken kiss a girl who looked a lot like Beth Ann Codington at the Sea View Theater last Saturday afternoon. It was dark so that he couldn't say for certain, but he said it sure looked like her."

Joey paused for a moment and pondered the situation, and then continued. "Wait a minute. Maybe Eddie wasn't really tutoring Beth Ann as he says. Maybe she was tutoring him, or maybe he's even copying her homework. She's the smartest girl in class. Why would she need a tutor anyway?"

"Tutoring him or not, I still think he's copying Beth Ann's answers to her tests," Lenny added.

After thinking about it for a while, Joey turned to Lenny and asked, "What if we're wrong?"

The recess bell rang, so they headed back to class. Eddie spotted them as they entered the hallway.

"Hey, where were you guys? I looked all over for you two," said Eddie.

"Stomach problems. I needed to use the boy's room," replied Lenny.

Joey chimed in. "Yeah…I…I…hah…I was in the next stall. It really stunk. Be glad you weren't there. I think Lenny clogged the toilet with his B17 mass-flying-turd bombing.

CHAPTER 2

THE CASTLE

Most every Saturday afternoon, the three boys, along with Jeff Baker and Ronny Baumgartner, ventured to their not-so-secret-anymore marble ring at the Sharp Park Golf Course. Lenny's little sister Lidia, or Liddy as he called her, always tried to tag along whenever Joey was with her brother. Lenny would tell her to get lost. He didn't want to hear her seemingly constant babbling about girly things. Sometimes, though, Lidia would sneak off to the golf course to spy on them, especially keeping her eyes on Joey. When their game was about to end, she would hurry back home, so they would never see her.

Joey, who had too few marbles to play, would just watch as the other boys played two or three games of ringer. Lenny received a weekly allowance of twenty-five cents, so he had an endless supply of marbles. The games all ended the same, with Eddie as the undefeated champion.

***

Anderson's store was out of marbles, so Lenny wanted to buy some more from one of the stores up in the Manor, a growing community about a mile north of Salada Beach. The Manor had one of the largest grocery stores on the north coast. It was the big Super X Market. The Manor also had a hardware store next to the Pacific Manor School, where Lenny thought he might be able to find a large steel ball bearing to replace his cat's-eye shooter.

Like it or not, both boys knew that Eddie looked at them as his best buddies. It was an awkward situation, but Joey was actually getting used to having Big Eddie around. He also felt sorry for the big guy because the girl Eddie liked was not interested in him. He just couldn't see it, even though it was as plain as day to everyone else. Lenny, on the other hand, still had a way to go before he would ever trust Eddie.

As they walked through the parking lot in front of the Super X, Joey saw a shopping cart lying on its side. As he picked it up, a paper bill flew into the air. He quickly grabbed it.

"I'm rich! I'm rich. Oh wow," he exclaimed as he held out a five-dollar bill in front of the other two. "I'm going to buy the biggest and best bag of marbles they have."

"Great," responded Eddie. "That's more for me. When we get back, let's play another round of ringer."

The large grocery store didn't have any marbles. It only had groceries, so the boys crossed the highway and went to a small general store on the other side. The smaller store was located next to a barbershop and the hardware store, where Lenny had wanted to go.

Right next to the cash register was a rack of baseball trading-card packages, and next to the cards were five small bags of assorted glass marbles, and one double-size bag. Joey purchased the larger bag of marbles along with three Snickers and three packs of baseball trading cards. As they left the store, he gave Lenny and Eddie each a Snickers candy bar. Then Joey opened three of the trading-card packs and shared the gum tucked in the back of each pack with Lenny and Eddie. As they sat on the curb eating their candy bars, Joey looked back and noticed a pendant with a small cross on it in the store window. His mother's birthday was just one week away, and he had never ever given his mom a real birthday present. Now was his chance. He quickly turned around, went back inside, and asked the man at the counter how much the pendant cost.

"Well, young fella, that'd be four ninety-nine plus a penny tax."

Joey's heart sank. He only had two dollars and seventy cents left in his pocket. "Here's the marbles and the trading cards back. I want to buy the pendant instead."

"Sorry, son. No returns. Besides, you already opened the trading cards and removed the gum that was inside them." The old man looked down at Joey and realized the boy's disappointment. "I tell you what. I'll take the pendant out of the window and hold it for one week. If you can get the extra cash, I'll sell it to you then. OK?"

Dejected, Joey nodded his head and left the store. *How will I ever come up with that much money?* He went home, lay on his bed, and stared at the ceiling, feeling sorry and disappointed. Every day for the next week after school, he walked to the Manor and searched for spare change in the Super X Market parking lot and the surrounding gutters. He found a total of thirty-eight cents over the course of the week. He was still two dollars short, so he resorted to prayer.

"God, please, I love my mom and pop. It's her birthday tomorrow, please." But, as much as he prayed, time had run out. He knew he had failed.

Lenny came by early the next morning. Joey didn't want to go out and asked his mother to let Lenny know he planned to stay in today.

"It's important that I at least talk to him, Mrs. Gunderson," pleaded Lenny.

Reluctantly, Joey came to the door.

"Joey, you know that large old home that was built to look like a castle? On the hill across from Highway 1? Guess what? The caretaker wants someone to pull all the weeds and trim the bushes in the garden. He'll pay us two fifty each if we do a good job. Bring gloves and a pair of scissors."

Excited, Joey quickly put on his canvas tennis shoes, grabbed Mama Morales's gardening gloves, and his mom's scissors. "I'm going to make some money," he shouted to his mom as he ran out the door. The boys ran nearly all the way to the hilltop castle that overlooked all of Sharp Park and the Salada beach. Mama Morales had once told Joey to never go anywhere near the castle on the hill. Joey had overheard Mama tell his parents that the place was once, among other nefarious things, a house of ill repute—whatever that meant. Joey wasn't sure. As much as he respected Mama Morales, he needed the money. The road up the hill that led to the castle was very steep, so they walked the last part of the way.

"Maybe we should have asked Big Eddie to come help us," said Joey.

"No," Lenny snapped. "Then we'd have to split the money three ways."

They reached the top of the hill, and an iron gate blocked their entrance to the ornate castle door. It was locked, but Lenny said he could climb over the wall and unlock it from the inside.

"Give me a boost," Lenny asked Joey.

Joey put his hands together, and Lenny placed his foot within the hands. Joey then lifted Lenny high enough to climb over the wall. Lenny flipped the latch and opened the gate for Joey.

"We should knock on the door and let the caretaker know we're here," suggested Joey.

"No need. He went to San Francisco early this morning. He told me to just start clearing the weeds by the old fountain and trim back the old rose bushes. He'd leave us the money under the back doormat. I assured him we'd do the best job he'd ever seen."

Ever cautious, Joey suggested that they first look under the doormat just to be sure the money was there. Lenny lifted the edge of the mat, and sure enough, there was an envelope. He peeked inside.

"Yes, it's all here, just like he said. Let's get started and finish this job before noon," urged Lenny.

As Joey worked feverishly at pulling weeds, Lenny sat back and just smiled. Joey was constantly urging him to work faster, but as much as he encouraged Lenny, Lenny continued to work at a snail's pace.

After about an hour, Lenny said, "We're done here."

"We are not even close to being done. Look at all the weeds below the fountain. We need to pull those, too," Joey responded in frustration.

Joey had already done nearly all of the work, while Lenny just kicked back and relaxed most of the time.

Joey shifted his work to the lower section of what had once been a nice garden. *He's hardly made an effort. How could he be so lazy? He knows how important this is to me,* Joey thought.

Lenny sat on the edge of the empty fountain and watched as Joey continued to pull weeds at a frantic pace. Then he started to sing a tune from the old Disney movie *Snow White and the Seven Dwarfs*, but he changed the lyrics. "Whistle while you work. Hitler was a jerk. Mussolini bit his weenie. Now it doesn't work. Yeah!"

"Stop, stop! Please, just help me!" Joey replied while trying to contain his laughter. "It's not funny, Lenny."

"Joey, it's good enough. I told the caretaker how much we'd clear out, and you've done more than he expected." With that, Lenny opened the envelope and handed Joey half of the earnings: two dollars and fifty cents. Lenny immediately folded the envelope and placed it in his back pocket.

Joey looked at the results of his hard work. "It really didn't look like anybody lived here anymore. Now it looks alive once again."

Lenny chuckled.

Once they reached the bottom of the hill, they decided that Joey would head to the Manor store, and Lenny would make his way home. As Lenny turned quickly toward home at the bottom of the street, the envelope he carried fell out of his back pocket. When Joey reached down to pick it up, his thumb slid into the envelope, revealing it to be empty.

"Lenny!" he yelled. "Your money's gone."

"No, I have it. I took my share and put it in my front pocket before we left!" Lenny shouted back as he continued on his way.

Later that evening, right after dinner, Mama Morales came out of the kitchen holding a beautiful cake with one lit candle on top, and everyone began to sing "Happy Birthday" to Ruth. Joey watched the smile on his mom's face and thought, *this is better than even Christmas.*

Joey took his mom by surprise when he handed her his newspaper-wrapped gift. She opened it, leaned over, and kissed her son on his cheek. "Thank you, Joseph." Her voice cracked as she spoke, and he felt a teardrop run down his neck. She quickly turned away and went toward the mirror at the end of the hallway. Roth followed her and gently helped her place the pendant around her neck. They never said a word, and she stayed there, just looking at the small, inexpensive cross for what seemed to Joey like a long time. Joey didn't realize it then, but his mother would wear that little cross around her neck for the rest of her life.

Just before bedtime, Joey's dad asked him where he got the money to buy the pendant. Joey explained all that had happened, even telling his dad about his prayer. His dad was satisfied with his explanation and was proud of his son.

"So, you really cleared the weeds out of the castle garden?" his dad asked.

"Most of them," Joey replied. "It sure looks a lot better now."

"And I thought that the owner moved out of that place months ago. I guess I was mistaken," his dad said as he turned off the bedroom light. "Good night, son. I love you."

Joey pondered what his dad had just said. Not just about the owner moving out, but the last thing, the love-you part. It was the first time he had ever heard his dad say those words to him. Joey slept well that night. Perhaps it was from his hard work, the good food, an answered prayer, or maybe it was because of the love he felt from his parents, and the kindness of his best friend, Lenny. For you see, Joey was now convinced that the envelope had only ever held two dollars and fifty cents. Maybe there was no caretaker at all. *Lennard Leibowitz, you are so cagey,* he thought as he drifted off into a deep sleep.

CHAPTER 3

MORI'S POINT

The school year was coming to an end, and unseasonably warm weather hit the coast. The sky was clear, with none of the lingering fog that was typical on the coast that time of year. The average temperature in Sharp Park and the Manor region rarely rose above sixty-five degrees, and it usually hovered in the low sixties a good portion of the year.

It was another weekend with marbles high on the agenda and maybe even some baseball-card trading as well. It was considered a scorcher outside, with the temperature expected to reach over eighty degrees. Jeff Baker came by, and the whole group headed to their marble ring.

Once Lidia spotted Joey leaving with Lenny and the other boys, she decided to tag along. Lenny spotted her and walked her back into their home. Lenny gave Lidia his sternest look. "You, stay here. Got it?"

"I'm not Odin," Lidia replied.

"Mom, Liddy's being a pest. Tell her to play with Bridgette Dubois, or tell her to go in the backyard and play with the puppy.

Odin needs to be housebroken. She needs to teach him where to go potty."

Sofia told Lenny to be on his way and then urged Liddy to play with friends her own age.

"But Mama, don't you know that Bridgette is one year older than me?" Liddy retorted.

"You know what I mean, Liddy. You need to stay here and let the boys play. It's warm outside. Maybe you should take a nap. I'm going to lie down now. You should do the same," was her mom's reply.

Liddy quietly moved from her bedroom after her mom fell asleep and sneaked off toward the golf course.

It was amazing. Joey played the best keepsie game of ringer ever. Even Lenny was surprised. Joey still lost—but only by two marbles. However, because the game was for all the marbles, Eddie won all the marbles played in the match. Even so, Eddie was a bit upset that he had come so close to losing.

"And still the champion," Eddie boasted as he slid all the marbles into an old blue sock. Their friend Jeff and the other boys returned home, defeated once again.

Eddie sat at the top of the sand mound and looked at the ocean. The tide was high, the waves were large, and they roared loudly as they broke against the shore. *Maybe the ocean is as mad as I am*, he wondered. *Maybe the warm weather messed up my game. Still, I won, so it's a nice day anyway.* His thoughts then turned to Beth Ann. His tutoring sessions with her had long since ended, but he just couldn't get her out of his mind.

They were well on their way home when Lenny had an idea.

"Hey, let's take a walk out to Mori's Point," Lenny declared as he started walking back south along the sandbank. With nothing else to do, both of the other boys followed after him.

"You know how I like everything Nordic. I believe the Vikings sailed all over the world. Maybe they even traveled over the Arctic Ocean and into the Pacific," Lenny commented as he briskly walked toward the point.

"Well, there you go. That explains why you save Prince Valiant comic strips from the Chronicle and have a Viking headdress over your bed. I'm surprised you haven't yet finished making a copy of Val's magic sword, Flamberge," Eddie opined.

"That's my next project, but it will have to wait. I'm nearly done reading the book my parents gave me. It's called *Viking Tales*, and it's really, really good. I know everything about them now. You guys should read it when I'm done," Lenny offered.

"You must be kidding. No way the Vikings ever made it into the Pacific. There's no conclusive evidence of Vikings around here. Lenny, I thought you were smarter than that bit of nonsense," Big Eddie replied.

"I know, but I'm a big dreamer." He pointed to the south. "Just look at that first large rock off the point. Doesn't it remind you of a Viking ship?"

"No," Eddie quickly responded.

Lenny continued. "If Sundays as hot as it is today, I'm going to climb out to that large, long rock at low tide and finish reading my book. I'll pretend I'm sailing my ship, the *Nordic Prince*."

"Wow, what an imagination. You name your marble shooter Thor, your puppy, Odin, and suddenly you think you're a Viking. No way are we going to let you venture out onto that rock. Besides, low tide this Sunday is at four a.m., you fool," Eddie responded.

"How do you know when low tide is?" asked Joey. "By the way, conclusive is a big word. My dad uses it sometimes; I don't think I've ever heard a kid use it."

"I read the newspaper every day. I'm a whole lot smarter than both of you guys realize. Believe me, I know these things. I'm Eddie the brain. That's what you guys should call me from now on," Eddie said half-jokingly.

Joey thought to himself, *Maybe Eddie is really that smart.*

Lenny was starting to believe it, too.

Eddie and Lenny walked onto Salada Beach slightly ahead of Joey. They walked back up to the higher sandbank after they smelled the stench from the large waste pipe that emptied onto the beach. Once past the waste pipe, the two headed back down onto the shoreline. Joey chose to stay on the higher ground, well away from the waves.

Joey's dad had warned him that Salada Beach was good for fishing and sightseeing, but not much of anything else. The water ran deep right offshore, and it had a reputation for riptides and strong undertows. If the locals wanted to swim or sunbathe, they'd head a few miles south to the crescent-shaped beach located at the mouth of the San Pedro valley, in the community of Linda Mar. Its shallow waters and wide beach made it the ideal place to swim and relax. Salada Beach was no Linda Mar Beach, not in the slightest.

Eddie called out to Joey, "Come down here, on the beach."

Lenny looked over to Eddie and informed him that Joey was deathly afraid of the ocean. He never learned how to swim. "Every year, my mother offered to take Joey with my sister and me to Fleishhacker Pool for swimming lessons. You know the saltwater pool by the San Francisco Zoo? But he would never come."

"What a coincidence," Eddie remarked. "That's where I learned to swim as well."

Eddie and Lenny continued walking and talking on the beach, well ahead of their friend. Joey continued walking farther back on the higher dunes, away from the water rolling up on shore. Joey stopped for a moment, realizing that he had never walked this far south before. He looked at the green grass of the golf course off to his left. It nearly surrounded a lake, and it was a stunning sight.

Then he recalled what Mama Morales had once told his family about the early community of Salada. She said that long before the Sharp Park Golf Course was there, a large lagoon covered much of the area, and it was even more beautiful than it looks today. The early Spanish settlers called it the Laguna Salada, which in English translates to the Salty Lagoon. Then, the lagoon was nearly three times its current size and had a small stream that carved through the sand and into the sea. The ocean waters would sometimes wash through the stream and into the lagoon, creating its brackish water. Joey stood there, trying to imagine how it once looked. By chance, he looked back the way he had come and noticed something or someone off in the distance, very near the water rolling on the shore.

About the same time, Lenny began to have a dark foreboding feeling inside that he just didn't quite understand.

"Let's rejoin Joey and get off the beach," he said as he looked at Eddie. With that, they both turned around and headed back toward Joey and up to the higher sandbank.

To Joey's horror, he realized what he was seeing. It was a small girl walking by herself, much too close to the roaring waves. She was after something rolling on the beach. It looked like a piece of driftwood, and as she bent down to pick it up, a wave knocked her over.

"No!" he gasped. He immediately began to run back, but this time he ran down on the beach itself.

No, no, oh God, no! He ran faster than he had ever run before. It was little Lidia. She was in the grip of the wave and barely had her head above water.

"What's got into him?" Eddie remarked as they watched Joey sprint down onto the beach and back the way they had come. His actions caused both Eddie and Lenny to stop for a moment and look more closely down the long stretch of beach.

"It's Lidia!" exclaimed Lenny. With a pained look in his eyes, he realized he was too far away to reach her in time, and panic overtook him. He screamed out Liddy's name over and over again as he ran. Eddie took off following Lenny.

Lidia's only hope was a boy, deathly afraid of the water, who couldn't even swim. *How hopeless,* Eddie thought as he labored to stay close behind Lenny.

Joey didn't stop or hesitate. He watched as Lidia struggled to get out of the ocean's grasp. Then a large wave broke just behind her, and she disappeared below the surface. A huge wall of white water crashed on the beach as Joey jumped headfirst into the roaring surf. He opened his eyes. The salt water stung, but he kept his eyes open, held his breath, and began kicking his legs as fast as he could. He kicked so hard that he lost both of his canvas tennis shoes. Then, like something coming out of a heavy mist, he saw a small hand reaching out to him. The only thing he could see was that little hand, a hand he knew belonged to Lidia. He grabbed the wrist of the outstretched hand as firmly as he could and struggled to get his head above the water. Another wave struck him, this time pushing him back toward the beach, as if trying to separate him from Liddy. Still, he held onto her. He pulled her upward, and her head finally broke the surface. Her eyes opened wide, looking directly into his, and she took a deep breath. Joey's heart jumped. He didn't feel safe until his back scraped against the surface of the beach, and he saw Lenny closing in.

Lenny arrived, followed by Eddie, and they tried to get Lidia well away from the water, but Joey wouldn't release her from his grip.

"Let go! Let go!" Lenny shouted as more waves crashed onto the shore.

Impatiently, Big Eddie reached down and lifted them both off the sand. Lenny tried to help, but Eddie darted away, carrying the full weight of Joey and Liddy in his arms, to the safety of higher ground. Though utterly exhausted, Joey still wouldn't let go of Liddy's little wrist. She began to cry because his grip was so tight.

Lenny had to pry Joey's fingers from Liddy as she cried out, "Please let go, Joey, please." The sound of her begging brought only joy to Lenny's heart. She was loud, alive, and safe. Lenny pried the last of Joey's fingers from her wrist, and Liddy stopped crying.

At the top of the dune, Joey rolled over on his stomach and tucked his head in his arms, as if to rest. He didn't want the others to see the tears in his eyes as he lay there silently weeping.

Other than some bruise marks starting to appear on Liddy's wrist, she appeared quite well and was now very talkative, back to her precocious self.

"Did you swallow any seawater?" inquired Lenny.

"No, but my wrist still hurts, and I want to go home now," she replied. "I want to play with Odin."

Lidia turned and saw Joey lying face down in the sand. She walked over, sat down next to him, and placed her hand on his shoulder.

"Don't worry, Joey, I'm OK. You'll be OK too, she said softly. While the others hadn't noticed, Lidia knew why Joey was still lying face down.

"Oh God, what will I tell my mom? We all need to dry off and think of something, or I'll never be allowed to go near Salada

Beach or Mori's Point again." Lenny was worried. He didn't want to lie to his mother, but he also didn't want to tell her the truth.

Before anyone could say anything, Liddy asked if they had seen it.

"What?" they asked.

"It was a wooden arm with a hand holding some sort of blue glass thingy," she explained as they all turned to look back down at the beach. "Oh…it's not there anymore," she said with a measure of disappointment in her voice. Liddy then added, "Maybe if we wait here some more, it'll come back."

Joey finally sat up. "Are you kidding? You almost drowned. We almost lost you. You act as if nothing happened, you little, little girl!"

"I'm not a little girl. I'm almost seven now, and I know how to swim well, I'll have you know," was Liddy's terse response. But inside, she knew just how fortunate she had been to have Joey nearby. That day would remain in her thoughts throughout her life.

As Joey stood up to wipe off the sand clinging to his clothes, a large wooden arm rolled up on shore—only this time it stayed in the sand as the waters retreated. No one else noticed. All their attention was focused on Liddy and what to do next. Without hesitation, Joey walked slowly back down to the beach, as if drawn to the arm by some unknown force. He picked it up and peered into the blue glass cylinder held in place by its two large wooden hands. He touched the glass, and something rolled within it. He quickly dropped it and backed away. Finally, the others noticed him standing there as if frozen in place. A wave rolled ashore, covering his feet up to the ankles, and he watched as the arm returned to the sea, disappearing once again.

"What was that?" exclaimed Lenny.

"See, I told you so," Liddy bragged.

"I'm not sure exactly. It looked like it was once two arms, but one was partially broken off. Two hands held a glass cylinder with something inside it. It was warm to the touch. I can't explain it. It made me feel weird, like it wanted me to release it from its glass prison."

"Yeah, right," responded Eddie. "Given what you described, I guess that it was once some sort of ornament off the bow of an old wooden ship. Maybe a Chinese junk or an old Japanese vessel, and any type of glass would feel hot in this weather."

"A Viking ship," whispered Lenny in the background.

They sat on the dune for half an hour, drying off and hoping the mysterious arm would reappear, but it had vanished.

"Now what?" Lenny inquired.

"I've got an idea. We'll go see if Beth Ann is home. She'll know what to do." Eddie, ever clever, already had a few good options, but going to Beth Ann's was a ruse to visit with her once again. Eddie looked at the others to see if anyone disagreed.

"Sounds good. Let's go. Eddie, you know her best. We'll stay back while you knock on her door," said Lenny in agreement.

***

Bethie's brother Brian opened the door just before Eddie was about to knock. "Study time ended months ago, big guy. What do you want?"

Just then, Beth Ann rushed downstairs, smiled, and said, "Hello, Ed."

Eddie stood there, taken aback for a moment. *Well, that's something new. She had never called him Ed before. In fact, no one had.* It was as if Beth Ann had really missed him. Her eyes peered deep into his for the first time, and he felt good inside.

"I was wondering if you could help me, er...I mean us." He nodded his head in the direction of the others.

"Sure, why not?" she replied as she bolted past her brother, quickly closing the door behind her. She took Eddie's hand, and they ran together to join the others. She remained holding Eddie's hand as they stood in front of the other three. Lenny and Liddy both started to speak at the same time. Joey remained silent.

"Stop. One at a time," Bethie urged. She pointed to Lenny.

"Joey saved my little sister's life..." He stopped, looked back at Joey, and thanked him. "I'm forever in your debt."

Lenny went on to describe all that had happened. Beth Ann looked at Joey. He was barefoot, his blue jeans still soaked, a pair of wet socks in his hand, and his light brown hair matted down. She immediately let go of Eddie's hand. She stood there, not saying a word. She looked at Joey as if noticing him for the first time.

"And...uh...I picked Joey and Liddy up with my bare hands and carried them all the way up to the safety of the high dunes," Eddie quickly offered, hoping to gain a piece of the glory and to divert her attention back to him. He saw a look in her eyes, the same look she had just given him when he was at her door, but now it was directed at Joey. What had changed so quickly? She now seemed transfixed by his friend.

"That was very good of you, Eddie," Beth Ann finally responded, without taking her eyes off of Joey.

Eddie said nothing in response. *Very good of me? That's it? That's all? I'm back to being Eddie once again. I was Ed the man a few minutes ago.* Eddie hid his mounting anger.

"What will you do without your shoes, Joey?" Beth Ann inquired.

"I still have my old shoes. I'll just wear them," he replied, acting as if it were no big deal. He knew his old shoes were too small, but they'd have to do for a while longer. It would be months until new ones arrived.

Beth Ann turned her attention back to the group. "Lenny, you go home and get some better clothes for Liddy. Don't let your mom see you, and try to find a dress that's the same color as the one she has on. I'll fix her hair and shake the sand off her dress. Then I'll wash the smell of the sea off her face, arms, and legs." Bethie took a closer look at the now obvious bruises on Liddy's wrist. "Hmm…my mom has some gauze. I'll wrap some around her wrist. I suggest that you tell your mother that you grabbed Liddy's wrist a little too hard as she tripped and was about to fall. Oh, and I'll bring her clothes back to you after you let me know if this plan worked. OK?"

"OK," Lenny replied. He returned home, took off his shoes, and snuck in the back door. He did exactly as Bethie instructed. When he returned, Liddy's hair was freshly brushed, and her shoes were polished as well. She changed into her fresh clothes behind Bethie's garage. Beth Ann inspected her, and all looked well.

Lenny and Liddy walked home with Lenny reminding her of what to say all the way.

After saying good-bye to Beth Ann, Eddie and Joey walked back home as well. On the way, Joey realized the feat Eddie had accomplished when he lifted both him and Liddy to safety. He now viewed Eddie as a true and loyal friend. He regretted ever thinking of Eddie as anything else.

"Eddie, what you did back there…I mean, thank you. I'll never forget it.

Eddie nodded his head, acknowledging what Joey had just said. Joey talked, but Eddie never said a word the rest of the way home.

Lenny's mom was in the back room ironing. Liddy put her hands behind her back when she saw her mother carefully place the iron down.

She turned and gave Lidia a stern look. "When did you wake up from your nap, and where did you run off to?"

Before Liddy could respond, Lenny offered his explanation. "She went to Bridgette's house while you were sleeping. Liddy didn't want to disturb you, so she told me where she was going."

Their mother considered Lenny's explanation. She looked back at Lidia and spoke once more. "That's nice, but next time, you wake me up, little girl. Do you understand?"

Liddy looked at her mother with a sheepish look and softly replied, "Yes, Mother. I'll never leave without telling you. I promise. I'm really sorry." With that, Liddy started walking back to her room.

"Stop right there. What is that on your wrist? Come over here right now. What happened? Tell me the truth," their mom inquired in rapid succession.

"I was knocked over," Liddy responded. "Joey saved me."

Before she could continue, Lenny spoke up once again. "I grabbed her arm so that she wouldn't skin her knees."

"No, Joey grabbed my wrist. He's the one who saved me, not you," Lidia quickly countered.

"Who knocked you down then?" their mother asked.

"No one. She just stumbled. Can I go back out now?" Lenny pleaded. He had run out of explanations and hoped his mother had run out of questions.

Liddy regretted lying, even though Lenny had assured her the story was mostly the truth—just without the ocean part.

"Lidia, you go to your room and stay there. Your father and I will talk more about this when he gets home." Clearly, Sofia suspected that there was more to the story than her children were providing. Exactly what, she didn't know. Perhaps Benny could figure it out.

Liddy returned to her room, lay on her bed, and sadly realized that in all the excitement, she had forgotten to thank Joey.

***

Sofia's husband, Benny, returned home from the jewelry store just after six in the evening. His working on a Saturday, the Jewish Sabbath, was something he never wrote about in his twice-a-year letters to his parents back east. After closing the garage door, he checked the small box on the inside wall of the garage to see if any mail was pushed through the slot from the outside. Inside the box was a letter from the principal of Sharp Park School. He opened it as he entered the back door and went into the kitchen. He smiled proudly.

After saying hello and kissing her husband on the cheek, Sofia's next words were, "Benny, we need to talk about Lidia."

"I know, I know. Isn't this wonderful news?" Benny replied.

"What?" Sofia questioned.

"The principal and Lidia's teacher want to meet with us. They are recommending that Lidia skip the second grade and go right into the third."

"What? Really? Let me see." Sofia snatched the letter out of her husband's hand. "This is wonderful, but that's not..." Her voice tailed off as she thought more about the topic at hand. "Let's discuss this more. We need to make the right decision for our daughter."

For the next twenty minutes, they discussed whether or not skipping a grade would be the right thing for Liddy.

Sofia thought some more. "If Liddy skips a grade, she would be starting third grade with her best friend, Brigitte."

"Then I'm sure what Lidia's answer will be when we discuss this with her," replied Benny. "Was there anything else you wanted to discuss?"

"No. It's a minor thing. I'll take care of it myself. Let's tell Liddy the good news."

Chapter 4

Valhalla

After Joey returned with his parents from church the next day, he met up with Lenny and Big Eddie. They sat on the high sandbank, just off the beach street, across from Beth Ann's house. It was already getting hot, and it was obvious that it was going to be another real scorcher that day.

Lenny started the conversation. "You know…I know what happened with the arm and its glass cylinder. I had a dream last night. In it, I saw an ancient Japanese merchant ship. The ship's captain looked like an Asian version of Prince Valiant. He had—"

"Wait now. A Japanese version of Prince Valiant! Come on, Lenny. Get real. God…you have too much imagination. You need to grow up, Lenny," Big Eddie said in a serious tone.

"No. Let me finish before you discount what I have to say. Maybe he didn't look like Prince Valiant, but he was a proud captain who cared for his ship and his crew. He had a large wooden statue of a great warrior placed on the bow of the ship. The warrior had his arms stretched out from the bow, holding the glass cylinder within his hands. The captain believed that as long as the warrior was on the bow, his ship and its crew would be safe as they traveled from port to port around the island nation. He believed there was power within the glass cylinder the warrior held. He knew the waters would be calm wherever his ship sailed. One day, as he sailed to his next port of call, he saw a storm building on the horizon, so he stayed closer to shore, hoping to find a safe haven to dock his ship and protect its crew and cargo. As his ship rounded a bluff, there, right in front of him, was the largest fleet of Chinese warships he had ever seen. He tried to sail away but was immediately attacked by two of the Chinese vessels. One of the Chinese ships rammed the bow of his great ship, knocking the arms off the great warrior. Once the arms broke off, the captain's once magnificent ship was sent to the bottom of the sea. As the arms with their glass cylinder floated in the ocean around the Chinese flotilla. A great storm moved in, as if seeking revenge, and sank most of the invading fleet. The rest sailed back to China, believing it was a bad omen, a warning to never attack Japan again."

"And when did this all occur?" Big Eddie asked.

"Hundreds of years ago, I think. I don't really know for sure," answered Lenny.

"If it happened that long ago, the wooden arm would have become waterlogged and sunk to the bottom of the sea to be eaten away by tiny sea creatures, so that it couldn't have floated for so long. You can understand that, can't you, Lenny?" Big Eddie explained.

"Maybe what was in the glass cylinder protected it and kept it afloat?" Lenny offered this as a defense against the logic Big Eddie had presented.

"It was only a dream, a fantasy. It was simply a figment of your imagination. Something special that you wanted to be true.

Don't you see, Lenny? It was only a dream, but a darn good one, I must say. I almost started to believe it myself," said Joey.

"Enough of this nonsense. I'm going home to finish the rest of my homework." With that, Big Eddie got up and left. Big Eddie wasn't his normal loud, jolly self. Both Joey and Lenny knew something else was bothering the big guy.

The reality was that Big Eddie had finished his homework long ago and just used it as an excuse to get away from his friends. He needed time to think about what had happened between him and Beth Ann.

Lenny and Joey decided to head to the shade of the trees by the golf course, where they had frequently played marbles. It was there that Lenny informed Joey about his sister skipping her next grade.

"Can you believe it? And I always thought I was the smart one," Lenny quipped.

"That's great news, Lenny." Joey knew Liddy was very intelligent. She often talked more like an adult than a kid her own age.

"Did I mention that our mom talked to her this morning? She won't be following us for a while. She's been restricted to the house for three days. It's for not telling our mom where she was going yesterday. If you ask me, she got off lucky, in more ways than one. Anyway, today is *Nordic Prince Day*, you know. We will venture farther than ever before to parts unknown. We'll view what's beyond Mori's Point. We'll—"

Joey cut him off midsentence. "We'll stay off the beach and only follow the path up the bluff past the Mori's Point Inn." Joey pointed to the small Italian restaurant that sat halfway up the bluff.

Lenny had eaten there once before, on his mother's birthday. There was a narrow road just off the coastal highway that led directly to the restaurant.

Lenny pointed at the point. "We'll approach it from the smuggler's side. Rumor has it that in the twenties, during what was called Prohibition, ships from Canada would travel down the coast and offload illegal whiskey on a small dock. The dock was located near the first large rock, you know, my *Nordic Prince* ship."

"Yeah, most everyone around here has heard that story. But I don't think the dock is still there. At least, I don't see anything that looks like a dock from here. We'll only go where it's safe. OK, Lenny?"

Lenny didn't respond. Instead, he started following the sandbank and called out to an invisible horde, "All Vikings, move forth! Conquer and pillage all that you see!"

When they were well past their marble ring, they observed a larger-than-normal wave crash on shore. There, out in front of them, rolling high up on the beach was the mysterious wooden arm with its glass cylinder. As it rolled ashore, the sun reflected off the glass into the boy's eyes. They both squinted and looked away.

"You pick it up! No, you this time," they bantered back and forth. Finally, Joey ran onto the beach, fearing another wave would take it away once more, and tried to lift it up.

"It seems a lot heavier than before. Give me a hand with this, will ya?"

Lenny moved cautiously forward and grabbed the wooded arm, keeping his hands well away from the blue cylinder. They carried it away from the shore and down the other side of the dune facing the golf course. There, they dropped it onto a patch of ice plant. Lenny slowly moved his hand up the wooden arm, closer to the glass cylinder.

"Stop! Don't touch the glass," warned Joey as he carefully leaned down and inspected it more closely. "It looks so ancient." The wood had deep cracks in it, but the artistry was still readily apparent. "Look how it's carved. Imagine how it must have looked when it was new. If only the other arm were still there."

As Joey continued to talk, Lenny peered into the cylinder. He could see something round, slightly larger than a nickel in diameter. It was between two glass rails, within the cylinder. Just then, the arm slid a few inches down the ice plant. The object inside the cylinder rolled in a circle, and a faint sound could be heard.

"What was that sound?" Joey asked.

"It was a whistling sound, I think," Lenny replied.

The two boys sat there, pondering what to do next. Lenny suggested that they take it to his house and hide it in his backyard to let it dry out.

Lenny looked at Joey and asked, "See if you can come over to my house right after dinner. We'll decide what to do with it then."

It was already dark out when Joey headed across the street to Lenny's house. Everyone still had the windows open because of the heat that still lingered in the air. Liddy's eyes lit up when she saw Joey enter their home. Now was her chance to thank him for saving her life the day before, but before she could even say hello, the boys disappeared into Lenny's bedroom.

They talked and talked but couldn't decide what to do, or if they should even tell their parents. They decided they couldn't let their parents know that they had been on the beach that far away from home. After all, they thought, who knows what their folks' reaction might be. No, they would keep this to themselves, at least for the time being.

"I hid it on the top rail of the fence, on the side yard away from my mom's garden. We'll let it dry out more and check it tomorrow, right after school," suggested Lenny.

"Yeah, it's too dark now to see anything anyway," Joey responded.

They talked a bit more, and then it was time for Joey to go home.

Liddy had waited patiently by the door, hoping for a chance to thank Joey. The boys were still talking to each other as Lenny led Joey to the door. Before Liddy could say a word, Joey was outside and heading home. Liddy looked out the living room window, hoping to wave goodbye, but Joey never turned around.

She whispered, "Good-bye, Joey," as she slowly lowered her hand. She walked to her bedroom, closed the door, and buried her face in her pillow.

***

The next day, promptly after completing his homework, Joey went to Lenny's house. Excited, they both went out to the backyard to check on the strange arm and its glass cylinder. They rushed over to the fence rail where Lenny said he had placed the object, but it wasn't there.

"Look, down there behind that pointed rock, just below the base of the fence," exclaimed Joey.

Lenny reached down and picked up what was left of the wooden arm. As he lifted a piece, it fell apart. The boys reasoned that the old wood had dried out so much that it must have shrunk, causing it to fall off the fence rail. The more they tried to put it back together, the more it disintegrated into unrecognizable splinters of wood. The blue cylinder had apparently landed directly on the point of the rock below and now lay cracked in the dirt next to it.

Disappointed, Lenny picked up the cylinder but quickly dropped it. "Damn, it's hot. Why is it hot? It's cool today." Lenny just couldn't understand it.

Joey ran back to Mrs. Leibowitz's garden bench and retrieved a little hand spade. A small chunk of glass had fallen out of the center of the cylinder, where a small portion of a mysterious round orb could be seen. Joey stuck the point of the spade into the small hole and forced the cylinder to break in half. A marble-like object fell out from between the small glass rails that once held it in place.

"Look, it's beautiful. It's like nothing I've ever seen before. All the jewelry in my dad's store doesn't compare to this," Lenny declared as he held the little sphere in his hand. "Joey, look at it. It's like it's a little planet with white for clouds, blue for water, and shades of brown for land. The ball is so polished, it almost looks translucent, yet it isn't." Lenny stopped for a moment, realizing his hand was shaking. It was as if the little sphere was too heavy for him to hold any longer, so he quickly placed it back down.

Joey was spellbound by what he saw in front of him. He touched it with his finger, and it felt warm to the touch.

"Pick it up, Joey," Lenny urged.

Joey gently picked the sphere up between his thumb and index finger. To Joey, it felt not too heavy, not too light. It was just right for its size. To him, it was simply magnificent. The heat he felt earlier had dissipated, and the sphere was now cool to the touch. It was as if it were now content.

"What should we do with it?" Joey asked, still holding it in his fingers.

"To be completely fair," Lenny replied, "you saw it first, so you should keep it."

"No. It's yours as much as mine. Besides, it was Liddy who first saw it."

Then it came to Lenny, and he declared, "I know what this is. It's solid, the right weight, the right size…oh! I think this would make the perfect shooter, the best boulder marble ever. It's almost magical. Don't you agree?"

"I don't really believe in magic. It's just a beautiful round piece of stone or something," Joey declared. He looked around at the scattered pieces of wood. He picked one up that looked sturdier than the others and placed it in his back pocket.

"I want to name it." The volume of Lenny's voice increased. Then he declared with a shout, "Let's call it VALHALLA!"

"Valhalla, it is then. You keep it, Lenny. Your dad's a jeweler. You should ask him what he thinks of it. I'm sure he'll know. Tell him we found it across from the golf course. That's the truth…well, sort of anyway."

"I'll do it tonight," Lenny replied.

***

Lenny showed the colorful sphere to his father later that evening and asked him what he thought it was.

"Hmm…let me take a closer look at that." He held the orb in his hand and remarked that it felt much heavier than it looked. "It's very clean and shiny. Did you just wash this in hot water, son? This gemstone feels warm."

Lenny looked at his dad but didn't respond. Benny reached into his pocket and pulled out his magnifier loupe. He placed the loupe close to the small, round object and inspected it from all angles.

"Where did you find this?" Benny asked.

"Joey and I were on the dunes by the golf course, and we saw it roll high up on the shore. We didn't even need to go near the water. It was really close, so Joey quickly scooped it up, and we came right home. It was in a glass case, held in place by wooden hands. The wood disintegrated into little pieces in the heat of the sun. The glass cylinder with this marble-like thing was all that was left."

Lenny's dad looked at him, doubt clearly etched on his face. "Where is the glass container it came in?" Benny asked.

"The backyard. I'll get it right now. It's broken in half, though," Lenny quickly added.

"Get gloves on, son, before you handle it," his dad cautioned him.

Soon, his dad was examining the glass cylinder. "Glass this color could indicate that it's very old indeed." Benny continued to inspect it. "It looks like the glass container was all one piece. I've never seen anything like this before. It's formed with a design on the inside as well as the outside, and I can't find a seam anywhere. From the shape and markings on the glass, I believe it was shaped to look like a scroll. The polished stone that was held in the center must have represented the tie in the middle of the scroll. I wouldn't be surprised if it perhaps fell off an old ship and has floated in the ocean for years. Very curious," Lenny's dad observed.

"But what's the round ball?" Lenny inquired.

His dad continued. "I'd like to take this to work with me tomorrow and have my boss look at it. He's seen gemstones from all over the world. He'll know for sure, but I guess that this is an agate gemstone formed from a quality piece of chalcedony...or more simply, quartz," he explained, so his son could better understand.

***

Benny kept the gemstone all week, after which he handed it back to Lenny in a small white box filled with cotton.

"It's just as I thought. This is a high-quality agate gemstone. You should save it. I doubt if you ever find anything like this again. It's truly brilliant, one of a kind."

Benny looked at his wife and told her he had good news. He had just received a raise. "We sold more items this week than in all the years I've worked at Fairmont Jewelers. Let's go out and celebrate. I am feeling good." Benny reached over and did a short dance with Sofia, spinning her around.

Liddy giggled and exclaimed, "Daddy got a raise. We're all so happy for you. Daddy, now you can give me an allowance too, just like Lenny."

Lenny didn't see his dad's good fortune as a coincidence. Instead, he thought, *how interesting! He has Valhalla one week, and all sorts of good things happen. I don't believe this is just a coincidence. It's the power of Valhalla. I'm sure of it.*

***

The school year ended, and summer break began once again. Lenny met with Joey and explained his beliefs about their agate marble. Knowing Joey would be skeptical, he compared the power of the brilliant marble to the biblical story of Samson and Delilah.

"You see, Joey, Samson believed his long hair gave him enormous strength. Perhaps you were destined to find this marble so that it would give you a special power just like Samson."

"The marble belongs to both of us, Lenny, not just me."

"No, Joey. I thought about this all week. You were the first to pick it up. It came to you. I'm sure of it. I have vivid dreams sometimes. I don't always know what they mean, but this past week, I've had the same dream every night. In it, I saw you holding Valhalla, and you were glowing with happiness. It's meant for you, not me." After finishing, Lenny handed Joey a small silk pouch that contained the special gemstone.

"One day, you'll pass this on to someone else who is as deserving as you. Until then, keep it safe," Lenny insisted.

***

One Sunday afternoon, Liddy saw Joey sitting on the front porch of his home. He was whittling a piece of wood with a small knife. A huge pile of wood shavings lay at his feet.

She walked across the street and asked what Joey was making.

"I'm almost done, Liddy," he said.

Joey continued to shape the wood. When he had finished, he held it up to show Liddy. She looked at what he had carved and then down at the large pile of shavings.

"You whittled that little cross from all that?" she asked. "That's a big pile of wood for such a little thing."

Joey smiled and said, "Yes, it is. There wasn't much good wood left. Besides, I'm not going to hang it on my bedroom wall. I'm going to take a small skinny nail and drill a hole through the top part. I'll run a narrow round shoelace through it, so I can wear it around my neck. I'm going to leave it roughly cut, so it has sort of a unique character to it."

The small cross was about a quarter-inch thick, one and a half inches long, and an inch across.

Liddy was impressed.

When Joey was finished with it, he wouldn't show it to anyone else, not even Lenny or Eddie. He wore it under his shirt every day.

CHAPTER 5

RINGER ROCK

Lenny, Eddie, and Joey, along with some other boys from school, decided to celebrate their time out of school by having a marble championship tournament. It was mostly Eddie's idea, but everyone was looking forward to the challenge. They began to refer to it as the World Series of Marbles. Word quickly spread throughout the neighborhood that the coming Friday afternoon would be the day of the tournament.

Kids of varying ages were invited to participate. Jeff Baker, Ronny Baumgartner, Carlos Rodriguez, Little Georgie Kaufman, and Alex Smith, or Smithy as he was called, all showed up to participate. They played each game of ringer in groups of two, and every game was for keeps. They played for all the marbles. The winner of each game not only kept the marbles he knocked out of the ring, but all of his opponent's marbles too.

To everyone's surprise, Beth Ann Codington, along with her sister, Coleen, showed up to the once-secret place now referred to as Ringer Rock.

Eddie smiled when he saw Beth Ann. He thought, *I'll be the world champion, and she'll witness everything. I'll leave no quarter. They'll all fall at the strike of my steelie.*

They drew names out of a baseball cap to see which two would go first. The winners would continue on, and the losers would be out of the tournament. Just as they were about to begin, two more girls, Lidia and her friend Bridgette Dubois, joined the growing group of spectators. Coleen noticed how Lidia wouldn't take her eyes off of Joey. She turned to look at her sister, Beth Ann, and she also seemed fixated on Joey.

"This may be the biggest event in the history of Sharp Park," proudly proclaimed Smithy.

The first two names out of the hat were Joey and Georgie. Joey pulled out his old, worn commie shooter, but Lenny stopped him.

Lenny looked at Joey and said, "Did you bring it, like I asked?"

"Yes. But I don't want to mar it." Joey replied.

"Use it. It can't be hurt. Believe me."

Joey pulled the small silk pouch out of his pocket and rolled out Valhalla. Lenny smiled broadly. Everyone's attention was now on Joey's new shooter. "Can we touch it?" they asked.

Lenny responded for Joey. "You can look at it, but you can't touch it. We call this shooter Valhalla, after the Viking afterlife. I will tell you now before we begin that the holder of Valhalla can't be beat. It holds a special power."

"What a bunch of shi…manure." Eddie caught his words, remembering who was watching. "There will only be one winner, and you all know who that will be. Me," boasted Eddie.

Two by two, they played until Joey and Eddie were the last two remaining. To everyone's amazement, Joey easily won each of his matches. He had cleaned his opponents out, rarely missing a shot with his Valhalla shooter.

Just before Eddie and Joey were to begin their match, Eddie made a proposition. "We play this for all the marbles, including shooters. The winner takes home the marbles won, not just in this match, but for all of the preceding matches as well."

Beth Ann shouted, "You can beat him, Joey."

Liddy nodded her head in agreement. Coleen observed everything and just smiled.

Eddie looked at Beth Ann with disbelief in his eyes. Now he was determined even more to destroy his friend Joey. Anger consumed his heart.

"I agree, with one provision—we both keep our shooters. Otherwise, we just play for the championship and nothing else," Joey countered.

"What are you, chicken? Afraid because you know you're already a loser, before the game even begins? I tell you what. I'll trade all the marbles I've won so far just for your new shooter. That's how generous I am. Then we play a normal set of ringer for fair instead of keepsie. That's your speed anyway," Eddie replied sarcastically.

"No. Valhalla will always be mine. We play for all the marbles except for shooters. That was the shooter rule before the tournament began."

Seeing Joey's steadfastness, Eddie finally agreed, and they started the championship game. Joey won the lag, and Eddie would shoot second. Each of them placed thirteen of his best marbles in the ring. Joey knocked out twelve marbles in one series of shots. When he started to aim at the thirteenth marble, an easy shot, he suddenly stopped. *I could clear the whole ring. Eddie wouldn't even get a shot. I can't do that. It's just not right. This means everything to him. He's too proud. He didn't mean what he said to me. He's still my friend.* Joey aimed at the thirteenth marble and missed.

Eddie surveyed the remaining marbles carefully and quickly knocked out nine in quick succession before missing. Joey then knocked out all of the remaining marbles to win the championship. All the girls watching jumped up and cheered. Beth Ann jumped down and hugged Joey.

"Come and find me later," she whispered in his ear.

Eddie sat there for a moment, not quite sure what had just happened. *Did I just lose?* He put his remaining marbles in a sock and flung them at Joey, saying, "A deal's a deal. Here's all the marbles."

"Keep them, Eddie." Joey tossed the sock back in his direction.

Eddied turned, walked away, and left them lying on the ground. He never played marbles again. He reasoned, *what do I care? Baseball trading cards are better anyway.*

***

On the way back home, when no one was looking, Beth Ann kissed Joey on the cheek. On her birthday later that summer, she kissed him on his lips. From that point on, they were labeled as "secretly going steady," according to their friends. That summer would come to be known as the "Summer of Codington" in Joey's journal.

Joey and the other boys, minus Eddie, continued to play one or two games of ringer every week during that summer. Joey eventually grew tired of winning and would, more often than not, just watch the others play. He'd give words of praise when a good shot was made. When he did participate, he would only play for fair.

Eddie didn't come around as much anymore. Joey would knock on his door and ask him if he wanted to play, but mostly, Eddie kept to himself.

Good fortune seemed to follow Joey everywhere. He hunted for lost golf balls on the course near his home and sold those he found back to the golfers for extra cash. Even his dad's shoe-store business picked up—so much so that he finally gave Joey an allowance for completing his chores every week and purchased their first fourteen-inch black-and-white RCA Victor television.

Joey would watch his favorite cartoon program about Crusader Rabbit and Rags the Tiger every weekend. A few years later, he'd have his first TV girl crush for Annette Funicello, who was one of the stars on the *Mickey Mouse Club* TV show. Life was so good to Joey—TV, good friends, how could life get any better?

***

Beth Ann introduced Lenny to one of her friends who lived on the other side of Highway 1. Her name was Susan Prouder. She was tall and thin. Lenny stood taller than Susan, which pleased her because most boys her age were much shorter than she was. He had seen her in school before, but she never paid much attention to him. When Joey had enough money, they'd all go to the movies together. All was good in Joey's life.

Lenny was well aware that all the girls in the neighborhood seemed to have a crush on Joey at one time or another. Joey just never seemed to notice. Lenny wondered, *is it Joey's pleasant demeanor and good looks that serve him so well, or is it because he possesses Valhalla?*

By the end of the summer, Joey had outgrown playing marbles, but one special marble he would carry in his pocket long after storing his others away. Valhalla would remain with him wherever he ventured.

***

In late August, Eddie's parents, John and Elizabeth Davis, invited all the neighbors to a backyard BBQ. They had just finished adding a new office and upstairs bathroom to their home. The backyard had a new brick smoker and grill, and John was eager to show it off. His wife, Liz, was a tall, slender woman who, with her spiked high heels, stood well over six feet tall. She had all the right curves in all the right places, and all the neighbor men took notice whenever she came out to pick up her morning paper. Her clothes and mannerisms matched her high-class looks, which seemed out of place for the small community of Sharp Park. John, a man of six feet four, was an engineer by trade, and it was clear that Eddie's family had money. Today, their Cadillac, which was normally parked inside the garage, was out on the newly paved street. Inside the garage was a makeshift table—a set of planks lying across two sawhorses and covered with two tablecloths. That would be for the kids to enjoy. The backyard was reserved for grown-ups only. Throughout the BBQ, Liz held a cocktail in one hand and a cigarette in the other. She talked more with the men than she did with the women. More than one of the neighborhood wives gave their husbands a good talking-to after the party. All in all, the BBQ was a huge success, and everyone enjoyed the get-together, especially the men.

The party was also an opportunity for the boys to get back together. Eddie was gradually getting over his animosity toward

Joey and his frustration with Beth Ann. He longed once again to hang out with his first two friends in town.

***

Liz Davis would pick up the *Chronicle* every morning. She'd sit on her front porch with a coffee cup in her hand, smoking a cigarette. While the other women in the neighborhood wore long, heavy cotton robes to pick up the newspaper or the milkman's morning delivery, Liz would wear a rather sexy, thin silk robe.

Mrs. Miller, the lady who lived right next door to the Davis family, told Sofia and Ruth that what Mrs. Davis had in her cup sure wasn't coffee. She had stopped by the Davises' home early one morning to borrow some sugar, and Liz reeked of gin and tonic.

"Do you know that the milkman almost crashed his truck looking at that woman? I witnessed it myself," Mrs. Miller said with a disgusted tone in her voice. She went on to say that she heard from a friend of a friend who knew a man who worked at the same firm as Mr. Davis, the real reason they moved to Sharp Park. Apparently, they had a very nice apartment in San Francisco, but there were too many nightclubs and dance halls around the city. Mrs. Davis liked the nightlife a little too much, prompting John Davis to buy a home in the quiet little Sharp Park. Their first year in town was a quiet one, but ever since Liz's husband started working late, things had changed. Mrs. Miller said she could hear them bickering with each other and sometimes yelling very loudly.

***

At the end of summer, word got out that striped bass were running south along the coastline. Joey and Lenny spotted Eddie standing on the sandbank looking north, holding a long fishing pole. Eddie had learned to fish from his father and uncle. They fished the ocean and the delta region of Northern California at least twice a year and always took Eddie with them.

The boys, along with Odin, walked north from Salada Beach to Manor Beach and watched the fishermen on shore reel in large striped bass, one after another.

"Stand back," Eddie cautioned as he cast the line from his heavy fishing rod well past the waves. He had pitched his line farther than the adult men on shore. Surprised, a few of them turned and looked at Eddie. Try as they might, none could cast his line farther than the boy. The boys started talking, and before you knew it, all was forgotten, and they were best buddies once again. Eddie pulled in three stripers that day, with Joey right by his side. Odin barked and jumped with each fish Eddie reeled in. Eddie walked away feeling like a hero once again, or maybe it was just because his two best friends were with him. In the years to come, fishing became Eddie's great passion. Eddie never asked Joey about Beth Ann. He endeavored to put the sweet thoughts of her out of his mind. As time passed, it seemed to be working.

***

Another school year had begun, and Eddie was elated to hear that Joey had broken up with Beth Ann. Joey really liked her, but he reasoned, *what do I know about girls anyway?* They had mostly held hands, traded a few kisses, but really, they had nothing else in common. It was more of a status thing than anything else, and that wasn't what Joey was about. He liked just about every sport, and she was more into academic endeavors. The thrill of a first girlfriend slowly wore off for Joey. Maybe puberty just hadn't set in yet for him. He believed he needed to mature more before settling on any one girl.

Once word got out about the breakup, it was open season on Joey Gunderson. Although he liked all the girls' attention, he wasn't ready to go steady again. Nevertheless, every girl he knew invited him to birthday parties, beach parties, you name it. Some even invited him to fake parties. Many a girl set her trap for him, but eventually, they all had their feelings crushed by his rejections.

Ever since he possessed Valhalla, he had the nagging feeling he had already met the girl for him, but who? He could almost feel her. *She's there somewhere nearby, but where?*

Lenny could not understand why Joey couldn't settle on just one girl. Unknowingly, Joey had broken just too many hearts in Lenny's eyes. Lenny began to think that maybe Valhalla also carried a curse.

***

Two years passed by quickly. By the time Joey was in eighth grade, he had broken the hearts of several more girls. The sad part was that Joey couldn't even see how his casual rebuffs caused those girls so much heartache. Lenny saw it clearly. He suggested that Joey not carry Valhalla to school with him anymore.

Joey would laugh and say, "The marble has nothing to do with girls liking me. I can't help it if I'm a cool, good-looking guy."

"Joey, you have to admit that you started playing baseball a whole lot better right after you started carrying Valhalla. Surely you can see that, can't you?"

"I feel more confident when I have it in my pocket, that's all," Joey explained.

Each summer, the three boys played in a small baseball league. Eight teams from the surrounding coastal communities competed. Joey played left field; Lenny was the first baseman, and Eddie was the team's catcher. Eddie was the home-run leader each season, but Joey always won MVP, the team's most valuable player. This always irked Eddie. It seemed so unfair to him.

Lenny told Eddie not to worry about it so much. He explained, "It's only because he holds the power of Valhalla. If either of us possessed the great marble, we'd be MVP instead."

From that moment on, Eddie firmly believed the little orb held the power of good fortune for whoever possessed it. Several times, Eddie offered Joey increasing amounts of money to buy the prized agate marble, but Joey always gave the same reply. "Valhalla's not for sale. It can't be bought, not for any price."

***

In their last year at Sharp Park School, Big Eddie got suspended for three days. He and a few other friends were on the playground watching Lenny and Joey play basketball when he overheard Rich Brookmeyer, a tall, stocky kid, and Carlos Rodriguez talking about Beth Ann Codington. Rich was watching Bethie when a gust of wind blew her dress well above her knees.

"I'd like to get me some of that. She's got those long legs, just right to wrap around my waist. Look at those sweet perky boobs, hmm, and good enough to kiss. I know she'd enjoy my big—"

Before he could say another word, a large hand grabbed him by his shirt, ripping it half off, and hard he went onto the concrete. Dazed and confused, Rich got back to his feet, and as

Eddie approached him again, he shoved Eddie away. Rich was lucky enough to get off two hard punches to Eddie's face. The punches didn't faze Eddie at all. Eddie reached out and pulled Rich by the hair to keep him from getting away. Holding Rich by the hair, he pounded his face with punch after punch. All sorts of whistles started blowing, and before the two boys knew it, they were restrained by three of the male teachers. Mrs. Burk, Eddie's prior fifth-grade teacher, stood between the two boys. She shook her head at Eddie, disappointedly. Rich's nose and lip were bleeding all over what was left of his shirt.

As Eddie and Rich were carted off to the principal's office, Beth Ann walked over to Joey and Lenny, where they stood mystified by what had just happened.

"I can't see what I ever saw in him. He's such a jerk, nothing but a bully."

"Who, Rich?" Joey asked.

"No, Eddie. Didn't you see what happened?" Beth angrily replied. "He just blindsided poor Richard Brookmeyer and ripped his shirt to shreds without giving him any warning. What kind of person does that? All Richard tried to do was defend himself, and for that, Eddie just beat his face to a bloody pulp. Richard has never done a bad thing to anybody for as long as I've known him. How could I have ever been so mistaken? How could I have ever liked Eddie?"

Eddie was suspended from school for three days. His parents grounded him for a week, and they had to buy Richard Brookmeyer a new shirt. Additionally, Eddie also had to personally apologize to Richard before he'd ever be allowed back in school.

Eddie would only tell the principal and school counselor that Rich was foul-mouthing Beth Ann and would say nothing more.

Carlos Rodriquez, on the other hand, told the school counselor what he witnessed. He said that Eddie was completely mistaken about Rich's comments.

Carlos went on to say that his good friend Richard only said that Beth Ann Codington was a sweet, very pretty girl. "He wished he could just hold her hand," said Carlos. "She's always so perky. She brightens up a foggy day. He wished she would hug him, to wrap her arms around him, like when she greets her girlfriends. That would make his day. When Rich was about to say she'd probably enjoy his…company, Eddie jerked him off the bench and threw him to the ground. It looked like he was going to stomp on my good friend. Richard's only choice was to defend himself. That's the truth, every word of it. I swear."

The guidance counselor met with Eddie and made it clear to him that there was no excuse for what he did. There were other, peaceful ways to resolve conflicts. The following week, Eddie was brought into the principal's office to personally apologize to Richard for his actions.

"I'm sorry, Richard. I should have taken a more peaceful course of action with you. I apologize for ripping your shirt and punching the hell…excuse me…I mean, hitting you so damn hard…I mean, hitting you at all, because of what I believed you had said. I will never cause you trouble again, I give you my word," Eddie said, trying his best to sound sincere.

"I accept your apology" was Richard's simple response. They both shook hands to seal things. Richard knew what he really said about Beth Ann and wanted this situation over and done with.

It would be over a week before Eddie could give a detailed account to his friends, Lenny and Joey.

***

"Eddie, Beth Ann doesn't know your side of the story. Everyone believes what Carlos and Richard said went down that day. You need to let her know," urged Lenny.

"What am I supposed to say? Repeat the words Rich actually spoke? No. It's Carlos's and Rich's word against mine. Besides, she's apparently already made up her mind about what she believes. I won't bow down to her anymore. Oh well. *C'est la vie.* We're graduating from eighth grade soon. I'll be looking forward to meeting some hot new chicks in high school anyway."

"*C'est la vie?*" Joey inquired.

Eddie replied, "I suggest you take French as your first language class."

The school year ended the following month, and there was one last summer of baseball before the boys headed off to high school in the fall.

CHAPTER 6

CALENDAR GIRL

The day before the start of high school, Joey asked Lenny to be sure to meet with Beth Ann. Bethie had been cool toward Joey ever since their breakup a few years before.

Joey urged Lenny, "I've thought about this a long time now, and it eats away at me. Tell her the truth about what really caused the fight between Big Eddie and Richard. She respects you. It will be up to her to decide, and not mince words. Apologize first, and then say the exact words Richard used, the same as Eddie told us."

"She'll slap the hell out of me if I use those words."

"Let her if need be. I know her well enough to know she'll give what you tell her serious thought," Joey pleaded.

Lenny did as Joey requested. Beth Ann didn't say much of anything, but she was clearly stunned by the words Lenny used to describe the event. When Lenny had finished, she simply asked him to leave.

***

It was during their freshman year at Westmoor High School that Eddie began giving everyone nicknames. He said it helped him to remember all the new names of people at their new school in Daly City. Westmoor High School was located about seven miles north. A school bus transported everyone to the recently completed and very modern high school. The first day was an exciting day.

That day, as the teenagers stood outside waiting for the school bus, a narrow eucalyptus leaf fell and landed on Lenny's head. His hair was slicked down with so much Brylcreem that he didn't notice. Lenny sat on the bus with the leaf on his head all the way to school. The leaf remained there until Joey laughingly picked it off his head just before entering his first period class. From that day on, Lenny was forever known as Lenny the Leaf, or simply the Leaf. Joey's nickname became Gunner, short for Gunderson. Lenny and Joey had already given Eddie the nickname of Big Eddie Davis while in grade school. Beth Ann was known as Beth the Babe by all the boys. Eddie named another local girl, Wanda Boothman, Wonder Boobsman, but most guys just referred to her as the Stacked One, for very obvious reasons. Wanda had matured significantly during the summer break.

May Jun, a tenth grader who recently moved from the city to the Manor, was one of the first Asian girls in that part of town. Eddie had seen her around town a couple of weeks before school was about to begin. He asked some of his Manor friends if they knew anything about her. They knew little except for her name and age. He knew he just had to meet her.

Eddie watched as she got on the bus at the Manor stop. She smiled in his direction as she came up the bus steps. Once Eddie found out her name, he quickly nicknamed her Calendar Girl. Her hair was as dark as coal but shiny as silk, and her eyes were the darkest of browns. She wore tight clothes to accentuate her blossoming figure but was careful not to be too provocative. She was a year older than Eddie, but apparently didn't care about any age difference.

She purposely bumped into him in the cafeteria the first day of school, right before Beth Ann was about to say hello to him. She immediately whisked him away from Bethie, apologizing for not looking where she was walking.

"I'm so embarrassed," she told him, but she wasn't embarrassed at all. She had been smitten with Eddie as soon as she saw him. *He's tall and kind of rugged, just the type of guy I like. My friends will never guess or even care that he's younger than me.*

They had lunch together in the cafeteria, and from that moment on, Calendar Girl had Eddie twisted around her little finger. Beth Ann was just a distant memory to him now.

Beth Ann sat two tables away with her friend Susan, all the while glaring at May Jun. Beth Ann had been going to ask Eddie to sit with her that day. She wanted to have a serious talk with him, but May Jun ruined everything. Beth Ann was secretly hoping to rekindle Ed's feelings for her, the same feelings she had begun to feel for him before the Liddy incident. She sat there and wondered, *why did I have to fall so quickly for Joey? I don't understand it. I normally choose who I like very carefully. It was like lightning hit me, and my mind turned to mush. I feel like such a fool, and why did I believe Carlos and Richard over Ed? I have to get him back. I was so wrong.* Her thoughts were interrupted by Susan, who began to gossip about that petite golden-haired girl, Bridgette Dubois.

"Susan, I don't want to hear anything about Bridgette. She's a friend of Liddy and therefore a friend of mine. I don't want to be known as a gossip, and neither should you." Bethie then went on to say, "By the way, I hear that May Jun smokes cigarettes."

"Ugh!" Susan moaned.

They finished lunch, and Beth Ann made it her goal to win Big Ed back. She couldn't stand to see him with that older girl, May Jun. *Hmm…maybe I should ask Ed to tutor me once again.*

***

They were seven months into high school when Joey noticed a gradual change in Big Eddie's attitude. He wasn't the easygoing big lug he used to be. As Joey opened his school locker, he wondered, *is it Calendar Girl's effect on him, or is it just Eddie growing up? He's moody and short-tempered with everyone, even his best friends.*

Lenny approached just as Joey was closing his locker, about to head off.

"Joey, did you hear?

"No, what?"

"I heard my mom tell my dad that the Davises are getting a divorce. She said they decided to stay together for now, but in separate bedrooms. They'll finalize everything after Eddie graduates from high school."

"And how would your mom know that kind of stuff?"

"Mrs. Miller, the Davises' next-door neighbor, heard them arguing about it the other day. She was in her backyard hanging laundry. Do you think Eddie knows?"

"Eddie's smart. I'm sure he suspects something. Maybe that explains some things," Joey replied as he hurried to his next class.

Lenny and Joey were sitting on a bench finishing their lunches and discussing Eddie's situation when May Jun wandered by. For some reason, Joey felt compelled to pull Valhalla out of his pocket right as she passed them. He stared at it for a second and then went to put it back into the pouch when he saw Calendar Girl turn around and look his way.

"What is that you have in your hand, Joey? May I see it?" May Jun's enticing voice was like soft music in his ears.

Joey let her hold Valhalla in her hands, but she quickly handed the shiny orb back to him.

"It's very hot," she commented. "My, my, Joey, what else is in your pocket that generates so much heat? I think someday I'll have to personally see what you keep in there," she said, very coyly and suggestively.

Lenny looked at Joey's face, which was turning a bright red. He thought, *wow, she oozes sex appeal. It's easy to see why Eddie likes her so much.*

Later, on the bus back home, Calendar Girl squeezed past Lenny and sat next to Joey. She placed her hand on his leg, asked how he was doing, and if he had a girlfriend. Big Eddie was one of the last teens to board the bus. He asked Joey to move so that he could sit next to his girlfriend. Joey immediately complied and headed to the back of the bus, where Lenny was sitting.

"May, where were you? I waited at our usual spot. I worried when you didn't show."

"Oh, Ed, I got out of class and decided to meet you at the bus instead." She kissed Ed and then turned her head back to quickly wink at Joey.

Big trouble was on the horizon, and his name was Big Eddie Davis. Lenny could see it plain as day. Hopefully, Joey wasn't blinded by Calendar Girl's wily ways.

Joey did his best to avoid May Jun. If he saw her coming his way, he'd turn and walk the opposite direction. During the lunch break, he started taking a roundabout route to the cafeteria just to avoid her. Lenny would be halfway done with his lunch before Joey arrived. Lenny was the one who suggested Joey stay as far away from Calendar Girl as possible.

One afternoon, when Joey rounded a corner on his way to meet Lenny, he found himself snatched by the hand of May Jun.

"Joey, I need to talk with you. I think you've been trying to avoid me. Haven't you?"

Joey shook his head no.

"Remember when Ed introduced me to you? I knew then that you were someone special. One time, when I touched you, static electricity rocketed through my finger, but not in a bad way. It just tingled, and I didn't want it to stop."

Before Joey could say a word, May Jun pressed herself against him and kissed him passionately.

"No, Cal…I mean, May Jun. You're Eddie's girl, and he's one of my closest friends. I can never be with you, even if you and Ed break up. Don't you understand?"

May Jun, still holding Joey close to her breast, whispered softly in his ear, "That's OK. Ed doesn't need to know. It can be our little secret. Just think about it tonight when you go to bed. Think about me."

Calendar Girl let Joey go and ran off to meet Eddie for lunch, just as she did every day.

Joey skipped lunch. Instead, he sat on the hill overlooking the football field, trying to decide if he should tell Eddie or not. He couldn't decide because the sound of her sweet whisper was still echoing in his ear.

Joey stayed close to Lenny for the rest of the school week. He never told Lenny what had happened the day he didn't show for lunch.

The weekend came, and the three boys, along with some other friends, headed off to play basketball at the Sharp Park playground. After playing a couple of hoops, Eddie excused himself and walked to the Manor to see his girlfriend. Lenny pulled Joey aside and said he knew something had happened between Calendar Girl and Joey.

"How?" Joey inquired.

"I could easily say my dreams, but I don't need those to see that she has a thing for you. I'll tell you right now. Big Eddie already knows something is up. Be on your guard, my friend."

"But I don't know what to do. I am afraid to tell Ed, and to be honest, I can't get May Jun out of my head. What should I do, Lenny? I really need your help."

"Don't bring Valhalla with you to school anymore. Understand? You may not know it, but I've heard other girls talk about you. You're playing a dangerous game, carrying Valhalla with you all the time."

"That marble has nothing to do with this. It has no power. It won't help at all to leave it at home," Joey declared.

"Then leave it at home if it doesn't make any difference."

Joey decided he'd leave the marble home on Monday, just to see if anything changed. Monday morning, he went through his normal routine and headed out the door, only to turn around and race back to his room.

Valhalla was in his pocket. Taking it with him every day had become automatic, a habit for him. He rushed back to his room to put the special marble back where he kept it each night.

"Not today, my friend," he said as he placed it back in his nightstand drawer.

***

It was near the end of their freshman year in high school. Everyone was getting anxious for school to end and the summer to begin. Joey felt anxious for other reasons; he couldn't shake the feeling that part of him was missing, without Valhalla. He had carried it every day for years, and it was unsettling to reach into his pocket, only to find it empty.

During a break between classes, Eddie asked both Joey and Lenny to sit with him during lunch. May Jun wouldn't be there. She had called in sick that day.

Joey was relieved. It was just like old times. Eddie and the boys were back together again. At least, that's what he thought. All seemed well until Eddie opened his lunch bag. Inside was a sandwich composed of two dry, stale pieces of Wonder bread, with a moldy piece of cheese in between. Also included was an overly ripe banana.

"Damn, my mother must have been half asleep when she made this last night," he muttered.

Lenny thought that *more likely she was half snookered with gin.*

"What do you have there, Joey?" Eddie quickly reached into Joey's bag, pulled out an apple, and took a bite out of it. Just as quickly, he grabbed Joey's sandwich and ate half of it before Joey could even protest.

"Here, Joey, you can have my lunch. I'll just trade mine for yours." Clearly, Eddie wasn't asking Joey's permission.

Lenny started to rethink things. *Maybe Eddie made that sandwich himself, especially for Joey.*

"You know, Joey, I waited a long time to meet someone as beautiful as Beth Ann Codington. Someone sweet and kind—and I finally found that in May Jun. She's really not like the person she makes herself out to be. It's all a front to gain attention, to be noticed. I've met her family, and believe me, she gets very little attention from them. They basically ignore her. When we're alone together, her real personality comes out. May Jun's really a shy girl, a good girl. That's what I like most about her."

Eddie paused and looked down, as if to gather his words carefully. He looked back up and continued. "I went to see her yesterday, and after her parents left to go shopping, we went into her bedroom for the first time. We started kissing. She was more passionate than I've ever seen her before. Just as things started to get interesting, she whispered in my ear, 'I love you…JOEY.'

"Can you believe it? I almost laughed. No, not really. Even after she said it, she had no clue. She didn't understand why I just got up and left. Maybe she realized it later. Perhaps that's why she's out of school today. I'm sick of you stealing my girls away. I thought you were my friend, but now I know you're just a backstabbing son of a bitch."

Eddie picked up the banana and smashed it on the table. "Oops…well, there's still a chunk left for you to enjoy." He stood up, pushed Joey's face into the moldy cheese sandwich, and walked away. Before exiting the lunchroom, he stopped, turned around, and said, "Lenny the Leaf, my good friend, a word of advice. Don't continue hanging around with such a low-life loser. He'll steal whatever girl you end up caring for, just as he does everyone else."

"Eddie, wait!" was all that Joey was able to say.

Eddie ignored him and walked out the doorway. Joey sat there, stunned and shaking. Joey dreaded his fifth-period Physical Education class later in the day. Big Eddie was in that class too. Nevertheless, Joey mustered up enough courage to speak with Eddie during PE. Scared or not, he needed to defuse the situation. Big Eddie just glared at him and shoved him away.

"Stay away from me. If you see me on the street, cross over to the other side. If I'm in the school hallway, don't even look at me. This is my only warning to you, Gunner, or should I just call you Ass Wipe from now on? Stay away. You know I mean it."

The eventful day finally ended, and as Joey gazed out the window of the bus on his way home, dismay and confusion filled his thoughts. *Is Valhalla the only reason Calendar Girl likes me? Would*

Eddie's reaction have been different if I had Valhalla on me? No, I think not…maybe, I'm just not sure. Joey did his best not to cross paths with Eddie again. He came to believe that Valhalla was as much a curse as it was a blessing.

Big Eddie Davis was never quite the same after his breakup with Calendar Girl. His home life was in shambles. His grades began to slip, and worst of all, he really missed the friendship he once had with Joey. On the other hand, he still considered Lenny the Leaf as good a friend as ever.

For the remainder of the school year, Eddie would get on the school bus and sometimes take Joey's lunch bag away from him. Eddie would toss Joey his lunch bag in exchange. Eddie's bag always contained something rotten. On the last day of school, Big Eddie took Joey's lunch once again and gave Joey a bag that contained Odin's poop, which Eddie had scooped up the day before, after he saw the dog do his duty in the sand. Joey never protested. He simply dumped the bag in the first garbage can he saw and went on his way. It was as if Joey believed he really caused the trouble with May Jun and Eddie, all by himself. He felt guilty about his desire for Calendar Girl. Lenny repeatedly tried to convince Joey he had done nothing wrong. The Leaf tried his best to get Eddie and Joey back together again, but Eddie wouldn't even talk about it. Joey didn't exist in Big Eddie's world anymore.

May Jun tried to win Ed back the entire last month of school, but without success. She would now sit on the opposite side of the cafeteria, far away from Big Ed. They just went their separate ways.

On the final day of the school year, Calendar Girl stopped by Joey's locker and asked him to meet her after school. She said it was important. Joey met with her behind the Sea View Theater, just as she requested, because she didn't want anyone to see them together. May Jun told Joey she didn't mean to hurt Big Ed, that she really cared for him. It tore her apart to lose him. She still missed him. Several times she'd tried to talk with him in the hopes of getting back together, but to no avail. May Jun expressed how sorry she was to see how Ed was treating Joey.

"Why don't you stand up to him? Don't let him humiliate you, Joey."

"May, Eddie's a big, very strong guy. The best I can do is ignore him and stay away from him. Besides, I've been taught to turn the other cheek in this type of situation. I'll do well to him, even if he does ill to me."

"That's crazy. Staying away from him makes sense, but treating him well after what's he's done to you? That's something I don't understand," May replied.

Joey stepped closer to May Jun. "May, Eddie was right about one thing. I wanted you from the beginning. I tried not to show it, but that obviously didn't work. You were always on my mind, and Eddie knows me well. He must have realized I had feelings for you early on."

May Jun leaned into him, placed her arms around his neck, and kissed him softly on the lips. "I want you to be my boyfriend, Joey. We'll keep it all a secret. You can visit with me all summer, here in the Manor. Ed doesn't come this way anymore."

Joey stood there, tempted and confused, but he remembered his words to her before. Even if she broke up with Eddie, he could never be her boyfriend. Joey stepped away but held onto May's hand.

"I can't, May. Remember when I said I couldn't be with you even if you broke up with Eddie? I can't go back on what I said. It's something I just don't do."

"Ed told you himself he's no longer your friend. There is no obligation to him anymore. Don't you see? What you promised was because of friendship. That's over now. Let's go to my house, where it's warm. I'm sure we can work this out." May smiled coyly and began walking back to her house, still holding his hand.

Joey walked with her to her front door. She opened it and called out to ask if anyone was home. No one answered.

"Good," she said, and she stepped inside, turning to invite Joey in.

"Good-bye, May. I really like you a lot, but if I go with you now, then everything Eddie said about me is true. It wouldn't just be in my thoughts as before. Eddie may not look at me as his friend anymore, but as hard as it is to understand, I still consider him my friend."

Joey turned and walked away. Halfway back to Sharp Park, he wondered, *why should I walk away from May Jun? I'm such an idiot. I should turn back now.* But he didn't because, in his heart, Joey knew that as much as he was attracted to Calendar Girl, she wasn't the one for him. Joey put his lust aside and stayed true to his word. Joey had now broken May Jun's heart, just as he had broken so many hearts before—only this time he knew it, and it hurt.

***

Beth Ann Codington viewed Ed's breakup with May Jun as an opportunity. Shortly after the breakup, she boldly sat next to him at lunch and asked him to tutor her once again. She was planning to attend summer school. Ed was tempted but didn't want to risk getting involved with Bethie again. He politely declined her request, and that set Beth Ann off on a tirade.

"I've liked you since grade school. That's the truth. I wanted you to tutor me during the summer, so we would have a chance to get together. I truly care about you, Ed. Can't you see that? I want to be with you."

Big Ed listened to her but didn't respond.

When Ed didn't respond, Beth Ann changed the subject to Joey. "You know it wasn't Joey's fault. May Jun was never good for you. I know she was the one who made a play for Joey, not the other way around. Joey rejected her advances, I'm sure of it. I'll admit that Calendar Girl has a certain charm and sex appeal, but that's where it all ends. Joey stayed true to his friendship with you. You're just too blind to see it. You know him. You know he'd never betray your trust. You pick on him, you bully him, and you cut him down every chance you get. Just stop it, please. He was your friend."

"Done?" Big Ed responded. "I'd like to finish my lunch now. See you later."

Shocked that he didn't seem to care, Beth Ann left, went into the girls' room, and cried.

***

The summer came and went too quickly, and the boys began their sophomore year. Big Ed continued where he had left off with Joey the year before. Big Ed's actions toward Joey sent a clear message to any punk in school that Joey was an easy target. To almost every guy, Joey now appeared to be a wimp.

Even after school, the other kids in the Carmel Avenue neighborhood viewed Joey differently than before. Some felt sorry for him, and others just decided they didn't like him anymore. Lenny and his sister, Lidia, always stayed true to Joey. Lenny's dog Odin, now called Odie by Liddy, always wagged his

tail whenever Joey was nearby. That dog would do just about any
trick that Joey asked of him.

Big Eddie was watching them play out of his living room
window one afternoon. He wanted to go outside, but with Joey
there, he decided it was best to just watch the three of them play
in the street with Odie.

Ronny Baumgartner came walking down the street and
stopped to see what they were doing. Joey considered Ronny a
friend. When Joey tossed a tennis ball to Odie, Ronny jumped up
and caught the ball instead. Unfortunately, he also accidentally
stepped on Odie's paw. Odie growled at him with disapproval.
Ronny glared at the little mixed-breed dog and kicked him. Odie
winced, and Liddy quickly picked him up and moved safely away.
Lenny shoved Ronny and told him to leave. When Ronny walked
by Joey, he grabbed Joey's shirt, and something snapped. Still
holding Joey by the shirt, he threatened to hit him for no good
reason. Joey just stood there and did nothing.

He looked at Baumgartner. "I thought you were my friend,
Ronny. I don't fight my friends."

Baumgartner was taken aback by Joey's calm response, and as
he walked away, he said, "I'm sorry I kicked your dog, Lenny.
Sorry, Joey." He then continued on his way.

In the street at Joey's feet lay what was left of the handmade
cross that he had spent hours carving. Liddy saw the look of
disappointment in his eyes. She reached down, picked up the
pieces, and handed them to him. In her heart, she felt his pain.

***

Joey went back inside his house. He could hear Mama
Morales talking to his mother in the kitchen. Mama was angry.

All the communities from the Manor to the San Pedro Valley of Linda Mar were now one city—the city of Pacifica.

"How could they vote for such a name?" Mama Morales lamented. "They gave the people a choice last year between a couple of names for the new city. Salada wasn't even one of them. Why? Long before the home developers came here, we already had a name that reflected the heritage of this land. Sure, Pacifica is a nice name, but Salada is the heart of all these communities. They know it, too. That's why they located the city hall and police department just a few blocks away from here."

She paused as Joey entered the kitchen. "Joey, you must never forget the name Salada, for it is your home. Do not let it fade from your heart."

"I won't," Joey replied as he passed by.

Joey went into the garage and placed the pieces of his cross on the old workbench. He sadly realized it was beyond repair.

Hanging on the wall of the garage was his dad's old guitar case. He took it off the wall, opened it, and strummed his fingers across the guitar strings. With fewer friends now, he sat in his garage week after week, learning to play the old guitar all by himself. It came naturally to him, and once he felt comfortable with the sounds he produced, he started to play the songs he heard on the radio. He didn't sing. He only hummed or barely whispered the words. Joey knew he didn't have a good voice. Because of this, he never sang in church, but sometimes he would move his lips and pretend he was singing with his favorite recording artists, the Platters. In the safety of his garage, the world was at peace, at least until the next day at Westmoor.

***

Big Eddie started hanging out with Cory Richardson, big Ralph Dunning, and Tom Jonas, his new buddies at Westmoor. One day, Cory, Tom, and Ralph Dunning, three of Westmoor's soon-to-be dropouts, decided to have a little fun with Joey. They squeezed in between Lenny and Joey during lunch.

"Hey, look what we have here. It's Gunner. No, it's Ass Wipe. Isn't that what they call you these days?"

Joey didn't respond. Lenny stood up and told them to get the hell away.

"Oh gee, Ass Wipe here is letting the Leaf speak for him. Sit down, Leaf, before we put you down," warned Cory.

Just then Big Ed sat down next to Cory and asked, "What's going on, guys? Can I get in on this? Oh, just one thing, leave Lenny out of it. He's, my friend."

The bell rang, and lunch ended before any damage could be done. Lenny told Joey that he needed to carry Valhalla to school once again, but Joey wasn't sure what to do. He told Lenny he'd think about it.

***

Cory Richardson overheard Lenny and Joey talking about hitting the basketball game between Westmoor and Jefferson High School that Friday night. Cory, Tom, and Ralph conspired to strip Joey naked at some point during a game break and shove his naked ass back into the auditorium for everyone to see. It'd be great for laughs, they told each other. Joey would never live it down. Maybe even afterward, they'd kick his ass a little bit to boot. That was their plan. They even asked Big Ed if he'd like to help.

"No, I'd rather just watch the game. You guys go and have fun. Don't lay a hand on my friend Lenny, though. Understand?"

"Sure, we have nothing against the Leaf," assured Dunning.

Lenny and Joey attended the basketball game, but nothing unusual occurred. The following Monday, the three stooges (as Lenny referred to Cory and his friends) showed up near the hallway lockers. Ralph had a Band-Aid on his cheek, and the makings of a black eye were clearly visible under his sunglasses. Wearing sunglasses on a foggy morning was a bit odd, even for one of the stooges. Tom and Cory didn't look so good either.

"I wonder what the hell happened to those guys? Looks like someone cleaned their clock," Lenny said to Joey.

Jeff Baker was next to them, opening his locker, and he helped clarify things. "Did you hear? Cory told some of his friends that just before the game last Friday night, five or six Jefferson seniors had jumped the three of them. Cory says they kicked their asses, but it looks to me like it was the other way around. Well, deserved, I think."

Months had passed, and another year of high school was nearing an end. Eddie didn't bother Joey as much as he did before. He'd still do the lunch bag thing once in a while, but not as much as earlier in the year. Eddie was back to studying hard to improve his grades. He tended to be by himself most of the time. He no longer hung around with the stooges. In fact, they seemed to go out of their way to avoid being anywhere near Big Ed, Gunner, or the Leaf. Joey started carrying Valhalla once again.

***

The summer after the end of their sophomore year was an eventful one, especially for Lenny. He and Joey decided to hike to Mori's Point. Odie followed right beside them.

Lenny was using a piece of driftwood as a walking stick. Over his shoulder, he carried a satchel that contained a long clothesline cord and a piece of cloth. Joey knew what that meant. Lenny was going to the point to stand on the first large rock offshore. He was determined to board the rock he had named the *Nordic Prince*.

Eddie noticed Lenny and Joey outside his window. He wondered where they were headed, so he followed them. It soon became clear what was about to happen. He watched as Joey, Lenny, and Odie walked along the low, narrow path that led to the base of the bluff. Eddie ran in an effort to stop them, but they were too far away, already near the base of Mori's Point. He knew he wouldn't reach them in time to stop Lenny. He yelled at them, but they couldn't hear him.

"Don't do it, Lenny," Joey protested.

"Here, just hold this rope," Lenny replied as he tied the other end around his waist.

"Stop! Don't do it. It's too dangerous. The tide's not low enough. The rock's too far away. Listen to me, Lenny."

Lenny had made it his goal to sit at the helm of his *Nordic Prince*. He had planned it out carefully. It was a cool day, the sky was clear, and the sea was calm. This was his best chance to fulfill a dream. In the dream, he saw himself standing on the rock, and he knew he would be safe. Lenny waited as the ocean water retreated, and then he jumped down into over a foot of frigid ocean water. He waded out to the first large rock and climbed quickly to the top. There, he pulled out a large cloth and tied it to the walking stick he carried. The cloth had a Viking dragon symbol with the words *Nordic Prince* written underneath the dragon's head. He had finally achieved his goal, and he felt satisfied. He sat down as the ocean waves lapped against the rock. The cool spray of water that whiffed gently over the rock made it feel like he was actually sailing a vessel.

By the time Eddie reached the point, Lenny was sitting on the rock, calmly reading a library book about Viking folklore.

"You dumb shit, why didn't you stop him!" Eddie shouted at Joey.

When Eddie shouted, Odie leaped out of Joey's arms and jumped into the sea below in an effort to be with Lenny. It was clear that little Odie couldn't get his paws high enough out of the water to climb the rock.

Joey handed the rope to Eddie and climbed down to retrieve Lenny's dog.

"Odie, come back here," Joey called out.

Odie turned and swam back to Joey. The outgoing current pulled Joey away from the ledge where Eddie knelt, waiting to help them out. Joey picked up Odie from the rising surf. He was now closer to the rock than the base of the point. Lenny had stopped reading and was now well aware of what was happening. As Joey and Odie reached the rock, he took his walking stick and held it down, so Joey could grip it. He helped pull Joey and Odie onto the *Nordic Prince*.

"Look how clear and beautiful it is. You can even see the Farallon Islands," Lenny exclaimed as he pointed to the tiny, barely visible islands well offshore.

Lenny felt a tug on the rope he had around his waist. He looked back and saw Big Eddie waving for them to get back onto the bluff.

"It's time to go back now, Lenny. The tide is already getting higher," Joey cautioned him as Odie shook the water off his fur and barked at the waves below.

Realizing it was time to go, Lenny said, "OK, when the next wave retreats, we all climb down and head back up on the bluff."

Lenny was the first to reach the ledge of the bluff. Big Eddie pulled him up at once. He then reached down and grabbed Odie from Joey's outstretched hands. Lenny quickly untied the rope from his waist and tossed it down to Joey. A wave rolled in, lifting Joey off his feet. Both Eddie and Lenny held onto the thin rope and pulled Joey back in their direction, where he was able to climb to safety.

"You're a real dumb ass, Joey. You should have stopped him before he ever reached Beach Avenue," Eddie quickly snapped at him.

"Don't blame Joey. I knew when I woke up this morning and looked outside, it would be the perfect day to sail on the *Nordic Prince*. Nothing was going to stop me, not even you, Eddie."

"You need to grow up, Lenny. You're too old to be dreaming of becoming a Viking. You're not a little kid anymore," Eddie retorted.

Lenny ventured out to the rock off the point three more times that month, without letting Big Eddie or Joey know beforehand. He pounded a wooden stake above the path at the lower edge of the bluff, where he tied a rope and used it to get back and forth safely. One morning, Eddie decided to take a walk on the shore of Salada Beach. Off in the distance, he could see a flag waving on the *Nordic Prince* rock. Next to the flag, the silhouette of his friend was clearly visible. Lenny was leaning near the top of the rock, reading a book. It took fifteen minutes for Eddie to reach him. Eddie waded out to the rock and sat there with Lenny.

"I guess if I can't stop you from coming here, I might as well join you. There's safety in numbers, you know, and if I'm not around, be sure to bring Ass Wipe with you."

In the weeks and months that followed, when the sea was at its calmest, all three would accompany Lenny. Eddie and Joey agreed there would be a peace treaty between them on the days they rode aboard the *Nordic Prince*.

It's for Lenny's safety after all, thought Big Eddie.

One time, near the end of his junior year, Lenny surprised both his friends by swimming all the way out to the farthest rock

off of Mori's Point. By the time he swam back to them, he was
shivering with cold and could barely climb out of the water. The
current was too strong, even though he was a very good
swimmer. He barely made it back safely. Never would he try that
stunt again.

Then, after a few earthquakes and rainstorms, the lower path
portion of the bluff collapsed into the sea, destroying the only
safe way to reach the base of Mori's Point. On a few occasions,
Lenny would take the long, steep path to the top of the bluff and
gaze down at the rock with fond memories. His Viking adventure
had come to an end.

***

They were well into their junior year, and Big Ed still
continued to ignore Joey. Several times Joey tried to regain
Eddie's trust, but Big Ed was stubborn and would never listen to
anything Joey tried to tell him.

Calendar Girl was now in her senior year. She had joined the
cheer squad the year before and was more popular than ever.
Eddie had gotten over her by then, but it had taken a long time.
He still picked on Joey but far less often. He now had his eye on
a few other girls.

Although Beth Ann had numerous boys interested in her, she
would never get too involved. She still had hopes that her Ed
would someday return to what he once was. First though, he
would have to let go of his grudge against Joey. Only then would
she try to win his heart back. She hoped all things would be
settled before the junior prom, or at least before the senior ball.
She knew she would only attend those events with one person, or
not attend them at all.

***

Occasionally, Eddie still would take Joey's lunch and give him a smelly bag in return but only on rare occasions. It happened far less frequently than before, and it only happened once the last four months of his junior year, but that was still too much for Joey. Joey started carrying an extra bag, which he kept in his coat pocket. The extra bag was filled with some rocks wrapped in newspaper. One morning as Joey was about to sit down after boarding the school bus, he saw Big Eddie cut in front of Lenny.

The big guy is going to sit right next to me and take my lunch. I just know it, Joey thought. Joey quickly put the bag with rocks on his lap. As he suspected, Eddie sat down right next to him.

"Hey, Gunner, I've been thinking." Before Eddie could get another word out, Joey handed him his fake lunch bag.

"Take it. It's yours. Enjoy your lunch. I made it special myself." Joey used the same words that Eddie had used on him each time he took Joey's bag.

"Here, then you can have my lunch," Eddie replied, as he motioned to Lenny to take his seat.

Eddie got up and exchanged seats with Lenny. When they got off the bus, Joey took the bag Eddie had given him and tossed it in the trashcan located by the bus drop-off point. Lenny happened to look behind as he and Joey headed off to class. Lenny observed that when Eddie exited the bus, he picked up the lunch bag Joey had just tossed into the trash, and then he dropped the bag Joey gave him into it. *How odd,* Lenny thought.

"Did I hear Eddie call you Gunner instead of his usual AW? You know, I think he reached in the trash and pulled out the bag you threw in there. I wonder why?"

"Maybe he just slipped up. I wasn't paying any attention to what he said to me anyway, and as for the lunch bag, he's probably saving it, so he can give it to me again tomorrow," Joey replied.

Later that same day, as Joey was headed to his next class, he rounded a corner, and ran smack into Calendar Girl. His books fell to the ground. May Jun, wearing her cheer outfit, stooped down to help him pick them up.

"I'm so sorry, Gunner."

"No need to be sorry, May. It was my fault. I was in too much of a hurry and wasn't looking."

"Well, it was sure nice running into you," May Jun said with a smile.

Joey said good-bye and began walking to class. He stopped when he heard May Jun running up behind him.

"Joey, you dropped this, too," she said as she handed him a note card.

It was a card he used as a bookmark and to keep class notes on. Joey thanked May once again and watched her as she scampered away.

Still so fine. The words came unbidden to his mind.

Big Eddie was standing farther down the hallway. He stood and watched Calendar Girl run up to Gunner and hand him a note.

Even though Joey felt that Eddie's resentment of him had cooled, he continued to stay far away from his old friend. For Joey, any hope of friendship ended the last time they sat together on the school bus. No longer would he even try to be friends. Now he disliked Big Eddie too much to even care anymore.

***

The school year ended, and during the summer, a traveling carnival came to town. It was set up in a corner section of the

Manor's Super X parking lot. A whole group of teens planned to hit the rides and games on Saturday night. Everyone from Sharp Park planned to be there. Lenny and Joey hurried there right after dinner. Lenny's friendship with Big Eddie had waned because of how Eddie treated Joey, but they still talked from time to time. As a courtesy, Lenny asked Eddie to go to the carnival with them. Big Ed told Lenny he didn't plan on going. Too much stuff to do at home was his excuse, but the real reason was because he didn't want to bump into Calendar Girl. He believed he was over her, at least as far as true love went. But sometimes when he watched her jumping around in her skimpy cheer outfit during school rallies, he yearned for her touch once again. He also didn't want to be in close proximity with Gunner, who he knew would be there.

Lenny was in a hurry to get to the carnival with hopes of getting Susan Prouder to ride the large Ferris wheel with him. He didn't want anything to wreck his chances of having fun, so Big Ed not coming was fine with him.

Beth Ann's mother drove the girls to the carnival and would drive them home afterward. They'd be leaving no later than seven thirty. Lidia and Bridgette were invited to go with the Codington's. Most of the other teenagers planned to stay until closing.

Everyone was having a great time. Lenny got his wish to take Prouder on the Ferris wheel. Lidia, Joey, and Bridgette all squeezed together and took a ride on it themselves. From the Ferris wheel, Joey saw a few guys arriving on motorcycles.

Susan Prouder knew who they were. She'd seen them before, a year ago at Nick's restaurant, just a few miles south of Sharp Park. It was Bo Harden, a young man six foot four inches tall. With him were Terry McHenry, Tubbs for short, who weighed close to three hundred pounds, and Mean Joe Pennington. About a year ago, all three had been arrested just outside of Nick's for being drunk and disorderly. Bo had just turned twenty-one, and their celebration got too out of hand. Bo resisted arrest, which added to his jail time. He was also told to never show his face in town again. Bo had long ago gained the reputation of being the biggest badass south of San Francisco.

"Why is he back here? There's only going to be trouble," Susan said nervously.

Mrs. Codington quickly gathered the girls together and drove them home.

Bo and his friends just wandered around the carnival as if looking for someone. It was then that Joey noticed they had one more guy with them. It was Ralph Dunning. Upon seeing Dunning, Joey asked Lenny if it was wise to stay any longer.

"Ralph only bothered us one time, and that was way back in our sophomore year. He never even came near us after that. Look at them. Right now, they're just hanging around, drinking sodas, and shooting the breeze. And look over there. A deputy sheriff is standing at the entrance gate. I don't think Bo wants any trouble, especially with him there." Lenny went on to say that if there were even a hint of trouble, they'd split the scene fast.

"OK, but let's keep our distance from them," Joey said cautiously.

Just as the boys were about to go on another ride, they saw Big Eddie enter the carnival. He walked up to Lenny and asked if he wanted to go into the fun house, completely ignoring Joey.

"I would if it weren't for the fact that Bo Harden, Ralph Dunning, and their friends weren't standing right by it. I prefer to stay as far away from them as possible. Oh, one other thing, I think I just saw Calendar Girl go in there with some of her friends."

Big Eddie didn't show any reaction to Lenny spotting May Jun. But after Ralph pointed at him, he walked behind the cotton-candy cart. Lenny followed him. Joey stayed where he was. He knew it was best to stay away from the big guy. He also wanted to catch a glimpse of May Jun. *She should be exiting soon*, he thought.

Eddie suggested to Lenny that they leave. "Gunner can come too. You can babysit him, so he doesn't get scared walking home in the dark." It was then that Lenny noticed a worried look on Eddie's face. No…not a worried look, it was something much more. Big Eddie Davis, the toughest kid he had ever known, looked scared. It was a new look, one he had never seen before, but why? It couldn't be Calendar Girl. It had to be something else. It had to be Bo and his friends, but they were just standing there, drinking sodas, and shooting the breeze. Sure, they looked tough, but they weren't causing any trouble.

"What's bothering you, Eddie?" Lenny asked.

"Nothing. Get your friend, and let's get out of here. I'm just not feeling well, that's all."

"Joey, we're going. Come on," urged Lenny.

Joey was now very confused. *First Lenny wants to stay, and now he wants to go just when I want to stay a little while longer.*

"Hey, Ass Wipe, stay here if you want, but the Leaf and I are leaving." Joey just shook his head when he heard Big Eddie call him an ass wipe once again.

"I'm staying here. I see some other people we know, and I'll just hang out with them for a while. I'll see you tomorrow." Joey might have left with them were it not for Eddie's remark. Joey was angry now. He didn't want to be anywhere near the big guy. The hopes he had to one day regain Eddie's friendship were now lost forever.

Lenny looked at Joey and nodded his head in the direction of Eddie, who had already started walking away. It was clear he was silently urging Joey to join them. Joey shook his head in response. Lenny turned and jogged to catch up with Eddie.

As they were walking, Lenny told Big Eddie he'd have to put his ill will for Joey behind him. Lenny had seen the look on Joey's face and knew what it meant.

"Joey's my friend. Please don't deride him anymore, or it will wreck the friendship we have. I don't want that, do you?"

"All right, I'll think of some other, less offensive name for him. Let's get going now. I wish I hadn't come here."

Joey watched as May Jun went on another ride with her friends. She looked really happy. He sighed and then decided to leave the carnival. By this time, Lenny and Eddie were out of sight. Joey could hear the sound of motorcycles starting up and then roaring past him. *Looks like the bad guys are leaving early*, he thought.

Then Joey noticed that the motorcycle engines stopped just up ahead, at the end of the street. He heard someone shout, "I told you who my cousin was. You didn't believe me before. You believe me now. Don't you, dirt bag? Bo Harden's my cousin, and he's the biggest badass around. I made a promise after what you did to us, and now it's finally your turn to cry. Not so big now, are you, Ed?"

When Joey got close enough to see, there under the dim streetlight was Eddie. He was being pushed back and forth by Bo, Tubbs, and Pennington. They taunted Big Eddie with foul and filthy words while pushing and punching him. Ralph Dunning was holding Lenny away from the action.

Joey yelled, "Stop, let them go. Someone has already called the cops."

Bo pushed Eddie to the ground. Eddie's nose and lip were already bleeding.

Fat Tubbs looked around and said, "Doesn't look like anyone's home? All their lights are out. Haven't you heard? There's a carnival in town? Maybe they're all there with their kiddies? It doesn't matter anyway. We'll be done here in a minute."

"Wait, is that Gunner? Oh yes, it is. I almost forgot. Ed here calls you his ass wipe. Come on over here. I think, given that you and Ed aren't really friends, you may enjoy this as much as I will," Ralph jokingly suggested.

Ralph walked over, put his arm around Joey, and walked him over next to Lenny.

"Continue on, cousin," Ralph called out to Bo.

Eddie tried to run away, but Pennington tripped him. He picked him back up and held him by one arm as Tubbs grabbed Eddie's other arm. Eddie struggled and almost broke free.

"You're pretty strong for a kid. Stop struggling or I may have to stomp on you after Bo puts you down. Hell, I'll probably do that anyway. That's why they call me the mean one." Pennington's low raspy voice rang in Eddie's ears.

Bo Harding stood directly in front of Eddie and told him to apologize to his cousin, Ralph. Tubbs pulled Eddie's hair, jerking his head back. "Look at Bo when he's talking to you, sonny."

Eddie didn't have a chance to respond. Tubbs and Pennington held him as Bo continued his assault on Eddie, hitting him in the face and midsection. Eddie's knees buckled.

Joey looked at Lenny and said, "This isn't right. It's not fair."

Then, all of a sudden, Joey jumped toward Pennington, striking him in the face. Pennington let go of Eddie's arm when he was struck. Lenny and Ralph couldn't believe what they had just witnessed. Pennington recovered quickly and knocked Joey down on the ground with one punch. Joey quickly got up to square off with Pennington once more, and again Joey hit the ground. Tubbs let go of Eddie to help his buddy out.

Joey called out Eddie's name and tossed him the red pouch that contained Valhalla. Eddie gripped the orb tightly in his right hand and blindly swung in the direction of Bo Harding's face. Bo didn't know what was tossed to Eddie. He hesitated for just a second. Eddie's wild overhand right fist caught Bo Harden directly on the chin. Bo's body stiffened, and he fell headfirst to the ground, out cold. Eddie kicked Pennington in the leg to keep him away as the mean one turned in his direction. Pennington went down, holding his right knee. He was obviously injured. Tubbs was breathing heavy. He looked almost exhausted. Lenny pushed Ralph away and tackled Tubbs. Joey regained his feet and turned to face Ralph. Pure anger was coursing through his veins. Ralph took one look at Joey's face, and he began backing away. He clearly didn't want any part of the action. Tubbs finally got away from Lenny, only to have Joey kick him in the nuts. The fat one dropped to his knees, cupping both of his hands between his legs. Harden still lay unconscious on the ground as Big Eddie walked over to Pennington and told him to get up.

"I can't. My knee is blown out. I need a doctor." When he said those words, everyone knew the fight was over.

A teenage boy had knocked out the twenty-two-year-old badass, Bo Harden. The tall, muscular teenager from Sharp Park would now be known as "the big badass, Ed Davis."

***

The fight was over, and the boys headed home. Lenny was about to ask Joey something, but before he could, Joey took off running without saying a word.

Lenny and Eddie walked toward their respective homes together. Lenny asked Big Ed why Dunning had it in for him. Ed would only say that they had a falling-out a long time ago, and Ralph was the kind of guy who just couldn't let things go. Big Ed made it clear he was done talking. After that, they hardly said a word to each other.

Early the next morning, Big Ed awoke in pain. His right hand was swollen and throbbing, so he soaked it in cold water, but that only provided temporary relief. Walking back to his room, he saw his pants lying on the floor next to his bed. He remembered that he had placed the pouch containing Valhalla in his pocket while walking home the night before. He opened the pouch and held the agate marble in his hands. For years he had wanted to possess Valhalla. He looked at it very closely. It was as shiny and as mysterious as ever.

Did it really have any special power? It was then that he realized that the throbbing pain he felt in his right hand was gone. The swelling had also disappeared, and his hand looked normal once again. He wondered whether or not to give it back to Joey. It was Sunday. Joey would be at church. Big Ed decided to stay inside all day. He felt on top of the world.

***

"Joey, get up. It's almost time for church," his mom called out to him.

Saturday night at the carnival seemed like a dream and nightmare rolled into one. He reached into his nightstand drawer to retrieve Valhalla, but it wasn't inside.

Of course, I tossed it to Eddie last night, he recalled. *Eddie blasted that guy so hard. What a sight to see. The big guy doesn't know his own strength.*

Later that afternoon, after church, Lenny came by with Odie following close behind. Joey informed him that he no longer had Valhalla. His enemy, Big Ed, still had it. The boys played with Odie for a while, but when Beth Ann, her sister, Coleen, and Susan Prouder strolled by, Lenny went off with them, so he could talk with Susan. He would tell the girls all that had transpired the night before.

Joey, now alone, opened the garage door and pulled out the guitar. There he sat playing his favorite songs.

Lidia and her friend Bridgette Dubois were sitting outside when they heard music. They followed the sound to Joey's house. He was sitting in his garage with his back turned away from them.

"Don't disturb him. I want to listen to him before he knows we're here," whispered Lidia.

Bridgette, now nearly fourteen and very pretty, was entranced by the sound of his guitar. When he had finished playing a song, she clapped her hands. Joey turned around and realized he had forgotten to close the garage door behind him.

Lidia walked up to him and asked who taught him to play the guitar so well.

"No one. I learned on my own," he responded.

"Sing, Joey. Please sing me...I mean...sing us a song," Liddy urged him. "Please. Bridgette wants to hear you sing, too."

"I don't sing. I just like playing the chords that I've heard on the radio. That's all. I'll play just one more song, and then I have to go inside. Tell you what, I'll play, and you two sing. Do you know the words to 'Bye, Bye Love,' by the Everly Brothers?"

The girls said yes, and he began to strum his guitar. Lidia and Bridgette knew every word, and the sound of their voices and the happiness on their faces lifted Joey's spirits. When they were finished, Joey placed the guitar back in its case and said good-bye to the girls. They begged him to play more, but he was done. When they left, he closed the garage door and thought, *that was actually kind of fun.*

Chapter 7

A Time to Remember

One afternoon, as Benny and Sofia sat on their backyard bench, they reminisced about their childhood.

Benny began. "I still remember ice boxes, and now we have electric refrigerators with freezers built in. Electric clothes dryers, instead of the old crank ringer, and clotheslines outside. We have three channels on TV, and I hear color TVs are out now too."

Sofia commented, "You know, Benny, I've come to really enjoy watching the *Mickey Mouse Club* each day after school with our children. Our Lidia looks so much like that pretty Annette Funicello. She could easily be mistaken for her cute little sister."

"Yes, the wonders of TV," Benny replied. "There are so many modern conveniences these days. How did we ever get along without them? Things are a-changing, and who knows what the future may bring."

"My mama always thought she knew." Sofia leaned on Benny's shoulder. "She would frequently remind my brothers and me that her dreams told all of our life stories. She said it was a gift passed down from her grandmother. My mama didn't see the same gift in any of her children, and that pleased her. It's not good to know such things, she would say. I think she told us that just to make us think we couldn't get anything past her," Sofia said with a chuckle.

"Well, I don't know how much truth there is to her gift. After all, she never predicted we'd get married and so fast after just meeting each other. How could a Jew marry a Roman Catholic? Who could ever envision such a thing?" Benny opined as he kissed Sofia.

"She did say that one day a man would take me far away from her. She was sure right about that part. But you know, deep down, our parents must really miss us. It's like clockwork. They each send us letters on our birthdays and special holidays every year."

The two of them sat there and continued to reminisce about their parents, the good old days, and how Sharp Park was changing.

"I remember when the streets around here were all gravel. Nearly all of them are paved now. By the way, did you know? According to John Davis, they're already building a freeway that'll come right through our little town." Benny was about to go on but stopped as he heard the sound of the mailbox's metal flap closing in the garage.

"I think I hear the mailman. It's time to get up." Benny went to check the delivery box, and sure enough, there was one letter inside. He quickly returned to his wife in the backyard.

"Sofia, surprise, surprise! It's a letter from your mother, and it's not even Christmas."

Sofia read the relatively short letter and was shocked to see that her mother and father wanted to visit them. They wished to make amends and see their grandchildren. The letter ended with these words:

We have been so wrong in our beliefs. We need to ask you both to forgive us. I have come to realize that all of us on this earth are God's children. Benny is as much our own son as you are our daughter. Please write back soon. We'll understand if you say no to our request, With sincere love, Mama and Papa.

A little over a month after Sofia received the letter, her parents, Agostino and Carmina Barzetti, arrived. It was arranged that they would sleep in Lenny's room. Lenny constructed a makeshift lean-to using a blanket, and he slept behind the living-room sofa for the week.

***

Joey came over to Lenny's house, and they went out to the backyard to talk.

"Lidia mentioned that you now played the guitar and that you are quite good at it. When the hell did this happen? I've never heard you sing or play any instrument."

"I don't sing, never have and never will. If you heard my singing voice, you'd understand."

"My sister believes she would like your voice no matter what, but what does she know anyway? Still, I'd like to hear you play sometime. How did you learn to play so quickly?" asked Lenny.

"I found the guitar in our garage. I listened to some songs on the radio and started strumming along. My dad heard me one day and helped me learn some chords using his good hand. It just came naturally after that. If I heard a song, I could play it with just a little practice."

"You had Valhalla with you, didn't you, Joey?"

"Yes, but I don't have Valhalla now, and I can still learn any song just by hearing it a few times. I don't need Valhalla anymore. I will live my life free from it."

"No, Joey. Valhalla was meant for you. You cannot let it go, at least, not until it's time."

"And when will that be?"

"Only you will know," said Lenny.

***

Lenny's grandmother came out to the backyard and wanted to be introduced to Lenny's best friend. She sat and talked with them for a while to get to know her grandson and his friend better.

"You have a special place, a rock. Sometimes I dream, and it seems so real. I've seen you standing on a rock surrounded by water, and you're always happy to be there. You have those types of dreams too, don't you, Lennard?"

"Yes, but how do you know these things?" Lenny inquired.

"You are all in my dreams. Your mama and papa, Lidia, you, and sometimes, even your friends, too," she said.

"And what else do you see in your dreams, Grandma?" Lenny curiously inquired.

She told them that of all the dreams she had ever dreamed, she understood all but two. "Lennard, perhaps you may help to clarify them. Would you like to hear them, boys?"

Both Lenny's and Joey's curiosity was awakened.

"Yes," Lenny quickly replied.

Lenny's grandma went on to describe a dream where she was on a hill, and below was a vast meadow that spread across this great land. In one dream, the meadow was covered with the greenest of grass, but in her next dream, the meadow was filled with a vast array of flowers for as far as her eyes could see. They were swaying as if in a gentle breeze. When she descended the hill to run among such beauty, she stopped because they were not flowers at all. Out of the ground rose millions of miniature porcelain-like hands, reaching upward, their little fingers moving in every direction. She could go no further and would always wake up.

The boys had no idea what the dream could mean. Perplexed that Lenny couldn't understand it either, the grandmother continued onto her next vision.

"I saw a great dragon sleeping in the west. To its north, a large beast roamed, walking back and forth, looking for something to devour. The beast was greatly weakened because a large fissure in the earth had opened, preventing it from reaching much of its food source.

"One day, the dragon awoke from its long sleep. It roared with power and great might. It was now well rested and ready to claim its place as the greatest creature on earth. When the dragon awoke, it saw its mortal enemy, a great winged creature of many tongues standing across a vast body of water. The great bird with many tongues had clipped its own wings, believing they cast too long of a shadow, and had grown too heavy. It saw the reach of its long feathers as more of a burden than a gift of flowing beauty. The great bird had grown a silver tongue and thought itself as reigning elite among all the creatures of the earth. But in reality, it had become elitist unto itself and no longer had an ear for the little creatures that once lived under its clipped feathers.

"The dragon saw its opportunity. With great skill and cunning, the dragon proposed marriage to the ugly beast of the north. It feigned its love for the beast so well, the beast accepted the proposal. They planned a grand wedding, and together they conspired to feast upon the great winged creature that lived across the waters.

"First, they offered to share their friendship, food, and wealth with the great winged one. The many-tongued bird was pleased, and they all lived in peace with one another for a season. The fearsome dragon built islands in the sea, to be closer to the great bird. The ugly beast forged alliances with the eastern sand devils to conspire against the great winged one.

"When the wedding date arrived, the great bird was given a place of honor at the banquet table. The servers brought out appetizers and great quantities of wine, placing them before the great winged one. *If the appetizers and wine are any indication, the entree will be fabulous,* thought the bird. The main course was long in coming, so the great one feasted on the bread and wine until it was gorged and drowsy. The servants gently lifted the bird, as if in great honor, but then quickly placed it on the hot grill in the center of the banquet hall, feathers and all. The once-great bird tried to fly away, but its clipped wings prevented its escape. The dragon from the west and the ugly northern beast ate of the bird until they were satisfied. They shared the heart of the great winged one with the other devil creatures of the earth. They all rejoiced in the demise of the great bird for the flavor of its meat was very satisfying to the tongue. The sand devils celebrated for a time until they too were devoured by the beast and dragon. Those creatures not invited to the wedding hid forever in fear.

Meanwhile, the ugly beast praised the dragon but secretly plotted its demise. This is where my vision ends." She shook her head.

"I believe the dragon, ugly beast, and the great winged bird with many tongues are different nations. That's the easy part to interpret. The dragon represents China, the ugly beast is the Soviet Union, and the great winged bird is the United States. But everything after that is too confusing. China is very much awake right now with Mao Zedong at the helm. The Soviets are strong, not weak, and the United States is the most powerful country in the world. No clipped wings on this great creature," Grandma Barzetti declared.

"Grandma Barzetti," Joey asked, "The great bird doesn't seem so smart to me. I don't think it's our country at all. The bird's fate was sad. Could it be saved?"

"Hmm…Lennard, your friend Joey has asked a very good question. Sometimes the dreams change, but that is very rare. Perhaps if the great winged bird remained true to itself and recognized the beauty of what made it a great creature, maybe then, but I don't really know. So, Lennard, what do you say? Interpret my dream."

"I'm not sure, Grandma. It's not my dream; it is yours. Maybe it's only a dream, nothing more."

"Or maybe its time has not yet come," his grandma answered.

After looking at the clouds in the sky, Lenny spoke again. "I don't believe the creatures just represent countries or nations. They are the different forces and beliefs of the people of the earth. Two-thirds of the world will plot against what was once seen as good. All that was right and good will one day be viewed as out of step, even bad, in the eyes of many. The clipped feathers are the good that will be cast aside. When the time of change comes to our people, a leader will emerge and be viewed as elite, with no need of counsel. Other future leaders will follow the same path and consider themselves above it all as well, but they will lack the wings of wisdom. Without the wisdom and influence of what once was good, the great one cannot prevail. In my heart, I don't believe there is any other ending."

Lennard looked down at the ground and continued. "In the first dream, the porcelain meadow has not yet grown, but sadly, its time is soon to come. There will be many with legs of plastic who will choose to walk the path through the valley. They will declare triumph and freedom as they crush their own souls. I do not see how this can ever happen in this great land. I hope your dream is false. It is best that I not say any more."

Joey just scratched his head, not knowing what to think or say.

Lenny's grandmother's tone of voice softened after hearing Lennard's interpretation of her dreams. She seemed enlightened by what Lenny had said. "Listen to your dreams, Lennard. Do not forget them. Seek to understand, for a dark time is coming. I love you."

She got up, said good-bye to the boys, and went back inside.

Lenny looked at Joey, shrugged his shoulders, and said, "Hell if I know what that was all about. I just took a guess as to what the dreams meant. It was a shot in the dark. I think Grandma actually believed it."

"It was just too deep and creepy for me," Joey replied.

Lenny quickly changed the subject. "Our senior year starts soon. That's all I can think about. Well, that and Susan Prouder. We made out at Ringer Rock the other day. She may not look it, but that shy girl definitely has a wild side, and I like it."

Both boys laughed.

Grandma and Grandpa Barzetti returned to New York two days later. Lenny was sad to see them go but happy to have his bed back once again.

CHAPTER 8

THE WAYWARD WIND

Shortly after the start of their senior year, Lenny asked Joey to walk with him and Odie to the top of the Mori's Point. The sky was clear, but the wind blew at a steady pace and chilled the air. A hike suited Joey just fine. After all, it was a good way to warm up. As they climbed the hill, Joey noticed the silhouette of someone sitting at the top, near the end of the bluff.

"Looks like someone's already enjoying the view up there," commented Joey.

"Well, yes. It's someone we know. He asked me to bring you here. He told me it was very important and promised that he only wanted to talk, nothing more. He just wants you to hear him out."

Joey knew right away whom Lenny was referring to. Just up ahead, he could clearly see that it was Big Ed Davis. *Why?* he thought. *What could he possibly say that hasn't been said before?*

Ed had given his word to Lenny, and as much as Joey disliked Ed, Joey knew that Big Ed would keep his word. Big Ed stood up as they approached. His hair blew wildly in the wind.

Big Ed said hello and then began the speech he had practiced all that morning. Odie sat beside Lenny and didn't move. It was as if the dog knew what was about to happen and didn't want to miss a word.

"Let me finish what I have to say before you say anything, Gunner. I've been thinking a lot since the fight. I couldn't understand why you helped me that night and at such great risk. You don't even like me anymore. You would never fight anyone for your own self. You would always back away. People started calling you chicken and a pantywaist behind your back. How could such a coward dive into the ocean without hesitation, not knowing how to swim, to save little Lidia's life? You put Liddy's life above your own. And Beth Ann, she was never really my girlfriend, so how could I blame you for taking her away from me? Just before May Jun graduated from Westmoor, she cornered me during lunch. You know how persuasive she can be…well, anyway…she said that you were the most honorable person she had ever met. Try as she might, she knew she could never have you, regardless of how you may have felt about her. It was because you gave your word and still counted me as a…as a…friend. How could I be your friend when all I did was trash you every chance I could? It is my character that is flawed. I was too proud to admit the truth to myself. You remained true to who you are…trustworthy and kind. I've kept Valhalla from you, but I haven't carried it with me until today. This belongs to you. I am not worthy enough to even hold it."

Big Ed held out his hand to Joey. In it was the silk pouch containing Valhalla. Joey started to reach for it but pulled his hand back and didn't take it from Big Ed.

"Take it, please. I do not know whether or not you will ever be friends with me again, but I give this promise. I will never stand against you, and if I ever hear anyone cut you down, they will have to deal with me."

Ed took a deep breath. He had said a lot but knew there was one more thing he had to say. "Joey, I am sorry. I don't expect you to forgive me. Heaven knows, I don't deserve it. I'm a big-time jerk. I ask now for your forgiveness. I want to be your friend once again. I know I don't deserve your friendship, but please, at least accept my apology. Valhalla is yours, please."

Big Ed extended his arm fully, holding the marble in its bag much closer to Joey. He hadn't lowered his arm since first offering Valhalla to Joey. Joey hesitantly took the red silk pouch into his own hand.

"Why have me come here to say these things? Why on top of Mori's Point?" Joey inquired.

"We made sort of a truce here some time ago. It was the proper place in my mind," replied Big Ed.

Joey looked down into his hands. He thought about all that Ed had said. Joey didn't reply to Ed's apology. Instead, he rolled Valhalla out of the silk pouch. The agate marble felt warm and heavy as it rested in the palm of his hand.

"You held Valhalla in your hand for a long time on this hill. Tell me, Ed. How did it feel to you?"

"The marble is as cool as the wind," Big Ed replied.

Joey knew it was time. "Big Ed, my friend, Valhalla now belongs to you. Not because you are strong. Not because you are now the big, badass Ed Davis. It is because you have humbled yourself. It is no longer mine. It is yours. The power it holds…is only the power that you already possess within your own heart. I came to know this, the more I held this great marble."

Joey handed the marble back to Ed, and then he held out his open hand. Instead of shaking it, Big Ed hugged Joey and thanked him.

Joey looked at Lenny and Odie and smiled. "Oh, I guess this means I accept your apology, my friend." From that day on, their friendship remained unbroken.

The three friends and Odie sat on the windy bluff overlooking the *Nordic Prince*. Lenny stepped very close to the edge. Big Ed pulled him back; afraid he would slip down the steep cliff into the surf below.

"Don't worry, Ed. I know my fate is not here or now. Why do you think I was never worried about the danger of the waters around the rocks below? I already knew my fate. It was in my dreams, and it was not here. I know my life on this earth ends on a warm day far from here. I see myself lying in the tallest grass I've ever seen. A gentle breeze sways the long stems back and forth. I close my eyes, and it's over."

Ed was concerned for Lenny. "No, your dreams are only dreams, nothing more. You could step off a curb and be run over by a bus tomorrow. You need to be more careful, Lenny."

"I know all of our fates, even yours, Ed. Do you want to hear?"

"I sure do," Joey replied instead of Big Ed.

"Gunner…" Lenny paused. It was as if he now regretted saying anything at all about his dreams.

"Go ahead, Lenny. I can handle it." Joey believed, just as Ed believed, that Lenny's dreams were nothing more than just dreams.

"All I will say is that the warrior will die the warrior way. The words of a song on his lips will end his day."

"Well, he must be talking about you, Ed, because I'm not a warrior, and I just don't ever sing." Joey laughed because it sounded so unlike himself. *Warrior? Sing? I never sing.* He sat there looking at the crashing waves toppling over the rocks far below.

"OK, that's just about the stupidest thing I've ever heard," Big Ed said with a grin on his face. "Let's get the hell off this windy hill."

"An old man will sit in his favorite rocking chair with his best friend by his side as a slumber overtakes his eyes. He will sleep the long deep sleep of no return and be at peace, knowing he is finally home. The marble lies covered but will return as music plays above the berm." Lenny looked at them both. "That's all I will say. I won't say any more. Perhaps I am wrong. Time will tell."

A huge gust of wind hit the top of the bluff as if urging them to move on, and they knew it was time to leave.

"The wind is restless and wild. It swirls as if not knowing which way to blow," Joey noted.

"It's telling us to get the hell off this damn hill," Big Ed replied as he hurried back down the bluff.

The boys would remember the words Lenny spoke that day even though they doubted every word. Lenny avoided talking about his dreams after that day. He regretted ever saying anything.

***

It was the boys' senior year at Westmoor High School. Both Lidia and her best friend, Bridgette, were now freshman, but they rarely saw Joey, Ed, and Lenny at school. The year the two girls started high school was the first year Westmoor began double sessions. Bridgette and Lidia attended classes in the morning session, while the three senior boys attended the afternoon session.

As the three buddies arrived, Bridgette and Lidia were finishing their last class and heading back home on the bus, the same bus the boys had just arrived on.

The two girls never graduated from Westmoor because the next year, a new school in the back of the San Pedro valley of Linda Mar opened in their hometown of Pacifica. Lidia took it hard. She had so wanted to graduate from the same high school as her brother, Lenny. What hurt just as bad was that she would not be able to hang around with Joey and her brother during school. Her best friend, Bridgette, was especially disappointed. Although they were in the same grade, Bridgette was one year older than Lidia, who had skipped second grade. Bridgette was a year more mature. She was hoping get to know Joey better. She had developed a huge crush on him.

Lidia and Bridgette were very much alike. They liked the same style of clothes. They dressed very similarly each day. They walked the same, sounded the same, and laughed the same. They had been best friends for so long, they had adopted each other's mannerisms and characteristics. They were both petite and smart. They liked the same things, including the same type of boys. It was almost like they had morphed into twin sisters.

They didn't look exactly alike, however. Bridgette stood slightly taller than Lidia and was more developed physically. She had light blond hair that barely touched her shoulders, which she carefully styled each day before school. It always looked perfect. Lidia had long dark hair and a more natural beauty about her.

***

About midway through the school year, Joey (or Gunner, as he was more frequently called in his senior year) was back on top of the popularity board. He made the cross-country team earlier in the year. He ran well and received his varsity *W*, which he wore proudly on his Westmoor athletics jacket, which was green with white sleeves. Lenny the Leaf joined Gunner on the varsity baseball team later that year and both earned their baseball block letter. Big Ed was more academically focused, hoping for straight A's in his effort to land a scholarship at a prestigious university.

All three friends had their driver's licenses, but Ed was the only one with his own car. His dad purchased him a used 1955 Chevrolet as a pre-graduation present. Once Ed had the car, it was so long to the school bus.

That year was a more peaceful one for the Davis household. Ed's mom and dad rarely argued anymore. His mom tipped the bottle a little too much at times. They still remained in separate bedrooms, but all appeared to be on the mend, at least in Ed's eyes.

Susan Prouder was now Lenny's steady girlfriend. Big Ed was studying with Beth Ann once again, and Joey, well, he just played the field, searching for his one true love. He needed to find her soon for the senior ball was less than two months away. He dated Gloria Martinez for a while, and after her, he moved onto Carolyn "Sweet Lips" Cain. Joey broke their hearts. One or two dates, and it was all over. Lenny caught Sweet Lips crying in the study hall. Carolyn had become good friends with his girlfriend, Susan Prouder. Susan was furious with Joey for hurting Carolyn's feelings.

Lenny consoled Carolyn, and afterward, he tried to convince his girlfriend that Joey really never meant to hurt Carolyn's feelings, but Susan wasn't buying it. Lenny and Susan had double-dated before with Carolyn and Joey. Susan informed Lenny that there wouldn't be any more double dates that included Joe Gunderson. Lenny confronted Joey after his breakup with Carolyn. He told him not to date anyone else unless he was sure things would last beyond just a date or two. Lenny just couldn't understand. After all, he and Susan had been a pair now for about a year.

***

One Saturday morning, as Lenny and Joey helped Big Ed wash his Chevy, Bridgette and Lidia walked by.

"Hi, Joe. Do you need any help?" Bridgette offered as she approached the guys.

They all responded in unison. "No, we got this, girls."

The boys looked at each other and stopped what they were doing. All of a sudden, Ed started squirting water from the hose at the girls. Joey and Lenny threw wet sponges at them. Both girls retreated across the street to the safety of Liddy's porch.

Bridgette leaned over and said to Liddy, "My parents said that I could start dating after I turn sixteen. Guess who one of my first dates will be."

"Eric Johnson?" Liddy answered.

"No, silly girl. It's that one right over there, standing next to your brother."

"Oh…" Liddy replied. She was silent for a moment and then asked, "But I thought you liked Eric?"

"Eric is nice, and I know he likes me, but look at Joe. He's so handsome, so cute, and so nice. How could a girl not like him?"

Both girls sat and just watched the boys fool around, throwing buckets of water at each other. Liddy looked down at her shoes, which were now soaking wet. Looking at them brought back an old memory. She thought back to the time Joey had saved her life. After all these years, she still hadn't thanked him. She said good-bye to Bridgette and walked back into her house.

***

After the boys dried off, they sat on the front steps of Ed's house and listened to his car radio. They were discussing the upcoming senior ball, when Neil Sedaka's hit song "Calendar Girl" started playing. Lenny mused that Sedaka must have met May Jun somewhere.

"Yeah, on a plane. She's a stewardess for Pan American Airways out of SFO. She was really something special, wasn't she?" Big Ed said with a smile and then burst out laughing.

They all had a good laugh and then settled back down to the topic at hand, the senior ball. Lenny was taking Susan. Ed had already made arrangements with Beth Ann, and Joey, well…he just wasn't sure whom he would ask.

Joey watched as Bridgette and Liddy said good-bye to each other and remarked on how much Bridgette and Liddy had grown up. Joey then made the mistake of commenting on how beautiful Lidia turned out to be.

"She's only thirteen, and she's my sister, for God's sake. What are you thinking? Are you plotting to date her when she's old enough, so you can break her heart too? Just like you do all the girls you get involved with?"

Joey had never seen Lenny so upset about such a small thing. "No, I was just complimenting her, nothing more," Joey replied.

"Remember, Bridgette is OK…someday. Lidia is not OK…ever. She is off limits. Just promise me that you will never date her, even after she turns sixteen. The day you do is the day you jeopardize our friendship. Got it?"

"I don't understand, Lenny. I would never do anything to hurt Liddy's feelings. Never, believe me."

"Just promise me, Joey," Lenny requested.

"I promise on my life," Joey answered.

Lenny calmed down after Joey had promised him. He knew Joey would never break his word. It just wasn't his nature.

"Why is it that when a guy breaks up with a girl, he's somehow the bad guy, but when a girl breaks up with the guy, it's no big deal? He's just supposed to take it in stride and move on?" Joey opined. "Maybe I should ask Coleen Codington to the prom?"

"Not a good idea," Ed quickly responded.

Big Ed and Beth Ann double-dated with Lenny and Susan for the senior ball. Joey decided to stay home.

He had the opportunity to take one of two other girls who were interested in him but decided not to ask anyone. Joey always believed he would be taking the girl of his dreams to the ball, but that was not to be. He thought about what might have been. *Too bad Calendar Girl is no longer around. If she were, I would have been tempted to ask her, or more likely, she would have insisted I take her,* Joey mused.

With nothing else to do, Joey sat down to complete his English class final, which was to write an original poem or short story. Being in a melancholy mood, he wrote a poem, while day-dreaming about the Calendar Girl May Jun, titled "The Elf with the Raven Hair." Joey never showed anyone the poem, except for Lenny, who sat next to him in the same class.

***

On graduation night, all the families sat together. Joey's parents, Lenny's parents, Beth Ann's parents, and Ed's parents all sat next to one another. Beth Ann and Ed both finished near the top of their class, and their families were so proud. It was a great night for everyone. After the graduation ceremony, they all went to Nick's, a restaurant in Pacifica. They danced and enjoyed the night away. Liz Davis got a bit drunk. John Davis smoked his cigar with pride. It was a night to remember.

The next day, John Davis moved out of the house, leaving Liz and their son, Edward, to get by on their own.

***

After high school, Lenny started an apprenticeship under his dad's tutelage at Fairmont Jewelers in San Francisco. Joey got a job as a metal worker in San Bruno, just over the hill from Pacifica. Big Ed received acceptance letters from three out-of-state colleges but decided to stay close to home to help support his mother. He worked for Western Electric Company during the day, just a short distance from Joey's job site. Ed attended junior college in the evening. He and Joey would spend lunch breaks together from time to time, and Ed convinced Joey to attend college with him. Joey eventually agreed.

Beth Ann Codington went off to attend UCLA in Southern California. She would be gone over four years. She spent three of her summer breaks traveling through Europe with her new college friends. Beth Ann only came home briefly during winter breaks. Beth Ann and Big Ed drifted apart.

Lenny and Susan were still together, and things were looking serious for them until November 1963, when Susan unexpectedly broke up with him. They had been together for so long that she felt she needed some space, time away to sort things out. The day after their breakup, John F. Kennedy, the thirty-fifth president of the United States was assassinated. It was a bad week for everyone.

***

Joey and Lenny got together every few months and went fishing with Big Ed, sometimes in the greater delta area, and other times along the rivers and streams of the central valley of California. They'd camp out, drink beer, build a fire pit, and eat the fish they caught. Ed had a favorite spot along the Stanislaus River where he always caught the biggest fish. He'd say it was because he carried Valhalla with him wherever he went.

The young men would sometimes talk about the hot young women who crossed their paths. They eventually toned that type of talk down a bit because it was evident Lenny still missed Susan Prouder.

Those days would remain fond memories in their hearts. They were good times, good places, and good memories. That's the way it should be among true friends.

***

By late April 1964, Lenny's sister Lidia was worried she wouldn't have a date to her senior prom. She was now in her senior year at another new high school that sat on the hill overlooking Sharp Park. Lidia had been asked by several other students to be their date for that special night, but she politely turned them all down. Her friend Bridgette Dubois had held out too. She had her sights set on her long-time target, one Joseph Gunderson.

Bridgette was very beautiful, and every chance she got, she would hang out at Lidia's house because, more often than not, Joey would also be there. One Saturday night, with no dates, they all played cards, ate popcorn, and watched TV together. Bridgette sat very close to Joey even though there was plenty of room on the Leibowitz sofa. She faked falling asleep, just so she could lay her head on his shoulder. It must have worked because Joey was enjoying her attention.

When Bridgette yawned as if waking up, she stretched her arms out and pushed her chest forward, forcing Joey to notice her fine figure. Both Bridgette and Lidia talked about how embarrassing it was not to have dates for the prom. Bridgette suggested to Lidia that she have Lenny take her as a last resort.

"But everyone would know he's my brother. That would be even more embarrassing. I so want to go, but I just don't care that much for the guys that have asked me, and time is running out," Lidia said, her urgency reflected in her voice.

"I've got a great idea. Your brother can pretend to take me to the prom, and Joey can say that's he's your date when he's really my date. We can all take turns dancing with each other, and no one will suspect that your brother is your real date. Brilliant, huh?" Bridgette said, trying hard to make it sound logical.

"Bridgette, that doesn't make any sense. Besides, we're too old to be attending your senior prom. It just wouldn't look right," replied Lenny.

"Lenny, you and Joe look so young, no one would even pay attention," said Bridgette.

Joey finally spoke up. "I'll go with your plan, as confusing as it sounds. I missed my senior ball. I wouldn't want either of you to miss yours. Lenny, look at your sister. She'll be crushed if she misses the prom. Let's do it. What harm can it cause?"

Before Lenny could reply, Bridgette jumped up and said, "It's decided then. I can't wait."

As farfetched as Bridgette's plan was, Lidia saw some personal benefit to her best friend's idea. "Please, Lenny, for me, please," pleaded Lidia.

Lenny couldn't resist his sister's plea. "OK, but once the prom is over, we come right home. I don't want any of our other friends seeing us around town with you two afterward."

Bridgette immediately hugged both Lenny and Joe, but she gave Joe a much longer and closer hug. Her plan couldn't have worked better—and right in the nick of time.

***

The boys in their tuxes and the girls in gowns, they ate dinner at the Top of the Mark restaurant on Nob Hill. The two couples enjoyed a night of dancing in the main ballroom of the Mark Hopkins Hotel. Bridgette and Lidia looked radiant. Lenny and Joey actually enjoyed the whole night. Any reservations Lenny had quickly vanished. The view of San Francisco was spectacular, and the dinner was excellent. For the most part, Bridgette and Lidia shared dancing between Lenny and Joey, but whenever a slow dance began to play, Bridgette would quickly take Joe's hand and lead him to the dance floor.

The night was nearly over when the band announced that they had received a special request from someone in the crowd. Before the band even started to play, Lidia took Joey's hand and asked for the next dance. It was as if she knew what the band was about to play. The lead singer introduced the song.

"This request is for an old classic, a favorite of mine and one I know you'll enjoy. It's called 'Only You,' by the Platters."

The Platters were one of Joey's favorite groups. He couldn't be more pleased as he danced the slow love song with Lidia. Joey was careful to keep a respectful distance between him and Lidia, ever mindful of Lenny's admonition to him about her. Lidia recognized that Joey was dancing much differently with her than with Bridgette. With Bridgette, he held her tightly and danced with eyes that spelled romance.

When the two were safely surrounded by other couples, Liddy pulled herself close to Joey and said, "Joey, there is something important I need to say to you."

Lidia's closeness to him caused his heart to beat faster, and he gently tried to get an inch or two separation from her but gave up quickly. He didn't even hear what she had said.

"Joey, please look at me," she said in her softest voice. "Thank you, Joey, so much."

Joey tried his best not to look nervous. He knew his face was now flushed, so he turned his eyes away from hers. He thought, *what if Lenny sees me holding her like this, and why is she thanking me?*

"Joey, look at me," Lidia implored once again. "Joey, remember when we were kids? You risked your life to save mine. I was almost out of breath. I reached out in desperation. I felt a hand take hold of my wrist. I couldn't see you, but I knew it was you, Joey. You wouldn't let go. I know in my heart you would have held onto me, even drowned with me. I knew you would never let go."

A tear rolled down Lidia's cheek. Joey gently wiped the tear away with the tip of his finger.

"I never thanked you. I tried several times, but always failed. You started going steady with Beth Ann, and I...I..."

"It's OK, Lidia. Please believe me. It's OK. You do not need to thank me. I knew what was in your heart when you placed your hand on my shoulder that day."

Lidia leaned her head on Joey's shoulder as the last few words of "Only You" graced her ears.

She whispered, "This is our song."

There was more that she wanted to say, but the song had ended, and they were still holding each other after the music stopped playing.

When Joey realized the song had finished, he quickly moved away from her embrace. *She's much too young. It was the song, my favorite song. That's what got to me. I just got wrapped up in the moment, that's all, nothing more*, he told himself as his heart pounded rapidly. *I won't break my promise to her brother*, he forced himself to reason.

For Lidia, her night was now complete. She had finally said the words she had wanted to say—most of them at least.

On the way home from the prom, Bridgette made sure she was sitting next to her Joe in the back seat of Lenny's car. Bridgette suggested they go straight to Liddy and Lenny's home to relax a bit to end the night.

After inquiring about how the prom was, Lidia and Lenny's parents left them to be by themselves. The four of them hung out together. They chatted awhile, and once they had finished, Bridgette asked Joe to walk her home.

Joe walked her to her front doorstep. He told her he had a great time and was glad they had all gone together. Bridgette didn't respond. Instead, she leaned forward, waiting for him to kiss her good night. Joey kissed her on the cheek, even though her lips were ready for his.

"You're very beautiful, Bridgette. I'd like to see you again."

"Next Saturday, at six p.m.," Bridgette replied without any hesitation.

"Next Saturday it is. I'll call you on Friday."

As Joey walked home, he kept thinking about how Bridgette and Lidia were so much alike. It was then he began to have the same feelings, the very same ones he once had for Calendar Girl, for May Jun. He felt alive inside once again.

Bridgette had danced so close to him, he could almost feel her heart beat. She would turn eighteen soon. *Maybe she's the one I've been looking for all this time, or is she? She must be. I do like everything about her. The way she walks, the way she talks, the ways she dresses, the way she looks, her mannerisms, everything. Why not go for it? Saturday seems so far away. I can't wait.*

Joey dated Bridgette on a regular basis after she turned eighteen.

***

A month after the dance, Gunner, Big Ed, and Lenny the Leaf moved into their own apartment, just over the hills near South City. They were kids no longer. They had jobs, their own cars, and wanted their freedom. The joy and freedom of living on their own, away from home, was short-lived. Little did they know that just one month later, their lives would forever change.

Lenny received his selective service draft notice in August 1964, with an order to report to the Oakland Induction Center in September.

Lenny decided to meet with an army recruiter to talk about his options, about conscription versus voluntary enlistment. The army recruiter told him he could choose his own military job specialty if he joined and might even have a preferred choice for an overseas assignment. None of those options would apply if he were conscripted.

Lenny talked about his options with Gunner at the apartment they now shared. Gunner suggested that because there was no war going on, it might be best to be drafted. After all, he would only need to serve two years instead of the three- or four-year requirements if he were to voluntarily join.

Brian Codington was already serving out his military service in Germany and would soon be returning home. His sister Coleen had told them that Brian was having a great time in Germany. Jeff Baker joined the navy shortly after graduating high school, and he was now stationed down in San Diego, California. Jeff had written his mother, telling her he loved the navy and planned to be in it for life.

Lenny wasn't sure what to do. Being able to choose his job specialty was important to him. He wanted to learn about electronics and not be just some grunt. Lenny talked with his parents as well as Big Ed before making his decision.

The next thing Gunner and Big Ed knew was that the Leaf had decided to voluntarily join the regular army. He would be leaving in three weeks.

During those same three weeks, Susan Prouder let Lenny know she wanted to get back together with him. She missed him. Lenny was elated, and for the rest of the month before he left, they were inseparable. On their last night together, Susan made sure it was a night to remember. They were closer now than ever before.

Lenny left home but returned months later for a brief period before being assigned to his permanent duty station. He had completed his basic and advanced military training. He was to report for more specialty training on Okinawa, an island just south of the Japanese mainland.

In the little time that Gunner was able to spend with Lenny, he asked him what his job would be in the army.

"Well, Gunner, I asked if I could have an overseas assignment in the Pacific, instead of choosing a job specialty. Surprisingly, the recruiter made it happen. Oh…yes…I also decided right after my intermediate infantry training that I would follow the way of Thor."

"What is that supposed to mean, Lenny?"

"It means that I'll be a sky soldier with the 173rd Airborne Brigade."

"Have you even told your parents, and what about Susan? Does she know?"

"I don't want to worry them too much. Jumping out of airplanes and stuff, well, you know. But after I'm settled on Okinawa, I'll let them know what's going on and that I'm doing well. Don't worry. We're not at war with anyone. It will be my great adventure."

Gunner couldn't believe it, but what was done, was done. He wished his friend well and told him to write often. That night as Joey lay in bed, he said a prayer for his best buddy, Lenny the Leaf.

"Watch over the Leaf, Lord. Let him always land softly and safe. Protect him, Lord." Gunner continued to pray but drifted off to sleep before he had finished.

***

Liddy hugged her brother and told him she would write him weekly. His parents and girlfriend cried as they watched Lenny's plane disappeared beyond the clouds in the sky.

In early December 1964, Joseph Gunderson received his selective-service notice. Gunner was drafted into the Marine Corps. A short time later, Big Ed was also drafted.

Bridgette and Lidia both cried when Joey informed them he was leaving soon.

Bridgette privately told Joe she wanted to spend the last night with him, but Joe said no, it wouldn't be proper. Sure, he believed he loved Bridgette, but his ultimate love would be for the one who would become his wife, no one else.

If nothing else, Joseph Gunderson was true to his beliefs. It was his nature, the way he was raised, his personal faith, and what he considered honorable. That would never change.

On the day Gunner departed, after saying his good-byes to his parents, he turned his attention to Lidia and his girlfriend, Bridgette.

"I will write to you every week, just like I do my brother. You better write back each time." Liddy was very emotional and could hardly contain herself. She nervously reached in her purse and pulled out a little box. "Keep this. I had my dad make it special for you. Don't open it until you're on board."

Lidia was afraid she would collapse if she became any more emotional, which was why she didn't want Joey to open the gift in front of her.

Bridgette kissed Joey passionately as Lidia watched. "I'll make sure he writes to us both," Bridgette said as she released Joe from her arms.

It was time for him to go, and a feeling of sadness filled the air for all who watched him leave.

As Joe's plane climbed to cruising altitude, he reached into his coat pocket and pulled out the small box that Lidia had given him. He opened the lid. A small, folded note lay on top of the cotton-covered gift. Joe unfolded the paper and saw it contained only four handwritten words. *This one won't break,* it read. He moved the soft cotton aside and underneath was a small silver cross. It was unique in that it had lines etched into its surface and sides, which gave the metal a wood-grain texture. The cross had small, ax-like cuts on some of its edges, similar to the ones on his handmade cross years ago. The cross was much thinner than his original wooden cross, and the fine workmanship was readily apparent. Joe looked at the shiny cross in the palm of his hand and remembered years ago when little Liddy held the broken pieces of wood in her outstretched hands. Her eyes expressed the sadness she felt for him. Joe looked out the window of the plane and thought, *she remembered after all this time. Sweet Lidia, oh sweet Lidia, thank you so much. She's just so thoughtful.* Joe placed the cross's silver chain around his neck, and there it would always remain. He closed his eyes and drifted off to sleep.

***

A couple of weeks passed, and it was Big Ed's turn. His mother, Liz, was a wreck, but she pulled herself together enough to see him off. Lidia Leibowitz and her family, along with the Gundersons, were also there to see him depart. Ed was about to board the chartered military bus when he heard someone calling his name. The sound of high heels clicking on the hard floor at an ever-increasing pace filled the terminal.

"Ed, Ed, stop. Please don't board yet," an almost out-of-breath Beth Ann Codington pleaded. She nearly tripped as she stepped over the boarding rope. Ed quickly caught her. She hugged and kissed him. She had come home for her Christmas break from college and panicked when she heard he was leaving the same day she arrived.

"I miss you, Ed. Don't forget me. Please write. It's been so long since we've written to each other. I won't let that happen again." She kissed him once more before the bus driver urged him to quickly board.

It seemed that all the boys who had grown up on Carmel Avenue in Sharp Park were disappearing.

CHAPTER 9

NOVEMBER THE EIGHTH

Lenny's time on Okinawa went by quickly. The 173rd
Airborne was deployed to the country of South Vietnam in
May 1965. Lenny wrote to his girlfriend, Susan, his sister, Lidia,
and his parents nearly every week. He was proud to be a sky
soldier. He wrote and told them not to worry, that Vietnam was
only temporary, and the 173rd was expected to be back on
Okinawa by the first of the year.

Lenny's parents worried because right before Lenny joined
the military, there was an incident where a US Navy ship was
attacked by North Vietnamese torpedo boats in the waters off of
Vietnam. There were no US casualties, but the short sea battle
concerned his parents. Hearing that their son was now headed to
Vietnam only heightened their anxiety. But, as the months passed
by, everything appeared to be OK.

In September 1965, Big Ed Davis also arrived in the city of
Saigon, South Vietnam. Ed was now part of the First Logistical
Command. His administrative job in the logistics group was his
first exposure to what were then very sophisticated computers.

The computers aided in the ordering and tracking of weapons, food, clothing, and many other important items for the increasing number of US military in that troubled country. He still carried Valhalla with him. Ed believed that the cushy job he had, away from any possible harm, was the work of the agate marble he carried.

Joe "the Gunner" Gunderson had written both the Leaf and Big Ed letting them know he would be stationed near Da Nang, South Vietnam, as part of a large marine division. Da Nang was located over six hundred miles north of Saigon. Gunner expected to arrive in Da Nang in late October.

The three friends began to make plans to meet at the Rex Hotel bar in downtown Saigon, on Saturday, November 13, 1965. It would be difficult for Gunner, but he would try his best to obtain a three-day pass and catch a military flight to Saigon. They made no promises, but each would try his best to be there.

All the boys wrote home regularly. They missed their family and friends. Gunner received letters every week from Lidia, just as she had promised. His girlfriend, Bridgette, wrote every other week, just as his parents did. Liddy would tell him about all that was happening in Pacifica. Her letters tended to focus on how his other friends were doing, how things were changing in their little town and in the United States as well. Liddy always ended her letters by saying she missed him very much, and how she prayed each night for his safe return, as well as her brother, Lenny, and of course, Big Ed too. Bridgette would write mostly about herself and how she was doing. She once sent him pictures of herself in a bikini to remind him of what he was missing. Joe missed them all very much. He often reread Liddy's letters until her next letter arrived. She provided so much information about the goings-on with just about everyone in town. He also looked at Bridgette's picture every night before bedding down.

***

It was the morning of November 8, 1965, when the Leaf and the 173rd Airborne moved toward War Zone D's Hill Seventy-Eight, just north of the village of Bien Hoa. Lenny still had the sound of the unit's battle song, "Rawhide," by Frankie Laine, on his mind. The captain ordered the song played just before they left their home base of operations. Lenny was singing potions of the lyrics in his head:

Rollin', rollin', rollin'.
Rollin', rollin', rollin'.
Rawhide!
Move 'em out, head 'em up,
Head 'em up, move 'em on.
Move 'em out, head 'em up:
Rawhide!

He hummed them over and over again as he cautiously moved through the thick brush on the hill. He heard heavy firing nearby, and the song quickly faded from his thoughts.

The battle was now real. It was terrifying, but he was certain he would unleash the hammer of Thor on any black-pajama-clad Vietcong (VC) that dared to cross his path. He named his M16 rifle the Hammer just after arriving in Vietnam. His M16 never left his side. It was as if it had become part of his anatomy.

From behind him, the Leaf heard someone running through the tall brush. He turned quickly and shot a VC dead just before the little bastard was about to stick his bayonet into one of his fellow soldiers. Another black-masked VC came at him from the front. The Leaf let loose a burst of fire that dropped the poor little shit before he could even fire his weapon. The battle continued toward their objective until his platoon leader relayed a message that they were to redirect their movement to Hill Sixty-

Five to aid Company C. All hell broke loose as they attempted to move in that direction. The air stank. It was as if Hell itself had opened up, and every black-clad Vietcong had crawled from its depths. Before he knew it, his whole squad was engaged in close-quarter combat. There wasn't time to think—only shoot and pray. His friends, the soldiers he had trained with, drunk, and laughed with, were wounded or dying all around him.

The Leaf continued his advance to Hill 65 but became separated from what was left of his squad. Up ahead of him, he saw a soldier from a different platoon fall into some high grass ahead of him. He could hear the soldier moaning in pain.

Shit, if he keeps that moaning up, every VC in the area will converge around us. Lenny crouched low and moved slowly forward. He entered the tall grass. It was at least four feet high and provided some cover for him. There, lying on his back was a soldier who looked so young, you'd think he'd just got out of high school. Lenny went down on one knee.

"Help me, please," the soldier moaned.

"Stay still. I'll bind your wounds. Just stay quiet, no matter how much it hurts. Otherwise, we're both dead," Lenny whispered.

The soldier had three wounds—one just below his left knee, another near his hip, and still one more in his left side near his rib cage. Lenny feverishly tried to stop the bleeding.

"What's your name, soldier?" Lenny quickly asked.

"Private Ronald Brown," the young man replied.

"My name is the Leaf…I mean, that's what my squad calls me. Lennard Leibowitz is my real—"

The Leaf suddenly put his finger to his lips, motioning for silence. He could hear movement close by. Then whatever it was moved away. Lenny moved forward toward the soldier's feet and peeled the high grass apart just enough to see a group of

Vietcong moving across the hill just below his position. He gathered some long grass and began to cover the wounded soldier.

"Please don't leave me," the soldier quietly begged Lenny, thinking he was about to leave to find more solid cover.

Lenny had planned to cover the soldier as best he could and try to get back to his unit for help. The young man's midsection was now covered with blood, and the Leaf didn't have anything more to stop the bleeding.

"Apply pressure here with both your hands," he urged the soldier.

"Please don't leave me." The young man was now crying. He believed that if the Leaf left, he would surely die.

"I'll stay here until help comes," Lenny whispered.

Lenny could see the man was dying. He would at least stay with him till then. Lenny didn't want the soldier to die on that godforsaken hill alone.

They could hear huge explosions close by, and the ground rumbled beneath Lenny's feet, almost knocking him over. He could hear running coming down the hill, racing away from the thundering bellows of smoke and fire.

He thought about the soldiers in his unit, those he knew so well, who had fallen wounded or dead trying to take the hill, and his stomach turned. More explosions followed.

Kill every one of those bastards, he thought as the blasts rolled across the hills.

Suddenly a VC stepped through the high grass in front of him. Startled, they each fired their weapons at the same time. Two pajama-clad enemies lay dead in front of him. The second Vietcong had been right behind the first one. He had killed them both with one long burst from the Hammer.

Lenny felt a pain in the middle of his chest. He could no longer crouch, so he slowly lay down. He laid his back on top of the soldier he was trying to save.

He could no longer hear the sound of battle or feel any pain, even though hell rained down all around him. He thought about his life, his love, his friends, his sister, and his mama and papa. The sky above appeared clear with only an occasional whiff of smoke passing by. The tall green grass waved back and forth above his head. *It is beautiful.* He closed his eyes and was no more.

***

Joe Gunderson had done the impossible. Just after arriving in Da Nang, he was given the opportunity to volunteer for a special temporary assignment, along with three other marines. They were to pick up some special gear that the marine unit commander said had been mistakenly directed to another officer, one he personally knew, who was located in Saigon.

"That SOB doesn't deserve that stuff," he said. The boxes of gear were located in a warehouse near the city. He gave the marines a letter of authorization to pick up the gear and fly it back directly to him in Da Nang.

The four marines flew to Saigon and retrieved two heavy crates that clinked like they held bottles filled with some sort of liquid. It would be another day and a half before they'd be able to fly back to Da Nang.

The timing was perfect. It was the day before the three friends were all to meet at the Rex Hotel's nightclub. Gunner woke up the next morning and headed for the Rex, hoping that both of his friends would show up as planned. Gunner ate lunch, and arrived at the bar just after 3:00 p.m. He ordered three beers and placed them on the bar, one bottle to his left and one bottle to his right. It was well past 5:00 p.m. when he saw the big, badass Ed Davis enter the room. Joey smiled as Ed approached. Ed did not react. Big Ed sat down next to Joe and chugged the whole bottle of beer before slamming it back down on the bar without saying a word.

"Is Lenny coming?" Joe inquired.

Silence followed. Ed looked straight ahead and avoided looking at him. Joe's heart fell. He knew something was very wrong.

Big Ed finally looked at Gunner. "Our friend Lennard is dead. He died in battle earlier this week. His name was on a causality list that I read shortly before coming here."

Ed could say no more. Instead, he ordered another beer and whisky along with it. Joey could not drink anymore. His legs felt weak. He leaned his arms and head on the bar and wept, much like he had done years before while lying above the beach of Salada. It was a little while before they spoke a word. Once Gunner was able to compose himself, the two began reminiscing about their childhood friend, Lenny the Leaf.

"Do you remember that dorky Viking helmet he used to wear? Man, he sure looked funny." Big Ed smiled as he thought about those days. "Lenny was so convinced I cheated in class and that I only received good grades because I always copied off of Bethie's papers. Oh, you two always made me laugh." Big Ed smiled fondly as he spoke of Lenny.

"Lenny was kind of like the glue that kept us together, even when it seemed we had fractured forever. He influenced us both in a very positive way, didn't he, Ed?"

Ed nodded his head in the affirmative. Hours later, they said good night and returned to their units. The war had become very personal to them now.

***

It had become a custom for each combat unit, at an appropriate time after a deadly engagement with the enemy, to conduct a ceremony to honor their fallen brothers. For each marine or soldier who died, a makeshift memorial was set up with his rifle, boots, and helmet set in a row. The man's boots were set in front of his rifle. His rifle, the bayonet fixed, was stuck directly into the ground, behind the boots. Then his helmet was placed on top of the rifle butt. Someone read a prayer, and a bugler played taps in the background to end the service.

As hardened as many of the troops were after battle, there was weeping in their ranks when taps were played.

Gunner remembered how soothing the sound of taps felt as it played to end each military day during his basic training back in the States. Now he began to hate hearing the bugle sound because to him, it now memorialized death. Gunner longed to return to the real world, the safety of his home.

Big Ed was now seeing orders for more body bags and caskets coming through the logistics channels. The dead would arrive in body bags, and then they were transported to a military hospital where the bodies of the fallen were carefully prepared for shipment back home to their loved ones.

"God, I hate this place," he often said as he processed and tracked the ever-increasing demand for the containers of death.

***

It would be months before Gunner received another letter from Liddy. Bridgette had written that Lenny's parents had received a telegram informing them of their son's death. She said Lidia didn't come out of her house for weeks afterward.

Benny and Sofia Leibowitz received a personal letter from Lennard's commanding officer. His words were warm and comforting to them, and they appreciated the written word, unlike the telegram they had received from the government a week before. Lennard's personal effects were returned to the Leibowitz's shortly after they received the officer's letter. His personal effects included one dog tag and pictures of him and Susan, Lidia, Odie, and his parents. In the family pictures, all were smiling and happy. Also included were all the open letters he had saved from friends and family. They were wrapped in one bundle with a rubber band around them. The top two letters in the stack were unopened.

The first unopened letter was from his girlfriend, Susan Prouder. It apparently arrived just minutes before he left on Operation Hump. Lenny's parents set Susan's letter aside unopened. They hoped to give it back to her after the funeral that they were planning.

Why hadn't Lenny opened Susan's letter? That was something Lidia just couldn't understand. Did he have a premonition, or was he simply saving it to read later? Lidia wondered about this as her parents put Susan's letter aside.

The second unopened letter was address to his parents. On the front he had written: *To be opened only upon my death.* The words sent a chill through his mama and papa.

The letter outlined what he wished to occur in the event he didn't return from Vietnam. He did not want a traditional funeral. Instead, he asked that his body be cremated and the ashes held until both Joey and Big Ed returned from military service. Lennard went on to explain that he knew both his friends would return home unharmed. He wanted his ashes to be poured out on the *Nordic Prince* rock just off Mori's Point. He asked that his parents, other friends, and Lidia remain on the top of the bluff, and that they let his best friends do the honor. They knew what the *Nordic Prince* was, he explained in his letter, and the safest way to it. Lenny asked that Joey say a prayer and read psalm twenty-three before Big Ed scattered his ashes. Lennard asked that it be done in late September, after his friends returned home safely. *The weather is always nicer, and the sea calmer on the coast that time of year,* he wrote.

The letter ended with the words *I love you, Mama and Papa. Lidia, my dear sister, a brother could never ask for anything more than a sister as kind and thoughtful as you. Let your grief be short and your loving memories of me be long. I love you all, Lennard.*

After reading the letter, they all sat on the sofa, held each other close, and cried tears of sorrow.

***

The next day, when both her parents were gone, Lidia gathered her mother's steam iron, a small towel, and the unopened letter from Susan. She placed the letter underneath the small towel and, ever so carefully, released the steam from the iron as she gently rubbed it across the towel. She hoped the steam would release the glued flap on the letter, allowing her to read it. She planned to glue the flap back together afterward, so no one would be the wiser.

Two months before Lenny's death, she had seen Susan with an older man. They were holding hands as they walked through Golden Gate Park in San Francisco. That Saturday, Liddy had got off work early from her job at Fairmont Jewelry. She decided to spend an hour or two reading at the park before driving home. At first, she thought the man was just a friend or relative, but when the two sat down on a bench down the path from her, they kissed. She waited patiently and followed them when they got up and walked away. They walked off the path to a nearby tree, where they embraced and kissed each other more passionately.

Lidia wanted to write her brother and let him know what she had witnessed, but she didn't have the heart. She knew how much Lenny loved Susan. Liddy planned to tell him in person, rather than in writing, after he returned home from Vietnam. Lidia despised Susan after seeing her with another man. She hurt inside. It was as if she had been betrayed as well. With her brother, Lenny, now gone, she now had to see what that skank Susan had written him.

She was successful at ungluing the envelope. A short half-page letter was inside.

Dearest Lenny,

Our time apart has been very difficult for me. You know I will cherish all the time we spent together, and I will always be your friend. I must tell you that I have met another man, whom I have fallen deeply in love with. We plan to marry next June. Please understand, I did not intend for any of this to happen, but it did. This will be my last letter to you. I wish you well. You will always be my friend.

Sincerely, Susan

Lidia read it with horror. *Sending him a Dear John letter while he is in harm's way? How could she be so unkind? Couldn't she have waited to tell him in person?* Lidia snorted. *Love! What does she know about love? I have loved…*

Lidia abruptly stopped what she was thinking about. She felt guilty. She shouldn't have thought of Susan as a skank. Lidia felt like a hypocrite and realized how wrong it was for her to snoop into her brother's private affairs. The letter was meant for Lenny, not her. Still, Lidia was glad Lenny hadn't opened it. She let the envelope flap dry completely and then glued it back in place. It looked like it had never been opened.

A week after reading Lennard's request regarding his funeral, his parents returned to Susan what they believed was an unopened letter.

CHAPTER 10

FOR GOD, AND SOMEONE ELSE'S COUNTRY

It was four months since Lenny's death before Gunner finally received a letter from Lidia. At the same mail call, he also received two other letters, one from Bridgette and the other from his parents. Gunner opened Lidia's letter first. In the letter she talked about Lenny's last wishes. She also said that her brother had assured her before his death that both his friends would return home safely.

Still, she admonished him with the words, don't you dare die. Promise me you won't do anything stupid. I have so much to tell you.

Lidia always referred to Joseph as Joey, never Joe or Gunner. To her, he would always be her Joey. Her letter was seven pages long and included a picture of herself. She wrote just about everything she could think of to tell him. She even wrote that some women were burning their bras at the Linda Mar beach, for some unknown reason. She wrote that she immediately went home, picked up several of her old bras, and joined the other women. She went onto say her bras were now much too small for her anyway, and she enjoyed the festivities quite well. Gunner quickly picked up Lidia's picture and took another look. Joey placed the picture of Lidia next to his picture of his bikini-clad blond bomb shell girlfriend, Bridgette. He would now look at both pictures before bedding down.

She told Joey, she missed him so bad it hurt. Lidia ended this letter with the words Love, Lidia. In all her previous letters, she had always ended with, Your friend always, Lidia.

Gunner enjoyed reading his other two letters, but Lidia's letters were the ones he kept rereading. *I just enjoy them so much,* he told himself.

***

Lance Corporal Joseph Gunderson had made friends with the other members of the squad in the First Platoon. He bunked next to fellow lance corporals Robert "Bobby" Wilkens, and Henry "Hank the Weasel" Hastings. The Weasel was a slim man with a pointy-looking nose. His nickname fit his physique well. Lance Corporal Kyle Perkins also bunked nearby. Their squad leader, Corporal Matt Akagi, was respected by his squad. He believed he led the best squad in the company. Corporal Akagi's real name was Mamoru, but he went by the first name of Matt. He had a hidden tattoo located high on the inside of his right arm showing a red tree with Japanese kanji writing of 赤 木 right under it. Corporal Akagi insisted that his squad take karate lessons from him daily—just a few, clever, what he called red-tree karate moves to go along with their marine training. Some tried hard to master them, and others didn't do so well. At least the extra training broke the monotony of everyday life at their camp.

In January 1966, another marine by the name of Private Andy Malone transferred into their squad when Kyle Perkins returned to the States after his tour of duty ended.

The First Platoon's sergeant's name was Mike Taylor. He was a tough but good leader.

Each marine counted down the days until he would leave Vietnam. The squad mates became very good friends with each other, forming friendships they believed would last long after the war. Gunner and Bobby Wilkens, a young black man, got along the best. Lance Corporal Wilkins was the first black man Gunner had ever met. They both carried small New Testament Bibles and read them every night. Bobby, a Southern Baptist, prayed before each meal, to the chagrin of Hank the Weasel. Hastings was an atheist. He just couldn't understand why Gunner and Bobby believed in what he saw as simple-minded mythology.

"You believe all that nonsense, Bobby?" Hastings asked as Wilkins was reading his little book. "The world was created in seven days, and all that crap?"

"The universe, you mean, and no, not seven days. It was six," Bobby replied.

"Hastings looked at Gunner and asked, "And you believe it too?"

"My dad once told me that a day to the Creator is not like a day to mankind. God isn't bound by how we calculate time or space. For all I know, a day to him could be a thousand, maybe a million years. It doesn't really matter. It's the fact that we're created beings, and he is the Father of all creation."

"What a bunch of horse manure. I'd say horseshit, but I wouldn't want to offend you guys. I just don't understand," Hastings went on to say.

Joey continued to explain. "Science and several religions of the world believe everything started from basically the same point. Something has always existed and had no beginning. What many scientists believe preexisted were molecules, gases, or some other elements. Some say a random explosion occurred, and the universe was formed. In my faith, an intelligent being that is not of this world formed the universe. One instance is by accident, and the other is by design. I choose to believe it was by intelligent design."

"I suppose you guys believe everyone goes to heaven or some other nonsense."

Gunner spoke up. "Only those forgiven by the son of the living God will see the gates of heaven. I have a personal theory. I believe that when the son of God rose from the dead, from that point on, all who died before and after his resurrection awake in the great day of God Almighty. The soul is released and is drawn to that day. I believe the great eternal one transcends both time and space. I don't know if that's how it will actually be, but it doesn't really matter. I know where my final home will be regardless."

"Yeah…it'll be six feet under in total darkness. Now just shut up about it, I'm not here to listen to a fantasy. Just let me sleep now. OK, guys?" Hastings turned his head away, and closed his eyes.

Bobby Wilkins was always happy, joked a lot, and sang all the time, which annoyed the Weasel even more. The new guy, Private Malone, was into all things motorcycle. Hank referred to Malone as "scooter," but it was all in good fun. Scooter Malone dreamed of a grand road trip where he'd ride his old '57 Harley-Davidson motorcycle, the wind blowing through his hair along route 66, from his home in Amarillo, Texas to the beaches of sunny California. Matt Akagi took a liking to Private Malone because they both loved their bikes and yearned to ride them once they were home. Gunner thought of Bobby, Andy, Hank and Matt as his best marine buddies.

Gunner would sometimes express how much he hated the Vietcong, or VC as they were commonly called. He hated the

North Vietnamese Army (NVA) regulars just as much. To Gunner, they were all the same. The only difference was that NVA were better trained and wore military uniforms, while the VC dressed like villagers or wore black pajamas with straw hats.

The Vietcong had killed his best friend, and Gunner relished the idea of killing them in return. Bobby was of a different mind-set. Sure, he hated the enemy, but he also believed all life was a gift of God. He did not look forward to killing anyone. He would fight to save his own life and those of his fellow marine brothers, but he would not relish the killing. Gunner began to rethink his hatred because it was at odds with his own personal faith.

Their company's master gunnery sergeant was a fellow by the name of Richard Hauk. Major Moore, one of the unit's senior officers, sometimes slipped up and referred to him as River Hawk.

The major had been a young second lieutenant during the Korean War, and it was believed that Hauk had been a member of his platoon. If anyone other than the master gunny's senior ranks referred to him as River Hawk, he'd dress them down very quickly. Master Gunny Richard Hauk was regarded as the toughest marine in the division. He was from Montana and had served with distinction during the Korean War. There was one rumor that the master gunny was part Native American, and his tribe had named him the River Hawk.

Corporal Matt Akagi said he heard otherwise. He said that the master gunny got his nickname when he was stationed in Korea during the fifties. Private Hauk and a group of other marines were crossing a body of water during the Korean War when they received fire from the opposite shoreline from the communist North Koreans. Although he was standing in nearly chest-high frigid water, Private Hauk leveled his M-1 rifle and calmly dispatched four enemies with only four shots, causing the other

North Koreans to flee and allowing the US Marines to cross safely. For his quick reaction and bravery, he was awarded the Bronze Star for valor. His commanding officer gave him the name "River Hawk" because he was such a hawk eye with his iron-sight rifle.

No one really knew for sure which story was true, or if neither was, and all were afraid to ask him. He was strong, tough as nails, and always had a stern look on his face.

***

From time to time, various units from the Second through Fourth Marine Battalions would engage what were believed to be NVA forces moving south below the Demilitarized Zone, or DMZ. Helping the US Marines were units of South Vietnamese forces known as the Army of the Republic of Viet Nam (ARVN). The US soldiers and marines hated the VC and NVA soldiers. After many hard-fought battles, they no longer saw their enemy as even human. Too many of their friends had died terrible deaths. Their hatred was so strong, some of them began referring to the Vietnamese as "little slant-eyed gook bastards." Bobby and Gunner never characterized the Vietnamese in such a way. They only saw the VC and NVA as a heartless enemy that must be stopped.

In mid-July 1966, various marine units moved to stop the NVA forces and push them back across the DMZ. It was a very hot and humid day, and sweat and grime covered Gunner's fatigues and face. He had trudged through high elephant grass for what seemed like hours. The First Platoon engaged in numerous firefights with enemy forces throughout the day. They were fortunate and suffered no deaths and very few casualties. When evening fell, they set up positions on a hill and dug themselves in for the night. Sergeant Taylor spread his platoon across the north perimeter of the hill with two or three marines in each foxhole. Corporal Akagi sent Gunner back to retrieve some additional supplies stored just a short distance from the commanding officer's (the CO's) location.

The CO, Captain Kean, and his fellow officers had just finished reviewing plans for the next day's operation as the light faded from the sky. Captain Kean was a tall man who always carried a side arm in a holster strapped low on his leg.

Just when the CO stepped out of his large dugout, enemy mortars began to fall. One mortar struck near the captain, blowing off a good portion of his right leg. The blast knocked Gunner down. Smoke filled the darkness of the night. He was stunned; his head was throbbing, and his ears were ringing. Gunner immediately reached for his M16, but it was nowhere to be found. He frantically searched for his weapon, crawling on his knees, all the while feeling around to his left and right for the rifle.

He thought he heard Corporal Akagi yell that the NVA were charging up the north perimeter of the hill. A flare went off in the sky just after the initial round of mortars ceased. To Gunner's horror, a group of NVA soldiers breached the north perimeter, firing into the holes where sat his platoon members as they pushed forward. Gunner's hand felt something to his left. It was what remained of Captain Kean's right leg. The captain's semiautomatic forty-five-caliber pistol was hanging out of the holster. Gunner quickly took it and turned to find better ground, but when he heard Bobby cry for help, he turned back in time to see two NVAs come over the hill in front of Bobby and Andy's position.

The flares went out, and now only flashes of light from rifle fire and exploding grenades lit the hill. It was as if lighting were striking all around him. Gunner rushed forward trying to fire Kean's pistol as he ran, but nothing came out. The receiver slide had not been charged. Gunner quickly pulled the slide back as he continued charging forward, firing at the two NVA in front of him. His heavy breathing, and the fact that he was running while shooting, ruined his aim, and he missed all the enemies who were now running through their lines of defense. Fortunately for Gunner, the NVA missed him as well. Another flare lit the sky, and Gunner saw one of the NVA soldiers start to thrust his bayonet into the hole where his buddies Bobby, Hank, and Andy were.

The pistol was now out of ammo, so Gunner threw the gun at the NVA directly in front of him. The enemy soldier ducked and then tried to aim his AK-47 automatic rifle directly at Gunner, but Lance Corporal Gunderson was too fast. He was on him before he could get off a good shot. Instead of firing point-blank at Gunner from the hip, the NVA soldier took too much time to aim, allowing Gunner to push his weapon to the side, causing the enemy soldier to shoot one of his own men, a soldier who had just breached the perimeter. Gunner kicked the NVA in the stomach, took his weapon, and killed a soldier to his right, who couldn't seem to get his bayonet out of Bobby's body. Then he looked down at the soldier he had kicked and shot him dead. He fired the AK-47 down the hill until it ran out of ammo. He then picked up Bobby's rifle, but it was jammed, so he threw it down and grabbed Private Malone's M16. He continued firing down range, killing more NVA and slowing the enemy advance on the north side. He ducked back down when he heard the artillery fire that had finally been called in to silence any further mortar fire and force the enemy to retreat. The battle was short, but it seemed like an eternity to Gunderson.

Private Malone would never feel the wind blowing through his hair on his grand road trip. Andy Malone lay dead, his body riddled with bullets. Hank the Weasel was leaning against the back of the foxhole, his rifle still in his hands. In the little light that was left from the flare that floated slowly down from the night sky, his face looked very pale. He had a hole in his chest and was barely alive. Bobby was on his back in the center of the hole with his hands wrapped around the bayonet still in his midsection. He looked dead. Gunner began to cry. He was too late to save his friends. He tried to stop the bleeding from Hank's chest, but nothing seemed to work. He yelled for a medic, but none were close by. He knelt beside Lance Corporal Hastings and began to pray. His tears fell on Hastings's forehead.

"You're not trying to baptize me now, are you, Gunner?" Hastings joked. He choked after he spoke.

"I'd like that, if you'd let me," Gunner replied.

Without saying any more, Hastings closed his eyes and died. Just as Hastings breathed his last, Gunner heard someone say his name.

"Gunner…" The weak voice of Bobby Wilkins called out to him.

Gunner had thought for sure Wilkins was already dead. It shocked him to hear Bobby's voice.

"Bobby, stay with us. A medic will be here soon," Gunner told his friend. Gunner had no idea what to do. The bayonet was still lodged in Bobby's midsection, and no medics were anywhere nearby.

"Are Malone and Hastings OK?" he said weakly. "We fought like hell, you know. Those poor NVA souls, we took a lot of them down."

"Just don't move, OK, Bobby? Don't worry about Malone and Hastings they're here with us."

"You're a good man, Joseph Gunderson. Tell my family…"

Those were the last words his friend Lance Corporal Robert Wilkins spoke. Gunner leaned back next to the dead body of Hank Hastings. It was then that he realized he had defecated and pissed his fatigue pants. He could feel the diarrhea still running down his legs.

If I had only stopped running and shot from a more stable position, I'm sure I would have killed those bastards before they killed my friends.

***

"Medic!" Gunner cried out again, not knowing even why he yelled. After all, his friends were already dead. Gunner slowly got up and started to head back to higher ground when a series of shots rang out all around him. Directly to his right lay a freshly dead NVA soldier, bayonet still in hand. Two more had just fallen dead to his left. Up the ridge was Master Gunny Richard Hauk. The River Hawk had killed them. He waved for Gunner to quickly race to where he stood. Master Gunnery Sergeant Hauk had just saved Gunner's life.

Just beyond the little ridge, the wounded lay on the ground, being attended by the medics. Corporal Akagi had a shoulder wound, but he didn't express any pain. He walked around checking on everyone else. When Akagi came by to check on Gunderson, Master Gunnery Sergeant Hauk told him to stay by the medics and rest up. He let Akagi know that three in his squad were dead. Akagi sat down and hung his head in despair.

Hauk kept everyone away from Gunner, even Sergeant Taylor. He had witnessed Gunner running and firing a pistol wildly at the enemy. He saw him engage in hand-to-hand combat with them. Gunner had informed him that three marines in the forward foxhole were dead when he first reached Hauk on the ridge. When it was safe, Hauk sent a squad out to retrieve their bodies.

"Lance Corporal, you stay in this position and guard the ridge," he ordered Gunner.

Hauk knew that Gunner had messed his drawers. He reeked with a foul smell. He would stay with Gunner, regardless of the smell, and would let no one else come near.

Gunner prayed that night for his friends, but he also prayed for rain. He wanted to wash the filth from his body. He knew he smelled like death itself, and he was ashamed.

Apparently, during a battle not too far away, two Hueys had crashed on a nearby hill, killing those aboard. The landing zone was too small for them both to land. They had been under heavy fire from the enemy.

Before they could attempt an evacuation from the hill where Captain Kean's company was located, a large enough landing zone had to be cleared for the medevac choppers, before they'd even attempt to land. Captain Kean was miraculously still alive—just barely, but nonetheless, he was still breathing. Unfortunately, heavy clouds hampered the rescue efforts, and it was late in the day before the marines were airlifted to safety.

As morning dawned, Gunner kept looking to the sky, hoping for rain. Only a thick layer of clouds was above him. The humidity was almost unbearable, and the stench around Gunner increased. Finally, he could feel raindrops falling from the sky. It rained steadily for only about fifteen minutes. Then the clouds disappeared. The sound of Huey helicopters could be heard approaching the large landing zone that had been cleared early that morning.

Just over the ridge, a small distance from Gunner, was a foxhole with two or three inches of water in it. He quickly removed his boots, and M16 in hand, he raced down to that little water hole. He stripped all his clothes off and knelt naked in the foxhole. He splashed the muddy water all over his body until very little water remained in the hole. He held his hands outstretched in the air, reaching for the last few drops of rain. When no more rain fell, he backed out of the hole and grabbed his soiled pants. He scrubbed them in the dark mud and what was left of the water in a failed effort to clean them.

Above him, he heard someone yell, "Get that son of bitch out of there, and put some clothes on the bastard. He's supposed to be a marine, goddammit. Who the hell is in charge here?"

The master gunny walked over to the lieutenant colonel, fresh off the chopper, who had called Gunner a son of a bitch and quietly had a word with him. No one could hear what they were saying, but the lieutenant colonel quickly backed away. He had a nervous look on his face and said nothing more.

"You heard him! Get down there and help Lance Corporal Gunderson. Get something to cover him and get him on the chopper as soon as the wounded are loaded." Hauk yelled out the orders to one of the squad leaders nearby.

The marines wrapped a blanket around Gunner and walked him to another Huey chopper that had just landed. He sat in the Huey as it lifted off, still in shock from the battle the night before. He knew his life would never be the same.

Gunner had suffered two small shrapnel wounds from the mortar shell that nearly killed the CO. He wasn't even aware of the wounds until a medic looked him over and patched him up. Before leaving Vietnam, Gunner was awarded the Bronze Star and a Purple Heart. Rumor had it that Master Gunnery Sergeant Hauk had recommended a Silver Star, but some jackass lieutenant colonel had reduced it to Bronze.

It didn't matter to Gunner. He saw his actions as a failure and was ashamed that he had soiled his fatigues out of fear. He returned home after completing his military service and was honorably discharged from active duty.

A few weeks after Gunner was discharged, Big Ed Davis, who never needed to fire a weapon while in Vietnam, returned home to Sharp Park as well. The war was over for the boys from Carmel Avenue.

Chapter 11
The Light

It was a quiet homecoming for Joe Gunderson. His mom and dad met him as he stepped off the plane. They all hugged. His mom cried, and when she dried her tears, she told him another surprise awaited him just around the corner. Near the exit, there stood his girlfriend, Bridgette Dubois. Many things had changed stateside while he was gone. Flower children roamed Golden Gate Park. Miniskirts were in vogue. Hairstyles had changed, and long hair was in for men not just women. Much had changed indeed. Bridgette looked even more beautiful now than when he had left years ago. She was wearing a short skirt and beaming at him, making little hops up and down, as he approached.

Bridgette looked at Joe. He looked older but so much more handsome in his dress uniform. She had waited out of sight, so his parents could enjoy the first moments of their son returning home. Finally, Bridgette ran to Joe and kissed him. It was the moment she had waited so long for. In the two years he was gone, she remained faithful. Bridgette loved Joe Gunderson—of that there was no doubt, and Joe knew it. He missed hearing her soft voice in his ears, her kisses, and her warm embrace. All the residue of war seemed to wash away once he held his girl in his arms. He spun Bridgette around. He just couldn't wait to get back to his hometown.

A special dinner was waiting for Joe. When he entered his home, the smell of Italian cooking was in the air. Pasta was his favorite food. When he was a boy, on more than one occasion, he had eaten at his friend Lenny's house. Sofia Leibowitz was a great cook. *Is it she who is in the kitchen?* he thought. But it wasn't Lenny's mom. It was Lidia. She had stayed behind to prepare a meal that she knew Joey loved—fresh, homemade fettuccini with clams, sauce, garlic bread, veggies, and wine.

Lidia took a deep breath as Joey entered the kitchen. She swiped at the apron she was wearing as if to dust away some flour residue. But that was not the real reason she brushed herself. She felt her knees shake at the sight of Joey and was trying to calm herself. She had to hold herself back from rushing into his arms. She probably would have if it weren't for Bridgette standing right next to him.

"Welcome back, Joey. It's good to have you home. We all have missed you more than you could ever know. I've prepared—"

Before she could finish her sentence, Joey walked around the kitchen table and gently and ever so briefly hugged her. He quickly kissed her on the cheek. "Hello, Lidia." She stood with her arms down, fearing that if she embraced him, she would not want to let go.

The dinner, as expected, was delicious, and everyone thanked Lidia for the wonderful meal. They talked and sipped wine for over an hour.

Bridgette wanted some alone time with Joe, so they went in his backyard. It was cold, something he rarely felt in Vietnam, where it was mostly hot and humid.

"Hold me, Joe. I am very cold," Bridgette softly said. Joe held her close, and the heat from her body warmed his very soul. "I love you, Joe. I want to be with you forever," she softly said.

After Joe and Bridgette went outside, Ruth Gunderson helped Lidia clean up in the kitchen. Lidia hardly said a word. Joey and Bridgette were still outside when she left to go home. A quick good-bye was all Joey and Bridgette offered her. They were too busy trying to keep each other warm.

In the months that followed, Joe and Bridgette were inseparable. It became very obvious to Lidia that her Joey was very much in love with her best friend, Bridgette Dubois.

It was Lidia's own fault. She had loved Joey Gunderson for as long as she could remember but could never tell him. She wanted to, but the words just wouldn't come out of her mouth. She was too young, or he was always dating other girls. Then he was with Bridgette, and it just never seemed right for her to let her true feelings out. Lidia was a beautiful woman now, but she was convinced it was too late for her to confess her love.

The more the months passed, the more it appeared Joey was going out of his way to avoid being around Lidia. When he did see her, he was always polite. He'd engage in small talk but not a hint of anything more.

Bridgette and she were so much alike, and they always got along so well. Bridgette was the best friend anyone could ever hope for. She was thoughtful, kind, and beautiful in every way.

Lidia thought, *If I can't have Joey, then Bridgette should be his love.* She wanted the best for both of them—at least, that's what she convinced herself. It hurt, but in her heart, she believed it was the best approach. Lidia resolved that she would do her best to find another man as good as Joey. To ease her heartache, she visited with Bridgette only when Joey wasn't around.

***

Big Ed came home to a party thrown by his best friend Joe "the Gunner" Gunderson. All the old neighborhood guys who were still around came by, and a great time was had by all. His mom, Liz Davis, was making an effort to quit drinking and smoking, but the boy's party wasn't helping. Bridgette, Liddy, and Coleen Codington also joined in the fun. Beth Ann was in Southern California just finishing up her master's degree, but she took time to phone Ed to let him know she'd be coming home soon. They all talked about their old friends, the changes in town, and about a new pier that was to be constructed on Salada Beach where the old waste pipe used to be. Everything was different and yet the same as before—except for one thing. For Gunner and Big Ed, the place didn't seem right without their friend Lenny by their side.

Two weeks later, Beth Ann showed up on Ed's doorstep. As soon as he opened the door and before even saying hello, she kissed him. Big Ed's dream had finally come true. Beth Ann Codington, the beautiful blonde, was back in his life once again. They went steady after she returned. Big Ed, for the first time, told her he loved her.

After he confessed his love, Beth Ann pulled herself close to him, kissed his ear, and softly whispered, "I love you with all my heart, Edward Davis."

The big, badass Ed Davis melted like butter in her arms. He knew then whom he would marry.

Ed still carried Valhalla with him wherever he went. He was convinced the agate marble had saved him from fighting in the war, and now Beth Ann would someday become his wife. *How much better could it get?*

* * *

In the first September after the boys had returned home, they made plans to fulfill Lennard's last wishes. They set a date and prepared everything for their final good-bye to son and friend, Lenny Leibowitz. The Leaf's ashes would be scattered across the *Nordic Prince* rock just offshore from the point.

Lenny's friends and family drove to the parking lot of Mori's Inn Restaurant. The restaurant had been closed for years and looked dilapidated. From there, they walked up a narrow path to the top of the bluff. Lenny's friends had placed folding chairs near the edge of the bluff for his family. A three-person military honor guard accompanied Lennard Leibowitz's ashes, which his friend, Big Ed Davis, carried. Behind Ed, Joe Gunderson carried a backpack filled with a rope, a large candle, a folded paper lamp, and an old papier-mâché Viking helmet. Lenny had been dead for about two years, but the funeral procession made it feel like he had died just days before.

Once they were all on top of the bluff, Joe began talking about his friend Lenny. He said Lenny was a kind soul. That was how he had been brought up. He had been raised in a home filled with love. He loved adventure, he loved his girlfriend, but mostly, he loved his family. After speaking of his best friend, Joe said a short prayer, asking the Lord to give comfort to all those who now grieved.

"I read you now my dear friend's last words to his family. Please remember and follow his last wishes as best you are able. Here is what he wrote. *Let your grief be short and your loving memories of me be long. I love you all, Lennard.*"

Joe's voice cracked as he read the words. He paused several times before finishing. After speaking, Joe turned his back and looked out to the sea.

The army honor guard performed a solemn flag-folding ceremony and presented a carefully folded American flag to Lenny's mother and father. A third soldier played a recording of taps in the background. Joe turned back around. Both he and Ed stood at attention and saluted. The honor guard slowly turned and walked in single file back down the bluff.

Ed and Joey proceeded down to what was left of the lower path that led to the Nordic Prince rock. The climb down was steep. Joe tied the rope from his backpack onto a stake he had pounded into the ground the day before. Both he and Ed slowly descended to the lower ledge. Once there, they jumped down into over a foot of ocean water and waded to the rock. Joe prepared Lenny's *Nordic Prince* ship. He popped open the round paper lamp. It was a Japanese-style lamp made of wire and thin paper. Joe placed the large, wide candle in the bottom of the lamp and secured the lamp to the rock with wire. He placed the old Viking helmet just below the lamp. Once he lit the candle, he nodded his head to Ed. As Ed poured Lenny's ashes onto the *Nordic Prince*, Joe recited the twenty-third psalm from memory. Lenny's sister and family looked down the edge of the bluff from above. By now, it was past five thirty, and soon the sun would be setting.

Ed and Joe climbed back up to the top of the bluff and watched the calm waves gently curl around the base of Lenny's Viking ship. They stayed until the sunlight was nearly gone.

Lidia decided to walk home along the berm by the golf course instead of driving. She asked Bridgette to drive her grieving parents' home. Joey decided to walk with Lidia because the sun was fading, and darkness would soon be upon them. When Joey and Liddy reached the bottom of Mori's Point, only the moon graced the dark sky.

A small flicker of light could now be seen on top of Lenny's rock. Lidia stopped, looked, and began to sob. Joey took her in his arms. Her body shook with sadness. He held her tight, not saying a word. They both stood and watched the light offshore for nearly an hour until the waves increased, and the flickering of light went out. Lidia had never been in Joey's arms for so long, not even when they danced at her senior prom, years ago. She didn't want to let him go. As Joey attempted to move, she stopped him.

"No, not yet, Joey. I want to stay just a little bit longer."

This was not the way she dreamed of Joey holding her. In her dreams, they embraced in happiness. Now she held him with sadness in her heart. She had never imagined it would be this way. Her sobs turned into many tears. By the time Joey walked her home, his shirt was completely wet, but he paid no attention to it. In his own heart, he realized he also didn't want to let Liddy go.

***

As part of the divorce settlement, Ed Davis's father had paid off Ed's childhood home, the house he had grown up in. His mom, Liz, worked as a part-time waitress at a small local restaurant. She earned just enough to get by. Ed had always sent her part of his pay when he was in the military. He continued to help support his mother after he found work in the South Bay Area.

Joe Gunderson's parents purchased the home they had rented for years from the now ailing Mama Morales. Mama's oldest daughter convinced her to live in San Diego with her family.

Mama agreed, even though she never really wanted to leave Salada. But she knew her health was declining and wanted to spend her last years with her own children.

Big Ed's data management position in the service, along with his associate's degree, served him well. He landed a job an hour's drive south at a large computer-storage manufacturing company in San Jose. His friend Joe was able to find work at a machine shop just ten minutes away from where Ed was now working.

The two friends decided to share an apartment in the Bay Area. Each weekend, holiday, and vacation time, they drove to Pacifica and stayed at their parents' homes, visiting with their girlfriends. Ed enrolled at San Jose State College and took evening classes to obtain his bachelor's degree in engineering. It took him a number of years to achieve his educational goal.

Ed and Beth Ann made plans to marry nine months after he had returned home.

Bridgette was pressuring Joe to settle down with her, even if it meant living together before marriage. That was not something Joe would even consider. He wouldn't live with her outside of marriage, but he also couldn't think of any reason why he shouldn't marry Bridgette. After all, he loved everything about her.

Something was holding him back from making the big decision. He wanted more time to think about it. Bridgette knew what she wanted. Her heart belonged to Joe. She practically asked him to marry her one night as they sat in his car, parked by the beach. Joe agreed that he would give thought to a formal engagement.

Somehow, that allowed Bridgette to believe that they were now officially pre-engaged, so she called her best friend Lidia to give her the good news.

"You can be my maid of honor. I'm sure Joe will choose Big Ed as his best man. It will be so wonderful," Bridgette cheerfully told Lidia.

"When…when do you two plan to marry?"

"The date hasn't been set, but I hope it will be very soon. I dream about how our honeymoon night will be all the time now. I can't wait. Isn't it wonderful? I knew Joe was the man for me way back when we were in high school. Can you imagine that? I've waited so long, and now my dreams are coming true. I'm so happy, Liddy. Please be happy with me. You're my best friend. You'll always be my best friend, Liddy, even after Joe and I are married."

"I will always be your best friend, Bridgette. Your friends are my friends, and my friends are your friends. That's the way it is and will always be. I am very happy for you and Joey," Lidia replied.

After ending her conversation with Bridgette, Lidia took a long walk on the berm leading to Mori's Point. Her heart was happy for her friend Bridgette and broken at the same time. She sat and watched the waves roll in and out. She remembered how, when she opened her eyes after almost drowning, there was Joey. She didn't know what love was back then, but she knew what it was as she matured. She only had eyes for one. She dated other boys in high school, but it was always one or two dates and done.

She laughed to herself. *That was the same reputation that Joey had, according to her brother, Lenny.*

***

Time passed, and it was time for Big Ed and Beth Ann's marriage. Coleen Codington was Bethie's Maid of Honor. Lidia and Bridgette were the bridesmaids. Joe was Ed's best man. Brian

Codington and one of Beth Ann's cousins were the ushers. Everyone danced the afternoon away. Joe toasted the newlyweds. Beth Ann threw her bouquet over her head. Her sister Coleen caught it, just as Lidia and Bridgette had planned. Big Ed removed the garter from Bethie's beautiful leg, and shot it directly at Joe, just as he had planned.

Joe watched Lidia anxiously waiting for the band at the reception to stop playing. When they stopped, she talked to the lead singer.

Joe heard the singer say, "I'm sorry, but I don't know that song."

Lidia looked very disappointed.

Why? She should be having a good time. The band is playing plenty of good songs. It troubled Joe to see her sad expression, in what was such a happy event.

The party ended, and Big Ed went off with Beth Ann on their honeymoon to Hawaii. They wouldn't return for two whole weeks. Ten months later, Beth Ann had her first baby. They named their firstborn baby girl Alysia. Beth Ann and Ed would have three more children over the years, all girls—Bobbi-Ann, Carol-Ann, and Adelynn, who was born after Bethie turned thirty-nine. He gave up after Adelynn. Having a boy just wasn't in the cards.

***

A week went by and Lidia decided to go through some of her brother's old keepsakes that he always kept tucked away in an old cigar box. She found a sealed note underneath an old picture addressed to "Gunner" dated just before her brother was deployed overseas. It had never been delivered. For just a brief moment, Liddy thought of opening it just like she had done with

Susan's letter, but instead she kissed the envelope where the name Gunner was written. She walked to the Gunderson's, and knocked on the door, hoping Joey would answer. The door opened and there stood Ruth Gunderson.

"Come in, Lidia, I've just brewed some tea, please have some with me, it's been so long since you've been here."

"Thank you, I'd love too." They sat down just across from the fireplace and exchanged some polite small talk.

"I found this note from Lenny addressed to Joey and wanted to deliver it to him." As Liddy reach out to hand Ruth the note it slipped from her hand and fell into the open lid of the tea kettle. Ruth quickly grabbed the edge of the envelope and pulled it out. She ran into the kitchen, fetched a towel, and immediately pulled the note out of the envelope to dab it dry. There it lay, the ink starting to smear, but it was out in the open and still easy to read.

It was a note to Joe reminding him of the promise he made to watch over Liddy while he was away. Treat her like you're her brother while I'm gone my friend. Protect her from getting involved with any bad men. You said it years ago that she'd be a beautiful woman someday, and it's now come true. I fear her beauty is like Valhalla, both a blessing and a curse. I don't know why I'm sending you this reminder, because I already know you'd never let anything or anyone hurt her. You are my best friend, Gunner. There is something else I need to tell you. I had a dream that someday you'll be torn between a golden haired one and some dark-haired girl. I couldn't tell who these women were, but I'll just say your old poem "The Elf with the Raven Hair," gives you the answer to your torment. I know you will choose the one you truly love. Your friend for life, Lenny the Leaf.

"Who is the elf with raven hair?" Liddy asked Ruth.

"In Joseph's last year of high school, he wrote a poem, or perhaps it was more of a short story, I think. It was titled "The

Elf with Raven Hair," I heard him tell Lennard once he still thought about some raven-haired Asian girl that lived in Pacific Manor. I believe her name was May, but I'm not sure. He never let us read the story for some reason. I heard most of it for the first time yesterday. Joseph had the poem in his hand, and all the letters he received when he was in the Marines lay by his side. He sat in front of the fireplace, and it looked like he was going to burn the letters, so I grabbed them and quickly hid them away. When I returned, I heard him reading the poem out loud. The words were somewhat sad. It was about a love that could never be, and I wondered if, in some odd way, the poem was more about what he's feeling now. I don't think it's about the girl that lived in the Manor anymore. Then I watched him toss each page of the poem into the fire. He reached back to where his letters were, and looked up at me. I said, Joseph, I couldn't let you, please forgive me. I'll return them to you after you think more about what you're doing."

He said, "it's all right mom, you always knew what's best for me. Hold them for me, perhaps one day I'll be ready to read them once again."

"He said it was time for him to step up and bend the knee to the one with golden hair. He said he was going to the city to pick something up, and left without saying anything more."

"Bridget will be so happy," Joey's mom said in almost a whisper.

"What more did the poem say," Liddy inquired.

"Oh, Liddy, it was his poem, and only he can tell you. Maybe he also wrote it in his journal. But I just don't know. Joseph has taken the week off from his job to finish moving and tie up some loose ends."

"Did he mention to you that he moved into a new two-bedroom apartment further south of San Jose? Even though he lives in the south bay area for a while now, he always kept his room here just like it was years ago. We enjoyed seeing him on his regular weekend visits. Now his bedroom seems so empty. He removed all his pictures off the wall, along with pictures of us, you, Bridget, Ed, Lennard, and Odie. He boxed up his book collection, sport mementos, radio and all his other clothes. I know we won't be seeing him as much anymore, and we're trying very hard to appear as normal. But know this Liddy, someday when you have children, and they move away, believe me, you'll always worry for them, because they'll still remain forever as children in your heart. We will miss him so much. Roth and I knew this day would come, but just like when he was in the military, it doesn't make it any easier."

Liddy sat as if frozen, she politely finished her tea and walked home alone in her thoughts.

The next day Liddy walked to the Salada beach cafe where she purchased a cup of coffee. She sat down on a spot overlooking the beach, and tears began to well up in her eyes.

Joey decided to take a walk as well, because he had a great deal on his mind. He intended to just walk around the block, but when it came time to turn the corner, he saw Liddy sitting all alone. He stopped for a moment, and again started on his intended way. He stopped once again, turned around and made his way back to Liddy. He needed to speak with her, even if just for a moment. Liddy glanced back and saw Joey as he approached.

"May I sit next to you Liddy" Joey asked with all politeness.

Liddy nodded her head, and quickly wiped her tears away before really looking at Joey. "What is it, Joey?" Liddy's soft voice filled his ears.

Joey reminisced about their childhood, the good memories, and the fun they had over the years, how Lenny was the best of all friends. It was then that Joey's voice began to break.

Liddy looked into his eyes, and pulled Joey closer, placing her head against his shoulder. She felt a tear fall from his cheek onto her hand.

"Oh Liddy, Liddy... Lenny loved you so dearly. He once told me that you were a great blessing to the family. You would one day marry someone whose love was as great as yours. It would last forever. You know Lenny was a dreamer, and he believed his dreams, so it must be true. You can't imagine how much comfort this gives me. I've only made two real promises in my life, and both were to your brother. I promised him I would watch over you as a substitute brother while he was away. Little did I realize he would be gone forever. I feel I have been remised in fulfilling that promise this past year."

He was going to say more but Liddy put her fingers to his lips.

"You could never be my brother, substitute or otherwise. Never! Do you understand Joey?"

Shocked at the sternness of her words, Joey looked at the waves breaking on the shore, not knowing how to respond.

"I never meant to offend you; it wasn't my intent. Perhaps I should go. I've overstayed my welcome." Joey started to stand, but Liddy took his hand and asked him to sit for a while longer.

"You don't understand, my words came out the wrong way. You have kept your word to my brother, and I release you from that promise." My brother had dreams, but know that I sense things in others. I know you have great love in your heart. I feel it each time you are near. I know how that feels. You should know that I fell in love with a man years ago. We only had one date, and it was like a wonderful dream, but then I woke up and he was gone. He had fallen in love with someone else."

"Well, I guess that's one way to get over a relationship. You're better off without him. The man's a fool to lose someone like you." he replied.

As Joey called the man a fool, Liddy thought to herself, he's no fool. He could never be a fool in her eyes, for you see, Joe didn't realize that the man she spoke of was the one she danced with at her senior prom.

Liddy just smiled, paused for a moment and said, "You bought a ring a couple of days ago, didn't you?"

"How did you know. Both you and your dad where out that day."

"You know that we would have given you a huge discount if we had been there. I could have helped you pick out a ring I know Bridget would have loved. Why would you buy the ring in secret? Liddy curiously inquired.

"Please don't tell Bridget, please. There is so much going on in my mind, no, in my heart that I can't explain, especially to you her best friend." Joey implored her.

Liddy could feel the emotions welling up within him, and simply replied, "Okay Joey, I understand."

"I'm curious, there were numerous wedding sets on display at the jewelry store. Which one did you choose? Liddy's interest was piqued.

"None of them, they just didn't call out to me. I asked if there were any others, and to my surprise, there was one that was not on display. It was sorted of hidden. A simple set it was, but I felt something inside, so I through caution to the wind and purchased it. I have made reservations for Saturday, at a restaurant that Bridget loves. Do not mention anything to her, please," Joey stressed.

"Okay, Joey, you don't need to ask me twice, your secret is safe with me."

Liddy had hidden that ring set for two weeks, she loved it so, and didn't really want to sell it too just anyone. *What a coincidence, she thought. How perfect, the ring she loved was the same one Joey chose.*

"Bridget loves you with all her heart, and you will be the best husband a woman could ever hope for. Love her Joey, as you have never loved anyone before. I can feel the love within you. You two deserve each other, and that fills me with joy." *It did fill Liddy with joy for her best friend, but in the deepness of her heart a sadness dwelled.*

Liddy could sense that Joey was about to say good-bye, so she felt compelled to ask him one more question. It was like old times being around him. They hadn't really talked with each other for what seemed like ages and she cherished these moments. "You said you made two promises to my brother. What was the other promise you made to Lenny?"

As Joey gathered his thoughts, there was a long pause before he replied.

"Liddy, that's a promise that will remain between Lenny and me. I will only say that he was protecting you from what he believed would one day crush your heart. I will keep my promise to your brother, even if it destroys …." He abruptly stopped mid-sentence. "I must leave now. I'm glad we had this time together." *How lucky he thought, I almost uttered what I told myself must never be expressed.*

Liddy wanted to ask Joey more, but sensed an urgency within him. She held onto his hand and then very slowly released it, letting her fingers slowly slide away from his touch. Joey rose up, rubbed his hand against his leg and quickly walked away. Liddy watched him as he departed. She wondered if he would turn back and look at her. Joey stopped half way up the street, but didn't turn around. Instead, it appeared that he wiped something from his cheeks, and then continue on his way.

***

A day later, Bridgette and Joe entered Fairmont Jewelry. Joe's reason for stopping by was so he could speak with Benny Leibowitz. Both Lidia and her father were there.

After saying hello, Bridgette began looking at all the diamond rings. Joe walked over to Benny and thanked him for the cross he made for him years before.

"I always wear it. It's very unique," he said to Benny, as he pulled it out from under his shirt.

"Oh, yes. Lidia here…" Benny glanced over to Lidia standing a short distance away. "She gave me a set of detailed instructions as to how it should look. I brought three different versions home before she settled on the one you're wearing. She wanted—no, demanded—that it look just that way."

As her father spoke with Joey, her eyes looked down when he mentioned she demanded that it look a certain way. Joey continued to look at Lidia until Bridgette called his name.

"Joe, look. Isn't this the most beautiful ring you've ever seen?"

Before Joe could answer, Benny said that he would give them the deal of a lifetime if they wanted the ring. Lidia left. She went into the store's back room and didn't return.

Joe replied that the ring was very nice, and he appreciated Benny's offer, but it was getting late, and he and Bridgette had reservations for dinner on the wharf. He'd let Benny know some other time.

"Lidia, come out, and say good-bye to your friends," Benny called out.

Lidia peeked around the corner and waved good-bye to Bridgette and Joey as they walked out the door.

***

Bridgette called Lidia over to her house after she and Joe had dinner and returned to Sharp Park. Joe told Bridgette he needed to talk with his parents about something. It was a foggy, cold night, and it had drizzled on and off all day. Lidia quickly went to Bridgette's home right after she called.

"Oh…Lidia, I think Joe is going to tell his parents that we are going to get married soon. When he comes back, I believe he's going to talk with my father. Joe was so serious tonight. He was trying to tell me something important but couldn't. Our engagement will finally be official. I'm going to suggest we get married within the next six months, rain or shine."

Lidia was actually happy for Bridgette. Perhaps with Bridgette and Joey married, she could move on with her life. Bridgette was so happy. The happiness seemed to rub off on Lidia too. They both hugged each other with anxious anticipation of Joey's return, just up the street.

Joe knocked on Bridgette's front door and asked to speak with her privately. Bridgette stepped outside. A minute later, she burst through the door. Lidia jumped up to share in her best friend's joy. Bridgette ran quickly past her. She was crying.

"He broke up with me. We just had dinner earlier, everything was perfect…why…why?" she cried. The love of her life, the one she waited so long for, had now abruptly abandoned her and wouldn't say why, other than to remark that it just wouldn't be fair to her. Bridgette's heart was crushed beyond belief. Lidia couldn't take it to see her best friend like that. Her brother Lenny had warned her long ago that as good a friend that Joey was, he always broke every girl's heart sooner or later.

***

Bridgette watched as Lidia grabbed her long coat and rushed out the door in a rage. Lidia saw Joey walking to his car. He was obviously going to head back to his apartment in San Jose. She would stop him, and find out why he had suddenly become such a jerk. She couldn't believe what she ever saw in him. He destroyed Bridgette's heart, and with Bridgette's heart, he also destroyed hers.

Lidia caught up with Joey before he reached the car. She grabbed his arm, and turned him around. With one swift blow, she slapped him as hard as she could across his face.

"You! You…are not the man I thought you were. I once believed you could walk the moon, that you could do no wrong, but you have proven yourself to be heartless. You broke the heart of a wonderful woman and my best friend. My brother once warned me about you, but I refused to believe him."

Joey didn't respond. Instead, he pulled out the keys to his car.

"No, I won't let you go without telling me why. Bridgette deserves to know. You owe her that."

Joey opened his car door, still not saying a word. He had a blank look on his face. It was the same look he had worn when he was in a foxhole with three dead friends. He felt alone and cold inside. Lidia and Joey were standing under the streetlamp, and he could clearly see the hurt and anger in her eyes. What could he say to her? He just didn't know.

Lidia still held onto his arm, pulling him away from the car, preventing him from leaving. He could have jerked his arm away, but he couldn't do that to Lidia.

"Why? Joey, why? You owe her that, can't you see?"

Joey finally said, "I can't. It's too personal, and it will only hurt her more. Please just let me go, and I'll never return to Salada again. I made a friend a promise a long time ago, and it still plays over and over in my head. I wanted it to stop, but it never did. Please believe me, Liddy. I loved everything about Bridgette. She's loving, kind, faithful, thoughtful, playful, and beautiful. Her words are soft to my ears, but I can't marry her. I tried to convince myself I could. I thought we'd be perfect together, but there was just one problem. I realized too late that it was something I just couldn't get past. It was a constant reminder every time I came to Salada. As hard as it is to believe, it's better this way. It's best that I just leave your lives. I will miss you greatly. I must leave."

"NO!" Liddy started to slap him one last time but pulled her hand back. *Joey could easily stop me from slapping him,* she thought, but he wasn't making any effort to at all. Instead, he just stood there with no expression on his face. Her heart was pounding, and anger was still coursing through her. He didn't tell her anything. He still didn't say why.

He turned to go once again, but Lidia had always been a determined girl, and now she was an even more determined woman. Lidia wouldn't let go of Joey's coat sleeve. She tried to turn him around to face her once more, but he was determined to leave.

Lidia softened her voice; afraid he would go without an explanation. "Joey, please tell me why. I also need to know. Please, Joey. Why?"

Joey stopped and turned to face her, to look at her one last time.

"Because she's not…You!"

Lidia stood there, not understanding the full meaning of what he had just said.

"I love you, Liddy. You and Bridgette are so much alike. Everything I liked about Bridgette was because of you. I almost convinced myself that it didn't make any difference, between you and her, but I was only fooling myself. I was trying to keep a promise not to break a sweet girl's heart. Now I've only caused you both pain. Please don't tell her. I'm sorry. It has to be this way. It's for the best."

Joey stood there for a brief moment thinking about what he just admitted.

"Hard as I tried, I just couldn't lie to you. Now you know what I've hidden inside. I don't expect to be forgiven by you or Bridget for the pain that I brought upon you both. By telling the truth I broke a promise and I hate myself for that and everything else. You are the last person I ever wanted to hurt this way. Let me go. Please."

Lidia was frozen by his words. She let go of his arm. He took a step closer to his car. She knew if he drove away, she would likely never see him again. She quickly took his arm back and moved in front of him.

"Did you promise to never to break my heart? If you leave now, you will have broken that very promise, for my heart aches for you. It always has. Don't break your promise. Don't break my heart." Liddy's words were filled with compassion and love. "Joey, I have always loved you."

She put her hands up to his face and gently kissed his lips for the very first time. Liddy's demeanor had changed completely. She moved her body closer to his, while still caressing his face with her fingers. She would not let go. Her body shook and her knees weakened, but all she could think about were the words he had just spoken. She paused, and Joey slowly put his hands on her waist, and kissed her with a passionate love, and warmth that filled both their hearts.

Just after she spoke those words and while still in Joey's loving embrace, Liddy saw Bridgette by a tree across the street. Bridgette's legs seemed to weaken, and she slowly dropped to her knees on the cold, wet sidewalk. Bridgette had just seen them embrace and kiss each other with great passion. She was more crushed and angrier now than she had ever been in her life. What she saw was that her best friend from childhood had betrayed her.

When Joey turned to look, Bridgette was already up and running around the corner, back to her house. His heart fell, for he cared deeply for Bridgette. Joey was at a loss as to what to do next. Lidia tried to go after her friend Bridgette, but Joey held her back.

"Now's not the right time," he said as he pulled Liddy back into his embrace. She was warm to the touch, and she placed her head against his chest. She knew he loved her with all his heart and his entire mind from that moment forward.

Joey felt guilty for not realizing his mistake sooner. He should have broken up with Bridgette shortly after returning home from Nam. Somehow, he couldn't. She was so kind and loving. She had waited patiently for his return from war. He believed he could make things good, but in the end he realized, much too late, that he had only made everything worse. There was little he could do about his terrible mistake now.

Word quickly spread that Lidia, Bridgette's best friend, had secretly stolen Joe Gunderson's love from her. She had seduced him right under her own eyes. Bridgette's friendship would never be rekindled. It was lost forever.

All of Bridgette's friends, who had also been Liddy's friends, turned against Lidia, except for one. Coleen Codington stayed by

Liddy's side. Maybe it was because her sister was married to Joe's best friend, or maybe it was because Coleen had always suspected that Joey and Lidia were meant for each other.

Lidia tried every means to explain to Bridgette what had happened that night with Joey. She knocked on Bridgette's door, but no answer. She phoned a few times and was told to never call again. Finally, Lidia wrote Bridgette a letter, describing her long-time feelings for Joey. Lidia believed Bridgette always knew that she had feelings for Joey. In the letter, she explained what happened as honestly as she could. Three days later, the unopened letter was returned with the words *Return to Sender* written on the front. Joey also wrote Bridgette a letter, taking all the blame for what occurred between them. His letter was also returned.

Lidia Leibowitz was now viewed as a pariah in her own hometown. She felt sad for Bridgette, but what was done could not be undone. Lidia would always miss Bridgette's friendship, but her dream was realized, and she would never look back. Her life started anew when she kissed the man she loved that fateful foggy night. She would never regret it. Lidia and Joey were married three months later. It seemed that neither of them could hold back from their love a minute longer. Joey saw Lidia as the light of his world.

***

Fourteen months later, Colleen Codington informed Lidia that she had some good news. She just received a wedding invitation from Bridgette Dubois. It stated that Bridgette was marrying a Captain in the Marine Corps. The ceremony would be held in San Diego, where her future husband was stationed. *She always did like a man in uniform*, Lidia mused.

CHAPTER 12

RETURN OF THE LEGENDS

Lidia moved into Joey's San Jose apartment right after they were married in 1969. In the years to come, they'd own their own home. Three children—two boys and one girl—would soon follow.

On one weeknight in 1971, Joe Gunderson went to the San Francisco International Airport to pick up some in-laws who were coming to visit from back east. As he walked through the airport, he noticed a tall man in a marine uniform looking out a window. Although the man's back was to him, Joe knew instantly who the marine was. It was Master Gunner Richard Hauk.

"Master Gunny," Joe called out.

The marine turned around and without hesitation said, "Well if it isn't Lance Corporal Joe 'the Gunner' Gunderson. You sure haven't changed much, although you certainly look a lot happier since the last time I saw you. How's life treating you?"

"Couldn't be happier, sir. I have a beautiful wife and child, and we hope to have more soon. I was just heading to the other end of the terminal to pick up my in-laws. They are due to arrive

in about a half hour. It's great to run into you, Master Gunny."
Joe was practically standing at attention as he talked.

"Hmm…you're not in the marines now. Relax. I remember
you very well. I always wondered how you would do in the real
world. It's good to know you're doing well."

"What brings you here, Master Gunny?"

"I'm about to head out for my third tour of duty in Vietnam.
In a couple of years, this whole damn mess will be over."

"Why go back, Master Gunny?"

"Stop calling me Master Gunny."

"Sorry, Master Gunnery Sergeant," Joe replied.

"No, that's not what I mean. I always thought you were one
of our top marines. Hell, you were a damn brave marine. You
can call me River, River Hawk. I always liked that name, a whole
lot better than Dick Hauk. I'm going back because there are
some boys out there that still need all the help they can get. I may
be a little older, but I can still kick ass. I certainly scared the shit
out that desk-sitting, paper-pushing, noncombatant SOB
lieutenant colonel the day you ran naked in the mud. What a sight
to see. Hell, I was proud of you—not for the naked thing, but for
what you did the night before."

"I didn't save anyone that night, sir."

"The hell you didn't. You slowed the NVA advance up that
hill. What would have happened if you hadn't been there? No, I
saw what you did. You're a good man, Gunderson."

In Gunner's mind, he knew if he had only stopped running
and taken more careful aim, some or all of his friends might have
been saved that night. It was nice of River Hawk to say he was
brave, but Joe could still remember how he really felt that night.
He was literally scared shitless.

"Say, I ran into one of our marine brothers, Matt Akagi, down in San Diego a number of years ago. He was riding an old Harley and had reached the end of his road trip down route 66."

"Matt said that after he returned from overseas, he stopped by Malone's parents farm, just outside of Amarillo, Texas to let them know their son was very brave, but most of all Andrew was his best buddy. Andrew always talked about how much he loved his mom and dad, and how he dreamed of riding his old Harley-Davidson on a road trip down route 66. Andy's parents took Matt to their barn, and there covered with an old blanket was the Harley. Do you love to ride as our boy did? They asked. Matt said it was his dream to have ridden that same road trip with their son. The next thing he knew, they asked him to ride route 66 with their son's motorcycle. They were going to just give him Andy's bike, but Matt wrote them a check anyway. He stayed with the Malone's for a week and tuned the bike up in preparation for the grand road trip. Matt bought a stencil, and painted the name "Private Malone" on each side of the gas tank. He told me he rode feeling honored every mile of the way. Funny how such strong friendships are forged in such a small portion of our lives. I thought you should know that Andrew's dream was fulfilled by his friend Corporal Matt Akagi.

The boarding call was made. The master gunny took his bag and stood in the boarding line.

"Good to see you again, sir," Gunner said.

The master gunny gave him a quick salute and boarded his plane. Joe couldn't believe it. *River Hawk! I'll never forget him. The man's practically a legend,* he thought as he continued on his way to the inbound terminal. *He saved my life, and I don't even know if I ever thanked him. Maybe, but I'm not sure. Everything was messed up that night in Nam. I hope our paths will cross again one day.*

***

Gunner arrived at the inbound terminal only to find out that his relatives' plane had been delayed. It wouldn't arrive for another two hours. He was glad to hear that Matt Akagi made it home safe and sound. Joe was proud of what his old squad leader had done. *How could things get any better? He thought.*

He walked over to a snack bar and ordered a burger and fries. Gunner sat at the table and started writing in a small notebook he always carried. He wanted to capture the memory of meeting with River Hawk and their conversation for a later entry in his journal.

A small hand reached down and took one of his French fries.

"Hi there, stranger. Fancy meeting you here. God, you still look good, Joe."

Gunner looked up, and there stood May Jun, smiling down at him. Calendar Girl was smartly dressed in a blue flight attendant uniform, the top three buttons of her white blouse undone, and her pencil skirt short and narrow. She looked more beautiful now than she had ever looked in high school.

"May Jun, I never thought I'd see you again."

"May I sit down? I'd love to talk with you, Joey, I mean Joe."

"Sure, by all means, please sit down. I'd love to talk with you, too."

"I've always wondered how you were doing, Joe. The last I heard, you, Lenny, and Ed got into a big fight with Bo Hardin, Tubbs, Mean Joe, and Ralph Dunning on carnival night years ago. Did you know that Mean Joe Pennington now runs a rescue mission down on Mission Street in San Francisco? Who would have guessed that he'd turn into a preacher? You guys must have knocked some sense into him that night."

"As far as the fight goes, Big Ed did most of the fighting. I never did find out what Ralph Dunning had against Ed. The last I knew, he was still friends with Ralph and the other stooges at Westmoor."

"You don't know? God, I thought everyone knew. Ralph, Cory, and Tom Jonas planned to strip one of Ed's friends and push him naked onto the Jefferson High School basketball court during the big game. You and Lenny were there at that game. I saw you in the hallway just before Ed took those three jerks outside and beat the holy hell out of all three of them. I couldn't stand those guys."

"Was he trying to protect Lenny? That's the only other friend Ed had at the time, beside those three," Gunner asked.

"I don't think so. A friend of mine told me it was you, but I knew that couldn't be because you and Ed weren't friends."

"We mended our friendship shortly after that fight. Ed and I are good friends again. He's happily married to Beth Ann Codington."

"Good for Ed. Well, I'm still looking for the right guy. The man I marry will have to be kind, honest, and thoughtful. I used to just want a really a big, big man. Now I just want a good man. How big just doesn't really matter. Well, it does matter that he's big…I mean, big-hearted." May Jun smiled. "Joe, I notice you're wearing a wedding band. Who's the lucky woman? Anyone I know?"

"I don't believe you know my wife. She's Lenny the Leaf's sister, Lidia. I'm lucky, real lucky to have her. We just had our first child, a boy, not too long ago."

"That's so wonderful, Joe. I do believe that she's really the lucky one though. How is Lenny?" May Jun inquired.

Gunner paused. "May, I'm sorry to have to tell you this. My friend Lennard died in Vietnam on November 8, 1965. He was the best friend a guy could ever have."

May Jun was shocked to hear that Lenny had died. "Oh! I'm so sorry to hear that," May Jun sadly replied. They were quiet for a minute. "Well, I must be off now." May Jun stood back up. Then she bent down as if to take another French fry but instead kissed Gunner on the cheek.

"Umm…Joe, you still move me inside. If you ever leave that lucky woman, look me up, but do it soon, because I won't be available too much longer," she said in a voice as smooth as silk.

"May Jun, I'm married for life to the woman I love, but thanks, and good luck to you." Gunner smiled as he said those words. He knew they were true. As beautiful and sexy as May Jun was, Lidia was more beautiful, both inside her heart and to his eyes. For Gunner, that would never change. Still, it tickled his pride to know that he still looked good. *May Jun is still the Calendar Girl I remember,* Gunner thought as he watched her walk away. *The River Hawk and Calendar Girl, two legends in one night. Oh, what a night to remember,* Gunner would write in his journal.

***

The years seemed to just fly by for the Davis and Gunderson families. Ed and Beth Ann became the godparents of each of Gunner's children. Ed made sure Joe's kids always referred to him as "the godfather." Likewise, Joey and Lidia became the godparents to all of Big Ed's children.

Big Ed Davis rose rapidly up the ranks at the computer firm where he worked. Ed was an excellent engineer and had keen business acumen. In the early 1980s, he resigned his position to start up his own data-management firm with two other business partners. When the company transitioned into a software-development company, Ed Davis became its president. He renamed the new firm Valhalla Software. Its large logo looked very similar to the agate marble he always carried.

By the late eighties, Ed and Beth Ann were very wealthy.

Joe Gunderson did well too. He became a manager at a large tool-and-die-maker company. Gunner could build and shape just about anything out of metal—or any other material, for that matter. Lidia worked part-time on occasion to save extra cash for their children's college educations.

Three times a year without fail, Big Ed and Joey would go camping and fishing along the many lakes and rivers of Northern California. They had a favorite spot along the Stanislaus River. Ed Davis purchased twenty-five acres of land around the Stanislaus. He would never develop the land. That place was strictly for family and friend campouts, rafting, and of course, fishing. Gunner bought one acre from Big Ed a few years later. It was a spot on the Stanislaus River that ran shallow but flowed swiftly during the summer months. It was Gunner's favorite spot to fly-fish.

Big Ed believed he owed it all to the power of the little orb that he always carried. Joe believed he owed all his good fortune, even if it was much smaller than Ed's, to his faith and to his wife, Liddy.

Anytime the two friends went fishing on a Sunday, Gunner would pull a small, tattered Bible out of his dad's old metal fishing box. He'd read a verse or two before casting his line into the water. Other than reading a few verses and praying before meals, Gunner never tried to push his beliefs onto anyone else. He believed that if people had questions, they only needed to ask. Joe Gunderson was good-natured, just like his father.

From time to time, both families would visit Sharp Park to see their folks and to get away from the South Bay heat. Gunner refused to call the town Sharp Park or Pacifica anymore. He preferred to call his hometown Salada or Salada Beach. He had never forgotten Mama Morales's words to him from so long ago.

CHAPTER 13

THE WALL

The First Trip to the Wall

On November 15, 1984, the Gunderson and Davis families traveled to Washington, DC, to visit the Vietnam Veterans Memorial, which was commonly referred to as the Wall. The families wanted to pay their respects to all of the fallen. But mostly they were there to see the only monument that bore the name of Lennard Leibowitz. Joey also wanted to honor his friends who had died in a lonely foxhole during their battle with the NVA.

The memorial was a large, V-shaped wall made of highly polished black granite with a reflective surface. Digitally engraved on the Wall were the names of all the men and women who died or were listed as missing in action (MIA) while serving in Vietnam. The Wall contained over 58,000 names listed in chronological order.

They found Lennard's name on the east wall, where those who died near the beginning of war were listed.

Big Ed Davis knelt down and placed a eucalyptus leaf on the ground below Lenny's name. He placed a coin on top of the leaf to keep it in place. Lidia broke down and cried when she saw Big Ed kneel down to pay his respects to her brother, his friend.

Gunner stepped forward and rubbed his fingers across Lenny's name. He walked a short distance away and did the same to his three marine buddies—Bobby, Andy, and Hank.

A statue of three combat men had recently been added to the area, just before the family's arrival. The statue of the three stood a short distance away, just to the south of the Wall. After paying respects to those who had died, Joey walked to the statue. It was there that he finally shed tears.

Big Ed and Gunner made a pact that they would return to the Wall in early November every ten years. They would pay their respects to those who gave their life during the Vietnam War. To Gunner and Big Ed, their friend Lenny the Leaf would never become just a distant memory. Their visits to the Wall would ensure that his memory would stay very much alive.

***

The Second Trip to the Wall

In November 1994 the two men, now in their fifties, traveled back to Washington. Big Ed, just as before, placed a eucalyptus leaf on the ground below the Leaf's name. He placed a shiny coin on top of it. He knelt and stayed there for a moment, as if in deep thought, before he stood back up. Gunner touched each of the names of those he had known and served with long ago. Then he walked back and gazed at the entire wall. All the memories of war returned, but he didn't dwell on them for too long.

The Wall was less crowded during the month of November. He and Big Ed were the only two still left at the wall, so they decided to walk the length of the wall. As they passed by the names, their own reflections stared back at them. Gunner and Big Ed talked as they passed by name after name. On the west wall, where the names of those who died close to the war's end were listed, Gunner abruptly stopped. Big Ed continued talking to his friend as he continued to walk along, but it was soon obvious that Gunner was no longer beside him. Big Ed turned and looked back. Gunner was kneeling down to look at a name on the wall. He saw Gunner draw his finger along the letters of a name and then wipe his hand across his eyes. Gunner didn't say a word. The name on the wall before him was Richard Hauk.

River Hawk had saved his life. Gunner wondered how many other lives Master Gunnery Sergeant Richard Hauk had saved? How many other marines came home alive, not even realizing that they had been spared because of the leadership and bravery of that one man? The time of the River Hawk ended many years ago, but Gunner would never forget the legend. Big Ed and Gunner left the memorial just as flakes of snow began to fall.

***

While at the airport waiting for their departure, Big Ed pulled out a new silk pouch. He rolled Valhalla into the palm of his hand.

"Gunner, my friend, I'm a wealthy man. I plan on retiring early, so Bethie and I can travel the world. She always liked traveling to new places. I buy a new car every other year. I have a beautiful home in Los Gatos. I've received many great and wonderful gifts from my wife and children over the years. But you know what? The greatest gift I have ever received is sitting right here in the palm of my hand. Thank you, Gunner."

"What about your daughters? You're always bragging about them, especially your youngest one, Adelynn." Gunner smiled as he looked at Big Ed.

"Well, you have a point there, but other than Bethie and my family, Valhalla is the greatest gift."

Big Ed was about to slide Valhalla back into the pouch, but it missed the opening and dropped on the carpeted floor in front of him. A passerby accidentally kicked the marble under the seats to the row behind them. A young boy, about eleven or twelve years old, reached down and picked it up. The boy held the marble in his fingers and showed his mother. The boy had a recent scar under his left eye. He looked excited as he moved the marble from one hand to the other, as if he were holding something hot. His mother spoke with a Middle Eastern accent but dressed very much like a westerner.

Gunner pulled out a half-dollar coin and approached the boy. He knelt down, held out the coin, and said, "Here, take this as a reward for finding my friend's fancy marble. He accidentally dropped it just a minute ago."

Big Ed was standing beside Gunner and smiling. The boy was very hesitant to give the marble back. His mother spoke up, telling her son in some Middle Eastern language to give the marble back. She looked at Gunner and Big Ed and began speaking in English. "I'm so sorry. My boy does not need a reward. He will give the marble back to you. Won't you, Amir?"

Her son didn't respond. Instead, he closed his fingers tightly around Valhalla. Again, his mother spoke in her own tongue. Before she could finish, the boy suddenly dropped the marble. Gunner picked it up and handed it back to Big Ed. Gunner gave the boy the coin, told him to keep it, and thanked him once again. The boy then said a few words to his mother.

"My son only speaks a little English. He thanks you for the coin. He said to be careful because the marble is very hot."

Big Ed chuckled as he slid Valhalla back into the pouch. It was cool to the touch when Big Ed handled it.

"You know, Gunner, something good always happens to the person who holds Valhalla, like that boy did. I believe that youngster will have a very interesting time while in this country."

"Ed…never mind," Gunner commented. Their boarding time arrived, and they headed back home.

***

The Third Trip to the Wall

For the next ten years, life was grand for Gunner's and Big Ed's families. Big Ed had grandchildren now. Gunner also had a grandchild on the way. Life was good for the two friends.

Big Ed retired in 2004, at the age of sixty-one, after a much larger computer firm bought out Valhalla Software. Valhalla Software would be no more. The new firm changed the name of the company after the buyout. Big Ed owned a large amount of Valhalla Software stock, and he was set for life. Shortly after Big Ed's retirement, he and Gunner took their customary trip back to Washington, DC. They could now easily find the Leaf's name among the many thousands that graced the Wall.

When they approached the vast, impressive monument, they noticed a man about their own age. He was carrying a cane and standing in front of the spot where Big Ed always placed a narrow eucalyptus leaf. They stood well behind the man, patiently waiting for him to move on. The fellow had a cap on his head with the words *Vietnam Veteran* embroidered across the back. He wore an old green fatigue vest filled with military patches. The man knelt down and placed a medallion on the ground below the names directly above. Finally, the man turned around and slowly backed up with the aid of his cane, until he could view the entire wall. Gunner looked at the man's cap. Embroidered across the front of the cap were the words *173rd Airborne Brigade* with the unit emblem in the center and *Sky Soldiers* underneath. On the side of the cap was an airborne symbol. Gunner stared at the man as he walked past him.

Gunner then turned his attention back to the wall of names and reached out to run his fingers across Lennard's name. Once he stepped back, Big Ed placed a eucalyptus leaf down below the Lenny's name. Ed had forgotten to bring a coin to keep the leaf from blowing away, but he didn't need one. There before him was the medallion that the old man had placed in that same spot. Big Ed slid the leaf under the silver medallion. The medallion was engraved with the words *173rd Airborne Brigade* around the top of the coin. In the center was an emblem of a wing with a sword. The bottom was engraved with the words *Sky Soldiers*.

Big Ed quickly stood up and turned around to see if the old man was still there. He was, and the man approached both Gunner and Big Ed.

"Do you know any of the sky soldiers whose names are listed here?" the man asked.

"Yes, Lennard Leibowitz. We used to call him the Leaf. He was a childhood friend and my wife's brother. My name is Joe Gunderson, and this is Ed Davis. We both served in Vietnam during the mid-sixties."

"Good to meet you. I'm Ron Brown. I served in the 173rd Airborne with your friend. I recognized that you knew him as soon as I saw your friend place the leaf below his name. I didn't know him well, only for about twenty minutes. He found me wounded, lying in a patch of tall grass and bushes."

The man stopped for a moment. He got choked up, remembering that day long ago. "I'm sorry. It's still hard for me to talk about that day. He bound my wounds and told me his name was the Leaf…then clarified it with his real name, Private Lennard Leibowitz. The VC were closing in, but he never left my side. He could have, but he didn't. He saved my life by binding my wounds and covering my legs with dry grass…"

Ron's voice broke again as he tried to describe what happened next. "He exchanged fire with some Vietcong that came barging through the high grass. He killed them, but he was mortally wounded in the process. He laid his back across my chest and face. The weight of his body must have slowed my bleeding. More VC came through as they retreated. One of them shot Lennard again as he ran by, just to make sure he was dead. I heard the bastard laugh after he did it. They never noticed me lying underneath him. Your friend saved my life both when he was alive and again after he was dead. The next thing I remember was being airlifted out, and for me, the war was over. Whenever I'm anywhere near DC, I stop by to…thank him."

Ron's eyes were red, and he had to wipe his face and blow his nose. "To me, your friend, Private Leibowitz was a hero, not just a name on a wall. A couple years ago, I heard a women stand before the Wall and say what a shame it was for so many to have died in vain, in such a stupid war. It took all I had to restrain myself. If she had been a man, I'd have decked him with my cane. I walked over to her and said, 'You can say the war was the wrong war to fight, and you can even say it's sad to see that so many died for someone else's country. But, damn! Don't you ever say that they died in vain! Those soldiers died to protect the people of that damn country. Whether we should have been there or not doesn't matter. They were there! They served their country. They died protecting their brothers in arms, and one of them died protecting me. He didn't die in vain, damn you!' I told her to get the hell away from the Wall. She didn't deserve to have her face reflected on the granite that bore the names of the brave and proud. I guess I was a bit too loud because the park rangers came and asked me to calm down. That prissy woman gave me the dirtiest look. As I was being escorted out, I told that poor excuse of a woman to kiss my ass."

"Ron Brown, you're the man! I couldn't have said it better myself," Big Ed commented.

The two friends exchanged addresses with Ron. They thanked him and wished him well. That was a special day for Gunner and Big Ed—to hear the final story of their friend Lenny the Leaf and how he saved another man's life. It was a very special moment. They walked away proud of their friend. Gunner didn't say much. He had had a lump in his throat the entire time Ron was talking, and the lump was still there.

CHAPTER 14

THE ROAD ALL MUST FOLLOW

B ig Ed's mother died of liver failure in 1993, and by 2002,
Gunner had lost both of his parents. Joe Gunderson's mom
told him just before she died that she wanted him to share the
blessings he received in life with others. "Help the helpless, Joey,
no matter where they come from, or what faith they have or do
not have, regardless of color, creed, or even country. These are
the things that we are called to do while on this earth. Let others
see your faith in practice by ministering to the poor. Do you
understand, my son?"

"I will do my best, Mom. You know I will." Joseph
Gunderson gave his word three days before his mother passed
away.

Beth Ann's father and mother both died before the end of
2005. Big Ed purchased the Codington home on Beach Avenue
at full value from the Codington son and daughters, who were
the beneficiaries. He purchased the property to preserve the
Codington home. The old home, which was originally built for
about $14,000, was now worth over $450,000. Big Ed's family

now owned three homes in Northern California: the family home in Los Gatos, a vacation home just outside of Sonora near Yosemite, and now the old Codington house in Pacifica. Big Ed had the interior of the Codington home completely remodeled with a new kitchen, bathrooms, and new furnishings in every room.

Big Ed's youngest daughter, Adelynn, moved into the Beach Avenue home after she completed her veterinary degree at UC Davis. She was twenty-four and loved living on the coast. Adelynn would run each day along the nature trail above Salada Beach. She would fish off the old Sharp Park Pier with her father, Ed, whenever her father and mother came to visit. She insisted on paying rent. Big Ed only charged her for taxes and utilities. Adelynn worked at a veterinary clinic over the hill in San Bruno. She was a free spirit and loved her parents. As a teen, she would camp out with her father, Gunner, Gunner's sons, and a few of her own friends along the shores of the Stanislaus River. Just like her father, she was a great fisherman. Hiking, camping, and fishing were her joys in life. Of all his children, Big Ed was closest to Adelynn. Adelynn looked very much like her mother, Bethie, had when she was young.

In 2006, Beth Ann Davis, Ed's wife of over thirty-five years, was diagnosed as being in the early stages of Alzheimer's disease.

Adelynn convinced her father to move back to the house in Sharp Park. She wanted to help him care for her mother. Big Ed agreed. He and Bethie would live downstairs and Adelynn, upstairs. Big Ed purchased a mixed golden retriever puppy, and named him Rex, the Wonder Dog. He believed it would be good for Bethie to have a pet.

Big Ed and Gunner never fished along the Stanislaus after that. Instead, whenever Gunner had a chance, he'd fish with Big Ed off the Sharp Park pier.

***

"You know, Ed, I remember when there was just a waste pipe here that emptied onto the beach. After we returned from Nam, I was happy to see that they finally removed that pipe and built a sea wall and the pier. It's a good place to fish, isn't it?" Gunner looked at Mori's Point and remembered their friend Lenny. "It's good to be retired. Liddy and I walked all the way up to the top of Mori's Point last year and just sat there reminiscing about our youth and how everything is changing all around us. We talked about Lenny, too. I still miss him."

Gunner continued, not waiting for Big Ed to respond. "Everything has changed. What was once considered right and proper is now viewed as backward or even bigoted, and what was once wrong is now made to appear right. I'm getting too old for all this confusion. Life was very different and far less complicated when we were young. It was as if shades of gray did not exist. A change is soon coming to this land. I think I see the clipped feathers on the horizon."

"Where? I don't see any feathers out there?" Big Ed replied as he looked at the ocean.

Gunner laughed. He had forgotten that Big Ed had never heard the dreams of Lenny's grandmother. "Never mind. It's not that important. It's cold. Let's get off the pier," Gunner suggested.

"Wait, I hear that you are planning a trip to Africa soon. I want you to have this, Gunner," Big Ed said as he handed the pouch containing Valhalla to his friend.

Gunner had not held Valhalla in his hand since he was a kid. *Why does Ed want me to take this now?* he thought as he rolled out the warm marble into the palm of his hand. Valhalla felt much heavier than he remembered. The more he held it, the warmer and heavier it became.

"Thanks, but no, Ed. This belongs to you. It's not meant for me to carry it." Gunner handed the still-mysterious marble back to his friend. Gunner would be leaving soon for his trip overseas. The two friends said their good-byes.

***

At sixty-five years of age, Gunner had retired as a senior manager at the firm he had worked for most of his adult life. Shortly after retiring, Joey and Lidia purchased a home just outside the town of Riverbank in the central valley of California. Gunner wanted to be close to the local rivers and streams in the area where he and his best friend Big Ed used to go fishing.

Two years after retiring, Gunner volunteered to travel with a charitable organization to Ethiopia. There they with other volunteers would provide aid, helping refugees who were fleeing from war-torn Sudan to Ethiopia's west, the authoritarian rule of Eritrea to its north, and the lawless country of Somalia to its east. During this time Ethiopia was in the beginning stages of a severe drought, which only further compounded the poverty that existed outside of its larger cities.

Gunner was informed that cell-phone service, Internet access, and other media channels were typically only available near the larger cities of Ethiopia, if at all. The refugee camps were in remote areas, and it was unlikely there would be any modern conveniences. The charitable organization recommended that volunteers travel with a backpack instead of luggage and told them to bring sleeping bags. The aid volunteers would have a shelter with bunks and some other amenities nearby. Also, an emergency satellite phone would be available.

Gunner was responsible for securing and assembling gas generators, some solar panels, and other necessary equipment to provide electricity for the volunteer shelter and, to a limited extent, for the refugees. He had volunteered primarily to fulfill his mother's last wish, but after seeing the utter poverty of the people, it became his personal goal to help as many as he could.

Problems developed with the delivery of equipment and then with the installation, so when the other members of his group were packing to go back to the States, Gunner informed them that he needed to stay at least a week longer to finish the job he started. Gunner asked one of the US volunteers to mail a letter for him when he reached the capital city.

"A handwritten letter, really? Don't you know it's the twenty-first century? I don't know anyone who still handwrites letters," said the aid worker as Gunner handed him the envelope. "Snail mail will likely take a week or more to reach its destination in the United States. You'll probably be done in another week. Heck, you'll be home before this letter reaches your wife." The man smiled and tucked the letter in his pack. "I'll see that it's sent out. Don't worry."

Gunner thanked the man. Early the next day, the other US volunteers headed back home without him.

***

Some of the refugees told of being persecuted by extreme militant Islamists. Non-Muslims were being systematically driven out of northern Sudan. It was especially rough for Christians, who were being singled out and made examples of what happens to infidels. They were either severely beaten or killed because of their faith.

The slave trade was still practiced in the neighboring countries, as well as in certain parts of Ethiopia. Female genital mutilation was a common practice that Gunner couldn't wrap his mind around. Rape was also all too common. All this had been happening for years, and yet the world press, and especially network news organizations in the United States, rarely reported what was happening in that part of the world.

It angered Gunner. It was obvious to him that the US press simply didn't see the persecution of many thousands of people in the Sudan by militant jihadists as that important. If the news didn't suit a network's supposedly unbiased view, they simply underreported it or didn't report it at all.

Look at what's happening to our world, you dumb asses. Don't you see the suffering? The jihadists are wreaking havoc. They have no souls, and it will only get worse. Get out of influencing politics for more than a minute and focus on what truly matters, Gunner ranted in his thoughts.

Perhaps it was just the frustration of seeing the suffering all around him that caused him to be so on edge. Gunner thought he'd be finished in another week, but one problem after another occurred, and he was in the refugee camp two additional weeks. When his work was finally done, and it was time for him to leave, he was informed that Arab and Sudanese slave traders were kidnapping young women not too far away from their camp. They looked at the slave trade as a way to make money, to help fund their jihadist activities in the western Mediterranean area. It was no longer safe for the group he was now traveling with, which included women, to travel back via the same route they had come. Instead, they were advised to take a roundabout route back to the capital city of Addis Ababa or to head directly to the city of Bahir Dar instead.

The aid volunteers would travel in two vehicles: one group in a small truck and the others in an old VW van. Each vehicle door was clearly marked with the refugee aid symbol, and Ethiopian drivers wore similar insignia on their T-shirts.

They all agreed they would travel the long road to the lakeside city of Bahir Dar in the hopes of catching a flight out of that city's airport, instead of out of Addis Ababa.

Gunner sat in the back of the truck wearing his San Francisco Giants baseball cap, daydreaming of coming home to his sweet Liddy. He hadn't shaved since leaving home for Africa. Gunner was in good shape for his sixty-seven years. He even liked his graying hair and the snow-white beard he had recently grown.

What will Lidia think when she sees me? I somehow feel she's going to tell me to shave the very day I arrive home, Gunner wondered. *Wait till she sees the pictures I sent her. She probably won't even recognize me.*

He was anxious to get home. The work he had done was rewarding, but he missed his wife, sons, and daughter.

The truck Gunner was in began to struggle as it drove up a small hill. The VW van in front of them crested the hill and disappeared out of sight. Near the top of the hill, the truck they were traveling in finally broke down. To Gunner, it just seemed like everything that could go wrong was going wrong. He couldn't shake the feeling that there must be some other purpose for him in that country. It was as if Ethiopia didn't want him to leave, at least not just yet.

***

Not too far away from Gunner and the other volunteers, two desperate men were heading their way.

Amir Hasani and Tareq Kandankulam were over a week late to their planned extraction point just outside of Tobruk, Libya. Because their original extraction point had been compromised, they were forced to flee south, pursued by the members of

Libyan leader Muammar Gaddafi's Khamis security brigade. They fled southeast with little food or water, as they struggled to reach the border of either Egypt or Sudan in order to escape from Libya.

Tareq had been wounded in an earlier exchange of gunfire. The bullet went clean through his left arm, but the wound didn't slow him down. The two had nearly died in the heat of Libya's desert while trying to evade Gaddafi's Khamis soldiers. Only their long hours of survival training and cunning had saved them.

Amir cleaned and stitched Tareq's wound with a sewing needle and thread from his clothing as best he could while on the run. They rested after safely crossing the border into Sudan, and Amir cleaned Tareq's wound once again. They stole a motor scooter just outside of a small gas station and general store in a Sudanese village and drove the rest of the way to Khartoum. They were weary, exhausted, and hungry when they reached the city. They rested there for two days.

After recuperating, they sent a cryptic text to their case officer, on a clean, never-before-used cell phone Amir carried. Unfortunately, they were informed that airport security in Khartoum was on the lookout for both of them. Apparently, a description of them had been given to Sudanese airport security. They were directed to slip across the border into Ethiopia and make their way to the city of Bahir Dar.

CHAPTER 15

THE RISE OF AMIR

Amir Hasani was of Egyptian and Jordanian decent. His
mother was Jordanian, and his father, Egyptian. Amir's
mother, Tania, was actually born in America to Jordanian
parents. Both of Tania's parents were attending a university in
the United States when she was born. Tania's mother and father
secretly planned for her to be born in America so that she would
have the rights of US citizenship.

Amir's father, Jibade Hasani, was a wealthy Egyptian
businessman working with companies throughout the Middle
East. His father married Tania when she was just seventeen years
of age. Tania's father, who had business dealings with the wealthy
Mr. Hasani, had arranged the marriage, believing it would be a
good match for his daughter. It was Tania's time, he thought. His
daughter was mature, intelligent, multilingual, and ready for
marriage. She was the perfect match for Jibade Hasani.

All was well for Tania and her much older husband while they
lived in her home country of Jordan, but everything changed
after Amir was born. Just after Amir turned one, Jibade decided

to move his family to Egypt. The first week after arriving in Egypt, Jibade beat his wife of one year for the first of many times. Her crime was that she had become too westernized. He didn't like her style of dress. She wasn't modest enough for him, at least not for living in Egypt.

She had given birth to Amir when she was eighteen. Tania began to cover herself from head to toe and always wore a veil to hide the bruises. It was almost as if her husband actually enjoyed beating her. Amir grew to hate his father.

On the outside, Jibade portrayed himself as a nice man whenever he and his wife were together with other people. He would shower her with fine, flowing clothes and jewelry. Everyone around Jibade admired him and his beautiful, obedient wife.

During one altercation with her husband, the then twelve-year-old Amir stepped in front of his mother to protect her from Jibade's fist. What his mother had done to deserve this, Amir didn't know. He only knew he must protect her.

"This is the proper way to treat a disobedient woman, Amir. Do not interfere," his father warned.

When Amir refused to move, his father gave him the back of his hand. The large ring on Jibade's finger cut Amir deeply just below his left eye.

Three days later, after many years of beatings, Tania fled Egypt with her son, Amir. Tania had been planning her escape for over six months. She was more pleasant than usual with Jibade and told him she loved living in their fine home in Egypt, which was all a lie. She waited for her husband to travel out of the country on one of his regular business trips. Then Tania took advantage of his absence to return to her home country of Jordan with her son.

She left a letter for Jibade saying she was done with him and was going home to her parents. It would be best if he divorced her. She would rely on the protection of her brothers and her father if he tried to take Amir from her. After one week with her parents, she left for America. Tania was a US citizen by birth, and she still had a valid passport showing her maiden name. She had also secretly obtained a passport for her son, Amir, listing his home address as her parents' home in Jordan, where he was born. She would travel using her maiden name.

Once in the United States, she actively looked for a new husband. It was important to her that she legally change her last name and that of her son. She lived for a time with relatives who had immigrated to America many years before. In America, Amir would be safe, and she would be free from the reach of Jibade.

After arriving in the United States, Tania moved to Virginia and began working at the Norfolk naval base. Tania met a US Navy chief petty officer by the name of Nicholas Montgomery. He wasn't very handsome, but he showed a real interest in Tania. He treated Tania and her son well. Nick fell in love with Tania, and she hinted at marriage. It worked, and soon, CPO Montgomery asked her to marry him.

She was more anxious to take his last name than anything else. Nick was a nice man, but Tania wasn't really sure if she loved him, or any man, after what her husband Jibade had done to her. Tania had told Nicholas that her ex-husband abandoned her and Amir and that they were now divorced.

Changing her last name and that of her son was a critical issue for Tania. She believed it would be nearly impossible for Jibade to find her and Amir once they had the last name of Montgomery. She urged Nick to adopt her son after they were married.

Tania received a letter from her father a month after arriving in the United States. It was to inform her that her husband, Jibade, would only divorce her if she gave up Amir to him. Jibade didn't know Tania was now living in America. He believed she was still hiding out in Egypt or Jordan. Five months later, Tania received another letter from her father informing her Jibade had died in a freak automobile accident. He attached a newspaper article that described the incident. Apparently, her husband was driving too fast on a road just outside of Cairo. He turned too sharply after passing a woman who was walking nearby with a young child. He lost control of his vehicle and hit an embankment, which startled a group of camels being fed nearby. One of the camels tried to jump over his automobile but instead fell on top of the car, killing Jibade.

Tania informed Nick that her ex-husband had been killed by a camel.

"By what?" Nicholas asked.

"It was a tragic death," she told him. "Thankfully, the camel survived. To die by camel is a fitting death for him," Tania emphasized.

It was now safe for Tania to return to Jordan, but Tania liked everything about America and decided to stay. She no longer needed to marry Nick but went ahead with it anyway because she believed CPO Montgomery was a good man and would make a fine father. Nick was true to his word and adopted Amir as his son.

Amir's name was legally changed to Adam Amir Montgomery, and he became a US citizen. He grew to love and admire his stepfather. Every chance they had, his stepfather took him hunting, camping, and sailing.

Adam Amir Montgomery joined the Navy just after he turned nineteen. His father and mother were very proud of their son. He passed the advance endurance training and became a Navy SEAL. Shortly thereafter, he was deployed to Afghanistan. He was a noted sharpshooter and an expert with a sniper rifle. Adam was a young but hardened veteran. His team occasionally worked alongside special operatives who engaged in cross border covert activities. Near the end of his second tour overseas, he was approached by a US intelligence agent.

"I understand that your birth name was Amir Hasani, and you spent a good deal of your childhood in Egypt. I'm told that you speak Arabic fluently. Is that correct?" the agent asked.

"Yes, and how did you know all this?"

"We're paid to know these things about the people we coordinate our efforts with. I've talked with your navy commander about the possibility of releasing you for a four-month temporary covert assignment in another country. You would need to volunteer, and the assignment would be extremely dangerous. Think it over, and let me know in two days if it's something you'd help us with."

Adam didn't need two days. He volunteered the next morning.

Adam met with his new intelligence team. No one used real names, only simple code names. Sky King was his team leader. Sky explained that the assignment was in the country of Libya. It would involve training a local asset in the proficient use of a modified OSV-96 Russian made sniper rifle. Adam's code name would be his real birth name, Amir Hasani. His Egyptian records would show he was a citizen of that country, and a few other documents would be needed to ensure his cover. Amir would hone his sniper skills using the OSV-96 while in Afghanistan and then transfer those skills to the asset in Libya. Amir would travel to Alexandria, Egypt, and set up a base of operations.

The OSV-96 rifle would be dismantled, packed in several boxes containing machine parts, and shipped by a merchant ship directly to Tobruk, Libya. Amir would be responsible for getting the rifle's ammo across the border from Egypt into Libya. The specialized ammunition would be placed under the hood of a truck carrying additional machine parts bound for Tobruk. The truck was registered to a tool business in Alexandria. A fake battery under the truck's hood would contain the special ammo. The only other weapon he would carry would be a pistol. That pistol and additional ammo clips were placed in a box behind the truck's glove compartment. The other part of his assignment was to train a skilled Libyan asset by the name of Tareq Kandankulam, code-named Tarred Candle.

Because the United States no longer conducted head-of-state assassinations, Amir would train Tarred Candle to perform the needed assassination. The covert assignment would last no more than forty-five days in country, which would be sufficient time to train the Tarred One.

US intelligence operatives knew that Libyan leader Muammar Gaddafi would soon convene a secret meeting with several Middle Eastern heads of state. Gaddafi was trying to secure support to help prop up his faltering regime. Gaddafi's meeting would provide the perfect opportunity to eliminate a key leader in the region.

Only the Tarred One knew which one of the leaders was to be targeted. Plausible deniability was the name of the game for those in the White House. A key White House official gave the CIA permission to conduct Operation Peacock. The wording in Operation Peacock simply stated that necessary measures should be taken to secure stability in the region, nothing more. To a select few, the word "Peacock" signaled the go-ahead for eliminating a particular head of state. No one else involved in the operation, not even Amir, would be told who the actual target would be. He was in country simply to train Tarred Candle. Amir was given clear rules of engagement, which basically meant that he was not to shoot anyone, except to preserve his own life.

***

Once word of the exact day of the conference reached Amir and Tarred Candle, they began camouflaging their position. They hid, half buried, for two days waiting for the right time. They knew an outside luncheon would be held right after the meeting. Amir had done his job in training Tarred Candle and could now return to Egypt, but he had become friends with the man and decided to stay with him through completion of the objective. Amir's orders were simply to train and then leave. But in Amir's mind, he decided the training wouldn't be over until successful completion of the mission.

After the conference of leaders ended, all the dignitaries were invited for food and drinks at a special location just outside of Tripoli. Tarred Candle had learned his lessons well, and he was ready to demonstrate his expertise with the OSV-96. Of all the ammunition Amir had smuggled across the border, only five rounds remained. One round, maybe two, would be all he would need to achieve his objective. Amir stayed with his now good friend, even though he could have left right after helping him set up his firing position far away from his target. Tarred Candle knew his target typically wore a brightly colored skullcap and would be easy to identify, even from the long distance he was shooting from.

Everything went as planned. The Tarred One took down the assigned target with one bullet. Amir wrapped the rifle in a sack and buried it in a hole over two miles away from the hidden sniper position. When he had finished burying the rifle, his partner spoke. "The mission is over. I consider you a good friend. You should know my real name. It is Tareq."

"Well, Tareq, believe it or not, my real birth name is Amir. I was born in Jordan and lived in Egypt for eleven years when I was young.

They made it back to their truck and began their travel out of Tripoli. All went well until they were stopped by a patrol on the long road out of town. One of the guards asked Tareq and Amir to step out of their vehicle. The guards checked the truck more thoroughly than it had been checked before. The top of the fake battery under the hood had jarred open, exposing the hidden compartment. Inside the fake battery box was a single high-caliber bullet. When the guard lifted his rifle and aimed it at Amir, he asked the other guard to radio for assistance. Tareq immediately pulled his pistol out from his back and killed the guard with the radio. Amir then took down two other guards with his pistol while Tareq dispatched the last remaining soldier. Tareq had been hit in the shoulder but was able to keep moving. It soon became obvious that their escape route back to Tobruk was compromised, so they headed southeast instead, in an effort to reach Egypt. Three times they evaded capture along the way, but each time they were pushed farther south, and Egypt was now out of the question. On one close call, they engaged in a close-quarter fight. They were able to escape, but now their pistols were nearly out of ammo. Any more intense gunfights and it would be over for them. The two ditched their truck and took the off-road military vehicle of the soldiers they had killed, continuing to push south.

After much hardship, Amir and Tareq abandoned the military vehicle they had taken and slipped across the border into Sudan. Exhausted, they found safe haven in Khartoum.

Amir had money hidden in a vest he was wearing, which, along with Tareq's cash, allowed them to buy some clean clothes, food, and a room for two nights. The two men slept for eleven hours before awakening to head out for some food.

They sat in an outdoor tea café with a TV that was broadcasting the daily news. To Tareq's surprise, the head of state he believed he had assassinated was alive and unhurt. He couldn't figure out what had gone wrong. The man he shot looked and dressed just like the person he was to assassinate. The newscast told how ruthless cowards had killed a servant at a children's party thrown by Muammar Gaddafi.

An older man at the small table next to them leaned over. "It is a very sad thing that such violence would happen at a party filled with young children. Who would do such an evil thing?" the man complained. He went on to say that Gaddafi had vowed to find those responsible, regardless of where they might flee. They would not escape, he boldly predicted.

"Was anyone else killed that day?" Tareq asked the man.

"No, just the poor servant, who was helping to feed the children, and some guards at a checkpoint were gunned down. Fortunately, no children were hurt. They say the servant was a father of five children himself. It's not right that a father should die that way," the man replied.

Tareq came to the realization that he had obviously killed a body double, not the intended target. There was no children's party that day. Only dignitaries had been at the luncheon. Amir and Tareq fumed inside about Gaddafi's clever lie. Amir kept looking at his cell phone, waiting for it to vibrate. Both men were anxious for a coded response from their case officer about where to proceed for extraction.

They watched as the TV showed a picture of two men by an old truck, pistols drawn, with four soldiers lying on the ground.

Someone had taken a cell-phone picture of the event, and now it was being broadcast on all channels. Only Amir's back was shown, but a side view of Tareq's face was in the picture. Fortunately for Tareq, the picture was taken from a distance, and a close-up of Tareq's face was too pixilated to clearly make out any distinguishable features. The newscaster was about to show an artist's drawing of what the two men looked like, based on eyewitness accounts, so both men got up and left. Their stay in Khartoum was over.

***

Unknown to Amir and Tareq, Muammar Gaddafi had placed a bounty on their heads. Gaddafi allowed a small detachment of his Khamis security brigade to cross the border into Sudan, dressed as faithful Muslim men. In Khartoum, they purchased weapons from the North Sudanese and continued their search for the men who had killed members of their security force and who had evaded them in Libya.

Tareq and Amir were back on the scooter, sunglasses on and shemagh scarves wrapped high above their chins. They followed a road along the Blue Nile to the city of Wadi Medani, where they stopped for gas and to eat. Tareq and Amir were sitting at a table when they heard a group of men arguing about which way to travel.

The Khamis were following a lead. They heard that two men had stolen a yellow motor scooter near the northern border of Sudan. The two men had tried to cross back into Egypt near southern Libya but turned back when they saw a black vehicle with small Libyan flags near the border crossing. They were last seen just outside of Khartoum.

When one of the men said he looked forward to torturing the man who killed his friend, Tareq and Amir realized they had picked the wrong place to eat. The men behind them were clearly Libyan. Another Arab man entered the café. He wore a black shirt and a gray-and-black-checkered shemagh scarf around his neck. To Amir, the man's accent sounded more Egyptian than Libyan. The Khamis greeted him, and it was obvious they knew him well. They discussed what had happened and gave their friend a description and an artist's rendering of what the two killers looked like. The black-shirted man said he was going to meet up with friends in Ethiopia, and he would keep a lookout for the two fugitives.

Amir had parked the motor scooter on the side of the small café. Nearly everyone in the café was Sudanese, except for them, the Arab, and the Khamis. The Khamis were engrossed in conversation with the other Arab man, so Tareq and Amir quietly paid their bill and left. They walked the motor scooter one block away before starting it and quickly tried to put some distance between them and Gaddafi's men. They would have to ditch the scooter in the very next town for fear that Gaddafi's men would catch up with them in the much faster passenger van that sat just outside the restaurant. A truck driver was pumping gas just outside of town. They parked the scooter behind the filling station and asked the driver where he was headed. The truck driver informed them he was traveling back home to the city of Ad Damazin. Amir offered to pay the driver if he allowed them to travel with him. The man agreed, but they would have to sit in the cargo bed all the way. They agreed. Both men were happy to get off the slow-moving scooter. The town of Ad Damazin was just across the border from Ethiopia.

They had finally eluded Gaddafi's Khamis guards and safely made it over the border into Ethiopia. It was now onto Bahir Dar, where they hoped for their safe extraction.

CHAPTER 16

THE WESTERN BRANCH

Tareq and Amir walked for over ten kilometers with a group of refugees making their way to a large refugee camp in Ethiopia. On the side of the road was a truck with some foreigners sitting nearby. Amir asked them if they needed any help. The Ethiopian driver started to speak, but his Arabic wasn't very good.

"I'm sorry. Our driver doesn't speak very good Arabic. If you can help us, please do. We'd much appreciate any help we can get," said a tall white woman with light-brown hair. She spoke Arabic very well. She was a South African journalist named Aba, traveling with her young female assistant, Katrien, and her videographer, Felix. They were covering the growing refugee crisis for a local South African news agency. Also in the group were Gunner, the only American, and a Sudanese woman named Hadria, with her young son, Abal.

The tall woman informed them that they had been on their way to Bahir Dar when the truck stalled going up the hill and would no longer start. "We've been trying to restart it for the last fifteen minutes but without any luck."

"My friend Tareq here is a good mechanic. Perhaps he can help you," suggested Amir.

"If we help you, will you give us a lift to Bahir Dar?" Tareq asked as he inspected the truck's engine.

"Yes, but please hurry. We were told Arab and Northern Sudanese slave traders are nearby."

After inspecting the truck and trying to start it, Tareq realized the problem was that the engine was starved for fuel. He removed the fuel filter and drained it. He tapped it with a small rock several times and blew into the filter. He repeated the process several more times before setting the filter down to dry out in the hot afternoon sun. Then he reconnected the fuel filter and pumped the truck's gas petal. He turned the key and continued pumping the petal until the truck finally started.

Aba, the tall South African woman, climbed into the front seat with her cameraman and the driver. All the others piled into the open bed of the truck. The engine ran rough, but at least they were moving once again.

A caravan of Land Rovers, pickups, and a large military truck with two small black flags was visible off in the distance, some way behind them. The Sudanese woman started hitting the back window of the truck to get the driver's attention.

"Faster, faster," she yelled. "They're coming." She had recognized the black flags and knew their meaning.

"Who is coming?" asked Tareq.

"They call themselves the Western Branch of the Levant. They are slave traders, rapists, and evil butchers. Do not let them catch us," she pleaded.

Will this ever end? Amir thought as the truck sped up.

Gunner asked the journalist's assistant, Katrien, who was also sitting in the back of the truck, what was going on. She told him bad people were coming their way. Suddenly the truck jerked, and the driver pulled to the side of the road. The left front tire had blown.

Another delay! These delays have become all too common, thought Gunner as he climbed out of the truck and looked underneath it for a spare tire. There was a spare, but it appeared to be flat as well. He was now convinced there was some other purpose waiting for him, something he had to do before he could find his way home.

A little way up ahead, just off the main road, was a narrow-rutted dirt road leading to what appeared to be a small village.

"We must hurry," the Sudanese woman urged the group. "Grab your bags, and let's get out of sight," Hadria told the others.

The group hurried a half of kilometer to the small village. What they found there was a group of abandoned makeshift shanties that were once used by refugees before the larger aid camps with food and water were built. Stacked against one of the buildings were various lengths of iron rods tied together with wire. *Someone must live here,* Gunner thought as he looked at how carefully the rods were tied together.

They hid in a small building with no roof as the caravan of vehicles stopped by their truck and then proceeded quickly on, as if in a hurry to catch up with someone.

After the slave trade vehicles had passed, the driver decided to go back to the main road and hitchhike to the next town for a tire pump and patch kit. As they waited outside the shack, an older man with a long white beard came walking down the dirt street. He greeted them.

"Welcome to my home," he said.

His name was Ibrahim. He told them that he had a small place just up the road, near a well. The eight of them were welcome to stay with him for a while and refresh themselves. Ibrahim was a Coptic Christian who had fled southern Egypt two years earlier, due to the ever-increasing persecution by militant Islamist factions. He told them he knew it was time to leave Egypt when the militants burned down the hundred-year-old Christian church that he once attended.

Aba, the South African journalist, quietly interpreted what the old man had said.

"Why doesn't the Ethiopian military stop the human traffickers?" Gunner asked Aba.

To his surprise, Ibrahim answered his question in English.

"Ethiopia used to try, but one particular group is too well trained and armed, and they usually travel in two separate caravans. They move quickly in and out of the countries around Ethiopia. Many of the border guards are paid off, allowing them free passage in and out of neighboring countries. They are more than just slave traders. Some of them are members of the Levant. They do not kidnap Ethiopians. They only go after infidel refugees. The Ethiopian military decided long ago that they would not engage with slave traders who left Ethiopians in peace," the old man explained.

"What is the Levant?" Gunner asked.

"The Levant is a growing group of extreme militant jihadists who believe in reconstructing the ancient caliphate of the Muslim world in the countries around the Mediterranean Sea. They will stop at nothing to achieve their caliphate dream. All infidels are worthless to them and are nothing more than pigs in their eyes," Ibrahim replied.

Amir spoke in English for the first time. "I haven't heard of them, and I've studied the Middle East very thoroughly."

"Then you need to study more," Ibrahim quickly answered. It was evident that the old man was well educated. He continued speaking. "One of their leaders resides in Egypt, or maybe Libya. I'm not sure which one. He always wears a black shirt or coat, with a vest of ammunition, and a black-and-gray-checkered shemagh. I have heard they have groups of small training camps in the hills near the Syrian border, in Sunni Iraq, and in parts of Libya and Egypt. Some of them want a worldwide caliphate. If you see them, run away," the old man warned.

"Do you have cell phone reception here?" Tareq asked Ibrahim.

"No. Not here. We are too far away from Bahir Dar. I have no need for such devices, but I do have a nice radio. I live in peace here and prefer to stay away from the noise and crowds of city people. There is a hill a few kilometers from here. Perhaps you could receive reception up there. It will be dark soon. I suggest you rest here tonight, in one of the other buildings. You can hike to the hill in the morning. It can be dangerous hiking along the narrow path at night. Oh yes, I have the business card of a friend in Bahir Dar who delivers me supplies each month. If there is cell phone reception on top of the hill, please call my friend and tell him to bring me toilet paper the next time he comes this way."

Tareq agreed that tomorrow morning would be the best time to hike to the hill in the distance.

"Hopefully, our driver will return this evening, and we'll be back on our way. If not, then we'll camp in one of the abandoned buildings for the night," Aba said.

All of them hoped they would not have to sleep on the dirt floors of the run-down shanties. Fortunately, all of them except for Hadria and her son had sleeping bags that they traveled with as part of the required aid gear. Ibrahim offered Hadria and her son blankets for the night and suggested the two sleep in his home because his iron wood-burning stove would keep them warm through the night. The others all slept in the abandoned building next door.

The next morning, Ibrahim cooked a small meal for them. They sat and talked while the radio played in the background. They enjoyed the simple hospitality of Ibrahim while waiting for their driver to return.

"Wait, listen to the radio," Amir shushed them. "You need to hear this because it concerns all of you. Something terrible has happened."

All were shocked to hear that what were believed to be mercenary soldiers had kidnapped a group of aid workers on the road to Bahir Dar. A ransom was being demanded for their release. To illustrate how serious the mercenaries were, the two drivers had been found dead. The ransom demand was attached to their bodies, which were hanging from a road sign. To the group's horror, they realized their driver was one of those found dead. Additionally, the names of all the missing foreign aid workers were broadcast on the news.

"I'm sure it was the Levant soldiers that passed by our truck yesterday who did this horrible thing," Hadria exclaimed.

"The truck and van were clearly marked as refugee aid vehicles. They know there are more of us than those they kidnapped. We need to hide the truck, so they think we are gone from here. Otherwise, they may come back to look for us," Aba explained in English.

The four men, Amir, Tareq, Gunner, and Felix, walked back to the truck. The truck's flat tire made it extremely difficult to move, but with great effort, they were able to move it down the narrow dirt road, until it was just out of sight of the highway. As they rested, leaning against the side of the aid truck, they all heard the sound of large trucks coming their way. The trucks went speeding past them down the hill. Then they realized the trucks were Ethiopian military vehicles.

Gunner thought what the others must have been thinking. *If they hadn't moved the aid truck out of sight, the Ethiopian military probably would have stopped and rescued them.* To Gunner it was just another sign he had another purpose for remaining in Ethiopia. He just didn't know what it could be.

Frustrated, Tareq decided not to waste any more time, so he headed for the large hill off in the distance. He ran behind Ibrahim's house, where he observed a large half-acre piece of land behind the home. Ibrahim had a garden. Four old tires filled with dirt lay on the ground. The old man was using them as planter boxes to grow herbs. Another old tire, this one empty, was lying on the ground with a shovel next to it. Long narrow iron rods were stacked against the wall. Some of them were twisted into the shapes of birds and other animals. Nearby was a large workbench with tools on it, and just past that was a brick stove. At the end of the garden was a pile of brush and pieces of wood next to a fire pit. Beyond the fire pit was a path that led in the direction of a large hill. It took Tareq over an hour to reach the top of the hill.

***

Amir, Gunner, and Felix were almost back to Ibrahim's house when they heard more trucks on the main road. They rushed back up the rutted narrow dirt road but stopped quickly as they saw the Levant truck with its small black flags stop near where the aid truck had previously been parked. A minute later, the caravan of vehicles went down the main road and disappeared into a group of trees, just off the road, in a valley below.

Amir relayed what had just happened moments before to the others at Ibrahim's house. Hadria clutched her son and began to shake with fear. Aba placed her arms around Hadria and her son to comfort them. Katrien suggested that they have a group prayer for the safe rescue of the captured aid workers, for themselves, and for the families of the slain drivers.

Amir immediately walked away and sat near the front door.

Aba volunteered to lead the prayer. She announced that she was a believer in the new Christian age of universal faith. Gunner asked her what that meant. Aba explained that in her new-age faith, all beliefs honor the same God.

"All religions lead to the same path, but by many different means. If all religions followed the same concept of a universal outcome, then there would be an end to war. All forms of ill will and discrimination would end under one universal outcome espoused in the multi-religious new-age belief. All would agree to be good stewards of Mother Earth. We must save our planet from the ill-informed. That must be our greatest goal. It doesn't really matter if you are Buddhist, Hindu, Muslim, Christian, or any other religion. We all are one. The tent is open to all in the faith of universal outcome. There are many Christians who believe just as I do. Please join us, Ibrahim, and Mr. Gunderson."

Ibrahim said he had already offered up his prayers as was his custom each morning. He then took a watering can and walked out to his garden.

Gunner stood by Felix, Katrien, Aba, Hadria, and her son, Abal. They all took each other's hands. Gunner stood between Hadria and Abal. As Aba started her prayer, Gunner let go of their hands and walked away. Hadria and Abal quickly joined their hands together as Aba spoke her prayer.

Gunner sat down next to Amir on the small step of the front door.

"So, you're not a believer either, I see, old man," commented Amir. Amir couldn't remember his fellow American's name, so he continued to call Gunner "the old man." Amir was usually good at remembering names, but for some reason, Gunner's name just slipped his mind. He was thinking about more important things. Besides he was embarrassed to ask after having been introduced earlier.

"It's a bunch of donkey poop and camel shit, isn't it? How could anyone believe in a God that allows such evil and suffering in the world? I have seen little girls die at the hands of suck-ass, supposedly godly people in Afghanistan. They call themselves holy warriors, but they are evil to the core. There is no God. How can there be? If there is one, then he must be evil as well."

Gunner didn't respond to Amir's comment. He was deep in thought about what Aba had just told him. Gunner looked at Amir and changed the subject.

"I came to this country to fulfill a promise, and my adventure here has been both frustrating and rewarding at the same time. I do not regret it, not even now, with all the uncertainty around us. But I just can't shake the feeling that there is another purpose for me being here."

"We all have a purpose. I know why I am here, but it sounds like you're not too sure of why you're still here, old man." Amir turned his attention back to Aba as she was finishing up her prayer.

"She calls it a universal-outcome belief…call it what you want, but I don't see much difference between that and what the jihadists want. They just have a more violent means of getting there." Amir looked at Gunner and asked him, "What do you think of all that garbage?"

"We live on this earth and are called to do good to one another. The rain falls on both the good and the bad. The world is both good and evil, and we choose the path to follow. Do not blame the one in heaven. Cast your blame and anger on the one from the pit of hell. A universal, multi-religious new-age belief? Many will follow because it sounds enticing to their ears, but I believe it is the easy and wide path that at its end, leads to the pit of emptiness." With that said, Gunner got up and walked away.

***

Tareq looked down to the valley below. He had noticed the caravan of vehicles that stopped near where their truck had been and then proceeded down the main road to park in the valley behind some trees. There was another caravan of Levant soldiers already camped there, waiting for the others to arrive. From his vantage point, he could easily see two large military trucks behind some trees. Two guards stood near the back of one of the trucks while others sat resting nearby. He counted at least eighteen Levant soldiers he could see, but there were probably more.

He saw three armed men dressed in dark clothing leave the larger group and begin hiking up the hill toward the dirt road where the aid truck was hidden. He watched carefully as the men reached the top of the hill and stopped near the hidden truck. They inspected it very carefully.

He saw one of the men point in the direction of the old man's house. Then he saw Aba and Felix walk back inside Ibrahim's home, unaware they had been spotted. Tareq checked the cell phone. It had one signal bar. He noted his geographic position from the phone, after which he quickly texted a coded message. He sat down and patiently waited for a response.

The three men at the top of the dirt road crouched behind the truck. One of them pulled out a military communication device and radioed for two addition men to assist them. Two black-shirted soldiers drove one of the off-road vehicles up the hill and parked it just behind the aid truck. Their leader was upset because he expected them to hike up the hill, not drive.

***

The old man had returned from watering his plants and sat down next to Gunner.

"I like your hat. It is very colorful. What do the letters mean?"

"It has the initials of my favorite baseball team on the front. They are called the San Francisco Giants." He watched as Ibrahim admired the hat. "Here, you may have it as my thanks for your kind hospitality. I have plenty of others like it at home."

Gunner handed the baseball cap to Ibrahim and thanked him again for the refreshing bread and water he had given to the group earlier. Ibrahim got up and opened a chest near his bed. He pulled out a light-gray shemagh scarf with white ragged edges at the bottom. He handed it to Gunner in exchange for his baseball cap.

"Thank you. Please take this as a gift from me," Ibrahim replied.

"This will go well with my gray shirt. Thank you, Ibrahim."

Amir smiled at Gunner. Then Gunner noticed a small scar below Amir's left eye.

"You look familiar. Have we ever met?" he asked Amir.

"Have you ever been to Afghanistan, Egypt, or Libya?" Amir inquired.

"No," Gunner answered.

"Then we've never met," Amir responded.

They were sitting and talking inside Ibrahim's little home when they heard the squeal of brakes. Amir peered through the slats of the old wooden front door. He could see the top of another vehicle just behind the aid truck. He had an uneasy feeling.

Aba, Felix, and Katrien were about to step outside, but Amir blocked them before they could exit. "It's them, the traffickers. They've stopped and are looking at our truck. They may have spotted you and Felix when you were outside earlier, but I'm not sure."

"Then we must hide in the hills out back," Aba said with a nervous urgency in her voice.

Amir was wearing a loose-fitting vest over his long shirt. He had kept his pistol hidden, but when he realized Aba might have been spotted, he pulled it out from under his shirt and checked its ammo clip. It contained just six bullets. Amir peered through a crack in the wooden door of Ibrahim's home. He saw three armed men coming down the narrow dirt road, and two others at the top by the aid truck.

Aba asked Amir what he intended to do.

"We need to stall them somehow, at least until Tareq gets back, or we will kill them if they start trouble," he replied.

"I'll talk with them. This is my home," Ibrahim replied.

Before they could discuss the situation further, Ibrahim was out the door. He walked confidently up to the three men and told them that only he lived in the abandoned village.

The man with the black-and-white-checked shemagh around his neck spoke. "We saw a tall, western-looking woman, old man. Who is she? We want to speak with her and the man she was walking with."

"They are my guests. She is an African journalist, and the man works the video camera. Aid workers were here earlier, but the Ethiopian military picked them up hours ago. The two you saw are here to interview me. I am an artist of some renown and live alone in the solitude of these hills. The Ethiopian soldiers are due to return soon to pick them up," Ibrahim told the man. He hoped that the man and his group would leave to avoid any confrontation with the Ethiopians. Ibrahim spoke in a loud voice, so those in the house could hear what was being said.

"Both of them have the right of sanctuary in my home," Ibrahim added.

"Is your home a mosque, old man? All I see is an old, run-down building."

"No, it is my home and my place of refuge from the noise of this world. As I've said, they are here to interview me for a news story and will soon leave."

Amir continued watching through the slats in the front door as the old man tried to talk his way out of a confrontation. *Ibrahim is a very smart man,* Amir thought as he listened to the old man's explanation.

"She should interview us, and her man should take our picture. We have a very important story to tell the world. Send her out with the cameraman. We will do them no harm. We will not leave until she speaks with us."

"What is your name?" Ibrahim asked the man who was doing all the talking.

"My name is Ammon. Send her out now."

The old man calmly walked back into his house and told them all that was said. Aba volunteered to speak with the man Ammon, but Felix refused and bolted out the back door. His fear was very evident to everyone.

Amir explained that he recognized Ammon, and that he and Tareq were not on good terms with the black-shirted men. If they saw him, it would only make things worse for everyone.

"I'll go with her. She can tell him that I don't speak Arabic, that I only speak Dutch," offered Gunner.

"And if one of them speaks Dutch, then what will you do?" Amir asked him.

"I know a few words, but really, what are the chances?"

If Felix would not accompany her, then Gunner was the only other option. Aba was very disappointed in Felix. Aba quickly showed Gunner how to hold and work the video camera.

"They're coming," Amir whispered.

Gunner immediately walked out the door holding the video camera. Aba followed closely behind him.

"The lighting is not good here," Aba said as she approached Ammon. "It's better if we are back by the first set of abandoned shelters. The sun is better suited for video at that angle."

Ammon agreed. *Good*, he thought. *They'll be even closer to my men at the top of road near the aid truck.* They all moved to the side of the first set of shanties.

Aba didn't want him anywhere near Ibrahim's home for fear he would see or hear the others. Amir watched as they walked to the far shacks and around the corner. He could only see Gunner with his video camera, not Ammon, Aba, or the other two Levant soldiers.

"No, no, I need to see all of you. Move back where I can see you more clearly," Amir whispered to himself. *Tareq, where are you? Hurry!*

Aba began the interview, as Gunner fumbled to work the video. Ammon and his men smiled. Ammon began to tell Aba about the dream of a worldwide caliphate and what it would mean to all Muslims.

"We will have peace and harmony throughout the world. We will live by a pure and righteous law," he went on to explain further.

The two guards by the aid truck started walking down the dirt road. When Ammon saw them, he grabbed his radio and angrily told them to remain by the vehicles.

"Do you kidnap women and sell them as slaves, or worse?" Aba boldly asked.

"My men are soldiers of the Western Branch of the Levant. We do what we must to fund our noble cause."

Ammon's eyes now shone fiercely at Aba. He looked at her light-brown hair, how tall and slender she was, and her mature, womanly look.

Aba noticed the changed look in his eyes. She tried her best to hide her nervousness.

"I have given you my time. Now you must give me your full attention. Please walk with me up the dirt road. Your cameraman can stay here while I will show you something very important."

"I am required to stay with my cameraman. Please understand. I must abide by certain rules too," Aba said in a shaky voice.

"As you wish. I can see you are nervous. Perhaps it is best that we talk right here after all. I want you to feel very comfortable with me. Please step inside this old house, where it is cooler, and I will speak with you in private. Please go inside. First, I must talk to my men."

Gunner started to go inside with her. He did not understand what Aba and Ammon had been saying. Ammon put his hand on Gunner's chest and shook his head no, continuing to talk in Arabic. Gunner immediately understood that he was not to follow Aba inside. Ammon took his two guards aside and briefly talked with them. When Ammon entered the shack, he closed the rickety door behind him. One of his men took position in front of the door. The other man came up behind Gunner, took his arm, and led him a short distance away from the shack. All of them were now completely out of Amir's sight.

CHAPTER 17

THE RUTTED ROAD

Gunner heard the sound of a slap and then a muffled cry from Aba inside the shanty. He could see a portion of her through a missing board on the door. Aba was on the floor, and Gunner could see that her pants were being pulled down to her ankles. He could hear her fighting Ammon, but her voice was muffled by Ammon's hand across her face. Gunner heard the sound of Ammon's fist striking the poor woman's face and then silence.

The guard in front of the door smiled as he noticed the concerned look on Gunner's face. "Don't worry," the guard said in English. Gunner tried not to react to the guard speaking in English. "You don't look Dutch to me. I think you are an American. I was educated in America, and I know how all American pigs smell. I will tell you now what will happen. The woman will make a fine whore. We will sell her for much money. Unfortunately for you, we don't need you. Yes…I think you understand me. Americans are better off dead than offered for ransom." The guard raised his weapon.

Gunner tossed the video camera in the guard's face and was immediately knocked down by the butt of the other guard's rifle. The side of Gunner's face was cut badly, and he fell to the ground, semiconscious. As he lay there, one of the soldiers shoved a boot in his face. They poured dirt on his head and into his nose. He choked, gasped, and snorted the dirt out of his nostrils. One guard laughed as the other one continued to kick Gunner. When Gunner appeared unconscious, they stopped. The heat of the afternoon was not conducive to fighting. Sweat dripped from the guards' faces.

"We will rest and then beat him more when he regains consciousness. Then you can shoot him. First shoot him in the legs and arms before you finish him in the head." The guard switched back to English and said, "Do you hear me, pig? Soon you will die."

Gunner's face was gashed and beginning to swell. His gray hair was now the color of the dirt, and although his eyes were closed, he was not unconscious. The shemagh he was wearing was smeared with his blood. He opened his eyes ever so slightly and could now see under the door across from where he lay. He became enraged by what he saw. Though beaten severely, he rose up and punched the closer guard in the lower abdomen, dropping him to his knees. The guard lay there gasping for air. Gunner grabbed his rifle and struck the other guard hard in the forehead, knocking him out instantly.

Amir couldn't see anything. Gunner and Aba were not in sight, and the interview was taking far too long. He went out the back door of Ibrahim's house and began to sneak from shanty to shanty, trying to get closer and to see what was happening.

Gunner burst through the rickety door. There was Ammon, half naked, on top of Aba. He was holding her arms stretched out above her head. Ammon turned to look back at the now-shattered door. As he did, he released one of Aba's hands. She dug her fingernails deep into Ammon's cheek. Ammon struck her hard in the face and started to pull up his pants before trying to fend off Gunner. His drawers were only halfway up when he turned suddenly and knocked the rifle out of Gunner's hands. Gunner quickly grabbed him by his testicles and dragged him out onto the rocky street. Ammon rolled over holding his groin, his pants now back down to his ankles. Gunner stomped on his stomach. As Ammon released his hands from his groin to hold his stomach, Gunner then stomped on his groin for good measure. Ammon curled up into a fetal position and moaned like a small child.

Amir saw a guard get up and move toward Gunner. He fired off two shots, killing the guard. The other guard still lay unconscious on the ground. The two others at the top of the road raced down to help their fellow soldiers. One of them radioed for backup as he ran.

Ibrahim heard the shots and peeked out his window. He saw more Levant soldiers running down the narrow road.

Gunner ran into the shack where the now-unconscious Aba lay. Her blouse had been ripped off, and she was mostly naked. Gunner quickly placed what was left of her blouse to cover her and laid her pants across her lower body. She had a large welt on her forehead and a cut lip. He heard automatic fire from outside the shack. Another weapon was leaning against the wall of the house. Gunner picked it up and looked out of the mud-brick shack to see men firing down the road at Amir. Amir had been hit badly and was now lying face down on the ground. Gunner opened fire, killing the one of the Levant soldiers and forcing the other one to retreat. He ran back to help Amir and get him out of the middle of the road. Gunner dragged him off to the side behind a small pile of crumbled bricks. Amir had been hit in both legs with numerous bullets. He was bleeding badly.

More shots rang out. Gunner fired his weapon once again as he slowly made his way back to the first set of shacks to help Aba. Aba suddenly appeared in the doorway holding her clothes in her hands. She stopped as if not knowing what to do next. She stood there, not moving.

***

Tareq made it back down the hill and found Felix hiding in some bushes. He instructed him to pile the bushes and pieces of scrap wood onto the fire pit. Tareq told him to roll the rubber tire on top of the wood and to pour lamp oil over everything but not to light it until he gave the word.

"Why?" Felix asked him.

"Help will come, but it will take some time, maybe about an hour or two from now. The dark smoke from the fire will help guide them. We'll light the fire in about an hour, no sooner." Those were Tareq's last instructions before he stepped out the front door and began firing his pistol.

Four or five more Levant soldiers arrived and took positions up the road. Gunner moved from shack to shack, trying to reach Aba. Two of the soldiers moved closer, the others providing cover fire, but they were not shooting in Gunner's direction.

Just outside the doorway of Ibrahim's home was Tareq, carefully firing his pistol at the Levant soldiers. One of the bullets hit Tareq in the chest, and his body slid down the wall. He now sat with his legs stretched out in front of him, his back to the wall, his eyes closed. His arms hung at his sides. He looked dead, but it was hard to tell from where Gunner was positioned.

Gunner peeked around the corner of a brick wall and fired his weapon, but nothing came out. He was out of ammo. He was very close to where Aba was standing frozen, a blank look on her face. Gunner jumped out and picked up a weapon that lay nearby and began firing. He yelled at Aba to run as he moved closer to the other weapon that lay on the ground next to the unconscious soldier he had hit with the rifle butt.

The soldiers up the road had halted their fire, fearing they'd hit their leader who was now trying to stand back up.

"Run Aba. Now…go!" Gunner yelled.

Finally, she stumbled out of the shack. Gunner held out one of the weapons for her to take back to Amir or Tareq.

"Take this," he yelled as he shoved the weapon into her hands. She took the weapon, clutching it against her torn clothes and ran less than twenty feet before stumbling and falling to the ground. When she got back up, she left the weapon lying in the middle of the road, far from both Amir and Tareq. Aba continued to stumble as she ran haphazardly back to the safety of Ibrahim's home.

Shortly after Tareq had stepped out the door, a burst of automatic fire hit the side of Ibrahim's home. Inside, all but Ibrahim cowered in fear. They could no longer hear Tareq. A short time later, a nearly naked Aba burst through the door. Ibrahim told them all to hide in the bushes away from his garden. Hadria and Katrien helped Aba and covered her with a blanket. They quickly exited out the back door. Ibrahim took Abal by the hand and told him to hide with the others in the bushes far away. Felix pulled out a lighter and handed it to Ibrahim, telling him what Tareq had said. Felix ran and hid with the women and Abal. Ibrahim hid by the fire pit, waiting for the right time to light it. All were unaware of how the fight was going on the long dirt road in front of Ibrahim's home.

***

Amir tore his shirt and wrapped the strips around both of his legs. One was broken, and he could see the tip of a bone where a bullet had struck him. He could barely move. He looked back, wondering when Tareq would arrive to help. Then he saw his friend sitting against the wall of Ibrahim's home, his head slumped, and his pistol lying on the ground next to his right hand. If it weren't for the obvious hole in his chest, he might have looked as if he were just sleeping.

Damn, we were so close to being out of here, Amir thought to himself. *Damn. Damn.*

His pain was almost unbearable, but he tried to crawl and reach the rifle lying in the middle of the road well ahead of him.

Gunner ran out the back door of the shanty and charged up through the bushes. Four Levant soldiers were moving slowly forward, firing their weapons at the shack that Gunner had just left. Their leader, Ammon, was now back on his feet and moving slowly up the road as two of his soldiers ran up to help him. Gunner had outmaneuvered them and was now just a few feet away from a soldier crouching behind the aid truck. He took another step forward, and a twig broke under his shoe. The soldier turned, and Gunner took him down with a quick burst from the weapon, which was now close to being empty. Gunner picked up the dead soldier's weapon and gunned down the three soldiers that still had their backs to him.

Up ahead stood Ammon with his arms draped over the shoulders of the men on either side of him. They stopped as Gunner approached, his weapon pointed directly at Ammon. Ammon quickly reached down and pulled a sidearm from the holster of one of the soldiers next to him. He dropped to his knees, firing two quick shots at Gunner. One bullet clipped

Gunner's right thigh, but the other missed. Gunner opened fire, dropping all three of the men in front of him.

Ammon lay on his back, still breathing. Gunner kicked his gun far away from his hand.

Exhausted from the ordeal, Gunner knelt down and looked Ammon in the eyes, and said, "You lose, you sorry son of a bitch. You may now depart to see your seventy virgins, who will look very much like old wrinkled dead men in the lowest reaches of hell." Gunner watched as life left Ammon's eyes. The slaver lay there dead, his eyes still wide open. No more Levant soldiers appeared to be around. Now there was only silence.

***

Gunner took a deep breath as he shouldered two more weapons and limped down the dirt road. He saw Amir peering over the edge of some loose bricks. Amir nodded his head. He was happy to see the old man still alive. *What a skilled fighter the old man turned out to be,* he thought.

Another vehicle quickly stopped, and more men jumped out. One opened the back hatch and pulled out a rocket-propelled grenade (an RPG) launcher. Gunner turned around and hid next to a half-broken wall beside a bundle of iron rods leaning against it.

"Damn, how many are there?" he said out loud. He watched as the soldier with the RPG made his way down the road and aimed it in Gunner's direction. He had been spotted. Gunner moved away quickly as the projectile hit the iron rods and exploded, sending sharp pieces of metal flying through the air. They fell to the ground like chunks of metal rain. Gunner ran behind another shanty. Another RPG exploded nearby.

Gunner laid down fire at the two men hiding up the road. When the second Levant soldier loaded the RPG again, Gunner knew he had to move fast, but his legs were like rubber now, and he could only drop down to avoid the third RPG shell, which hit the wall he was hiding behind. Tiny shards of brick tore through Gunner's shoulder, arms, and cheek. They stung like hell.

Ibrahim and the others trembled with fear as they heard the sound of explosions and the raining pieces of metal hitting the tin roofs of the shanties up the road. *Surely we will die,* Felix thought as he lay prone on the ground, trembling with fear.

***

"Enough of this!" Gunner yelled. He popped up and rained down every bit of ammo left in his weapon. He reached down and picked up the last remaining rifle and did the same long rapid burst of fire. Then there was silence. Two more Levant soldiers lay dead.

Gunner could hardly walk. He was so exhausted. His mouth was as dry as desert sand, and his eyes were bloodshot. His hair was the color of the ground, and his face was almost unrecognizable, caked with a thin layer of dirt. He was too weak to carry the weapon any longer. He turned and limped back toward Amir, who lay about thirty feet away.

Before he took two steps, a shot rang out, hitting Gunner in the back of his left shoulder, spinning him around, as if in a slow-motion pirouette. He fell to his knees, his arms down at his sides. His knees landed on sharp pieces of the iron rods that were scattered along the rutted road.

Up the road were two older men and a teenage boy. They were Arabs and were dressed in more traditional attire. The two older men wore scarves wrapped around their heads, qalansuwas rising from the center of the folds of cloth, unlike the Levant soldiers who wore black shirts, scarves, and matching skullcaps. One was holding an automatic weapon. The other held an old, long-barreled rifle, and the young teenage boy, wearing a white skullcap, rested his hand on the handle of a long, curved knife that was tucked under his belt. The man with the long rifle took aim once again, but the other man grabbed the long barrel and pushed it down toward the ground. He clearly didn't want the man to shoot again.

They looked at all the dead bodies of the Levant soldiers but paid particular attention to the one called Ammon. The man with the automatic weapon stood guard as the other two pulled Ammon's dead body out of the road and into some shade. The boy appeared to be crying. The oldest man with the long rifle yelled what were obviously obscenities at Gunner. Then he appeared to offer up some sort of prayer for the dead man.

When he had finished, all three walked up to Gunner. He still knelt, both knees on the ground, his arms hanging at his sides. Blood was dripping from his shoulder and right arm where shards of brick had lodged.

Amir tried to crawl to the rifle between him and Gunner, but the pain was too great, and he had to stop. The three Arabs were focused on Gunner and believed the battle was over. They weren't paying much attention to anything else around them. Dead bodies were everywhere.

They continued to talk to Gunner in Arabic. The man with the machine gun handed it to the young teenager and pulled the boy's long knife out of his belt. The boy placed the weapon directly in front of himself with the butt of the rife on the ground, while he held the top of the barrel with both hands.

Amir fought through the pain and crawled closer to the rifle, which lay half covered in dirt just past a large dip in the road. The oldest man looked in Amir's direction. Amir quickly played dead in the middle of the rutted road. Once the oldest man looked away, Amir continued to crawl. Sadly, it became apparent that he would not reach the rifle in time.

Gunner was too weak to do much of anything. The man with the long knife pulled Gunner's hair back, exposing his throat and placed the blade of the knife against Gunner's skin. The knife blade was sharp, and the touch of the blade created a thin cut on the side of Gunner's neck.

Amir watched as the man looked up into the sky and yelled, "Death to all those who oppose Allah." Amir continued to crawl but knew he could do nothing to stop what was about to happen.

***

With what little strength Gunner had left, he wrapped his right hand around an eight-inch piece of jagged iron rod that was just below the dirt next to his hand. He quickly drove it up, striking the man in his lower abdomen just to the left of his groin. The rod went deep into the man's bowels. The man trousers were now drenched in blood.

Gunner reached out to grab the rifle away from the boy, but the kid moved, and Gunner's hand slipped down the receiver, his fingers sliding across the trigger. As the boy pulled the rifle away, the butt of the weapon bounced up and down on the ground, and it fired wildly into the air. One of the bullets struck the teenager directly under his chin, killing him instantly. It was not what Gunner had intended. He froze as he looked at the boy's dead body.

The older man with the long rifle was caught off guard by the horror of what he had just witnessed. He stumbled back a few steps, reeling at the sight of the boy's body and the blood oozing out of his friend who was now lying on his back. He shook as he leveled his old rifle at Gunner's head.

At single shot rang out. Amir closed his eyes, not wanting to see anymore. Amir could almost feel the round fly through the air over his head. The man with the long rifle crumpled to the ground. He had been hit in the temple and had died instantly. Amir looked back toward Ibrahim's home, and there sat Tareq, holding the pistol out in front of him. Tareq lowered his arm and looked at Amir. He slumped over and died. The severe pain Amir felt in his legs was now less than the pain that was in his heart.

***

Amir could see the old man still kneeling up ahead of him, just staring straight ahead. He could see the old man's lips moving, but he couldn't make out what he was saying. Amir continued to crawl until he finally reached the rifle in the road. His knees ached as he continued to make his way closer to the old man who had saved his life and the lives of the others. He could hear the old man but didn't understand his words.

"Old man, stay with us. Help will be here soon." A plume of black smoke was now rising from the back of Ibrahim's garden. "Just hold on, do you hear me, old man?"

Finally, Gunner turned and looked down at Amir, who was lying just off to his right. Gunner asked if everybody was all right. Amir told him all had survived except his friend, Tareq. Gunner's face was grim. A tear mixed with blood ran down his cheek exposing a thin river of skin, like a stream carving its way through the dirt.

"You wanted to know your purpose, old man. You saved us. You killed all of them. That was your purpose. You saved us. That is why you were supposed to be here," Amir explained.

Gunner's voice was weak, and a trickle of blood came out of his mouth as he spoke. "No. Look at the young boy, so much like my youngest years ago. No, that's not why I am here. May Almighty God have mercy on all who died today. How can I ever be forgiven? I came to help the needy, not to kill."

"You saved our lives. You had no other choice," Amir told the old man.

Gunner looked down at Amir. "I understand everything now. You are my purpose, not the dead that lie around us."

Gunner struggled to reach under his shirt. He had to pull at the chain around his neck twice before it broke loose. He dropped his hand, and the chain fell into the dirt. Gunner picked it back up and placed the chain with its now blood-and dirt-stained silver cross into Amir's hand.

The Arab man with the iron rod stuck deep into his body moaned and gurgled as he lay on his back directly in front of them.

Amir thought of shooting him just to stop the bastard's annoying sounds, but instead, he kept his focus on Gunner. Amir looked at the cross and started to wipe the dirt, grime, and blood off of it. The old man stopped him.

"No, not until it's time. It is yours now. I give it freely to you. Keep it as it is until its day."

Amir didn't understand what the old man meant. To Amir, the cross was nothing more than a trinket. But it had been given to him by a very brave old man, so he tucked it in the inside pocket of the loose-fitting Arab vest he wore.

The old man was now looking straight ahead again. Amir clearly heard him say, "Oh no, you never let go…"

The old man's voice was barely audible, but Amir caught a few more words. "You never let go of me."

no emotion, and those in the large chopper heard only a focused voice over the roar of the engines.

The smaller black helicopter landed in the street in front of Ibrahim's now-burning home. Two bodies were loaded into it, and it immediately lifted off and headed away.

Small-arms fire began raining around the remaining rescue soldiers. They returned to the large helicopter. It lifted off and flew away. Ibrahim could see his burning home in the distance. He placed his hands over his eyes. He couldn't bear to see his once-serene home become a pile of ashes.

***

An Ethiopian military unit soon engaged the remaining Levant soldiers who had taken refuge in the abandoned shanties near what was left of Ibrahim's home. They rescued the six other foreign aid workers who had been tied together in the back of the large truck, which was still parked in the valley below the main road. The Levant fighters numbered in excess of twenty-five men in the beginning. Gunner had taken down about ten or more himself before dying. It took three hours before the remaining Levant soldiers were defeated. Only one was taken alive. All the rest preferred to die in battle.

The Ethiopians loaded all the dead bodies of the Levant soldiers into the back of the truck. All the dead were dressed in black shirts, except for two older men and half of another one, who was missing the upper portion of his body. A youth was also lying nearby. One older man wore a bloodstained light-gray shemagh. He was lying on his back near the edge of the hill. His shirt was burnt, and his legs were disjointed. His face was filthy and bruised beyond recognition. His white beard was stained a rust color from dried blood, and his hair was matted down and coated with dirt. One of the Ethiopian soldiers remarked on how bad the man's face looked.

"From the large hole in the street, I'd say he ate a grenade. He looks like shit."

"No, more like jerky," the other remarked.

"Grab his legs, and help me throw this garbage in the trash with the rest of them."

With that, the battered body of Joseph Gunderson was tossed unceremoniously alongside those of the dead human traffickers.

The bodies of the dead soldiers were later checked for identification, which only some carried. After that they were cleaned, photographed, fingerprinted, blood-typed, and DNA-sampled, each one received a toe tag with a number assigned to match his file. They were then carefully wrapped in white linen. Since the Ethiopian military believed all the dead were Muslims, they were lined up without caskets, each lying on his right side facing the approximate direction of Mecca, and buried in a mass grave two days later. A small wreath was placed on the grave, nothing more. Joe Gunderson's body lay at rest next to those he considered the evilest of all men.

CHAPTER 18

LOST MEMORY

Liddy Gunderson was on her way home after visiting with Big Ed and his very ill wife, Beth Ann. It would be the last time Liddy would ever see her friend. Sadly, Bethie died two months later.

It was during the two-hour drive back to her house when she heard on the radio that a group of twelve aid volunteers in Ethiopia had been kidnapped by mercenaries. One of the volunteers was believed to be an American. Liddy's heart sank. She hadn't heard from her husband in over two weeks, and he should have returned from his volunteer service already.

When she got home, she immediately called the US State Department, asking if they had any information about the kidnapped group in Ethiopia. She was told that the State Department was unaware of any kidnapped aid workers, but that they'd check and get back to her in the next day or two.

The man to whom Gunner had entrusted his letter two weeks before decided it would be best for him to mail it when he returned to the United States. He didn't trust the Ethiopian mail system.

Upon arriving home in Minnesota, and in all the excitement of his return, he forgot about Gunner's letter, which still remained in a zippered compartment of his pack. It was over two weeks later when he realized his mistake. He immediately dropped the letter off at his local post office. He felt guilty, but for all he knew, the man they called Gunner was probably already home.

Two more days passed, and Liddy called the State Department again. She was told there had been a kidnapping, and one American had been taken hostage. The State Department could not confirm if the American were her husband, Joseph Gunderson. The representative assured Liddy, they would keep her updated.

Liddy's son Abe searched the Internet for any news. Nothing was being reported on any of the US network news channels. It was as if one unconfirmed missing American overseas wasn't that important.

It was late at night when Liddy received a call from the government representative, saying he had just heard that all twelve of the foreign aid workers were rescued unharmed. He cautioned Liddy that the source reporting the situation, while generally reliable, could not fully confirm that her husband was part of the rescued group. Liddy felt a glint of hope. She hung up the phone and sat down next to her son.

"Look, Mom, on my laptop. They're showing the rescued workers." Liddy's son excitedly turned his computer screen, so she could see better.

Liddy looked and saw a man wearing a SF Giants baseball cap in the back of a group of people exiting a military helicopter.

They were quickly rushed onto an awaiting bus, and she just couldn't tell if it were her Joey or not.

"Dad wore that baseball cap, Mom. I'm sure it's him. Dad's safe!" Her son exclaimed to his other brother and his sister's families.

Liddy sat silently while her family hugged each other after hearing the good news.

"All are reported safe, Mom. You should be happy," her older son, Lennard, told her.

"Until I hold him in my arms, only then…" Liddy started to cry. Lennard held her and told her not to worry.

The very next morning, a letter arrived. It was from her husband, Joey. Liddy tore open the letter and tossed the envelope on the ground before she even reached the front door of her home.

The letter was dated over two weeks previously. Inside were two pictures. One showed a white-bearded Joey wearing his SF Giants baseball cap, standing with the other US volunteers. The other was him smiling broadly, surrounded by refugee children.

Yes, it must have been him they showed on the web. Liddy's heart was pounding with happiness. After looking at the pictures of her husband, she thought, *He will just have to shave that off when he returns home.* She put the pictures down and began to read the letter.

Dear Luv, my darling Liddy,

My work is not yet done here in Ethiopia. I will be staying another week, maybe more, to repair some needed equipment. I miss you greatly and can't wait to see you. Tell our children I'll be home soon. Give them my love.

Every time I think my work here is done, some other problem pops up. I'm beginning to think this country doesn't want me to leave until I fulfill another purpose. I will never forget these people and their children. I have no regrets and would do this again.

I had a vivid dream last night. In it, I was standing on a hill overlooking Salada, but there were no roads, houses, or the golf course. The hill had patches of green grass intermixed with small wild flowers. I could hear water rippling down a creek nearby, and the birds were singing. The Salada lagoon was large, and its water was clear as glass. The sun was warm, and there were no clouds in the sky. The Salada beach was golden, and the sea was so calm—it was the bluest of blues. This is the way it was meant to be in the beginning, peaceful and serene. This is what heaven must be like, I thought. And then I awoke and thought of you. You are my heaven, Liddy. I love you.

Joe

Liddy held the letter and read the last line again. She softly replied, "I love you too, Joey."

***

All twelve aid workers were given a full night and day to clean up, rest, and recuperate from their ordeal. For the next day and a half, they were debriefed one by one. When it was Ibrahim's turn,

an American official was brought in to assist with the
questioning. Joseph Gunderson's passport was on the table in
front of the official. He picked it up and looked at the picture.

"You don't look like the man pictured here, even if I imagine
him with a beard."

"I'm not the man you are looking at. My name is Ibrahim
Chenzira. I sheltered the foreign aid workers in my home, which
was destroyed by the murderous Levant. The nice man you see in
the picture gave me this hat. If the other rescue helicopter did
not pick him up, I fear he may be dead. I have not seen him here
with the others. I pray he is still alive."

The American official got up and left the room. Another
count of the aid workers was taken. Eleven were accounted for.
One was missing.

"Where were all the bodies taken?" the US official asked the
Ethiopian man in charge.

"Their bodies were taken to an airport hangar for processing
and identification."

"Get me there fast," the American replied.

***

Adam Amir Montgomery woke up four days later in a US
military hospital in Germany. His broken leg had been set. A
small piece of shrapnel had also been removed from the side of
his head. Another operation would be done the next day to repair
his left leg, which had suffered numerous bullet wounds. One
bullet still remained and needed to be extracted. His right
forearm was heavily bandaged. The arm had suffered lacerations
from the grenade shrapnel.

Adam had sustained a severe concussion and couldn't
remember anything past the point where he was looking through

the slats of the door to Ibrahim's home at the Levant soldiers as they walked up the street with Aba and the old man.

He remained in the hospital for another two months, rehabilitating his legs and trying to recover his memory. Then Adam was transferred back to the United States and continued the rehabilitation process at a hospital near the Norfolk naval base in Virginia.

As far as Adam's family and friends back home knew, his injuries occurred in Afghanistan. The world would never know about his secret mission in Libya and flight to Ethiopia with his partner, Tareq Kandankulam. There was no record of him training an assassin or even an assassination attempt in Libya. The secret would remain just that, a secret, and he was bound by it.

The doctors told Adam his memory might return in time, but there was a chance that his memory of that day might never return.

Adam Montgomery was awarded a Purple Heart and a Silver Star for bravery on the battlefield. The record would show that he and an Afghan soldier had been on a special covert assignment near the border of Pakistan when they came under fire. Montgomery and the Afghan soldier had been on point, according to the report, and separated from the other members of their team. The Afghan soldier, whose name was classified, was killed in action. Navy SEAL Trooper Adam Montgomery, who suffered numerous wounds, eliminated more than ten Taliban insurgents before being rescued by the other special operatives.

***

A report was also prepared regarding the events in Ethiopia. Two men, one named Tareq and the other named Amir, both last names unknown, were in Ethiopia, fleeing persecution in Northern Sudan. They stopped to help a group of six aid workers whose truck had stalled. Tareq fixed the vehicle, and the two men joined the aid workers traveling to the city of Bahir Dar. A flat tire caused them to take refuge in what was thought to be an abandoned village. A group of militants who call themselves the Western Branch of the Levant spotted the aid workers.

As best as could be determined, when it became apparent the militants might kidnap the foreign aid workers, the man named Tareq climbed a high hill and managed to call a friend in Bahir Dar for help. The local notified the authorities, and a rescue plan was put in place.

A South African journalist named Aba Govender concocted a plan to stall the militant leader and suspected human trafficker, who was called Ammon (last name unknown), by appealing to his vanity and proposing to interview him. An American man, Joseph Gunderson, posed as her videographer and accompanied her. The rest of the aid workers hid in a thick grove of bushes behind the home of the only resident of the village, a local artist named Ibrahim Chenzira.

When the man named Ammon took Aba aside and assaulted her, she resisted and was knocked unconscious. A medical examination the next day showed she had been raped and suffered a concussion.

It is believed that the militants killed Joseph Gunderson while Ms. Govender was being assaulted. Aba was not sure how, but she had been able to fight her attacker off and run outside. A man she believed to be Mr. Gunderson was lying on the ground with the large video camera next to his face. He looked dead. A half-naked man was crawling a few feet away.

One of the militants, who had been shot by either Amir or Tareq, was lying dead next to Mr. Gunderson's body. Another militant, who had been wounded in the face, was kneeling on the ground, a rifle held loosely in his hands. As she ran out of the building, she somehow was able to take the rifle away from the wounded man with the bloody, grimy face. She ran, while under fire from other militants, and made her way to Amir. She apparently gave the weapon to him and ran for the safety of Ibrahim Chenzira's home. Mr. Chenzira escorted her to the backyard where she hid with the others. Her recollection of these events is clouded by her concussion.

Piecing things together, it appears Amir and Tareq fought off the attackers, killing twelve to fourteen of them. It is believed that Tareq died during the early part of the battle. It is also believed that Amir was killed by a suicide bomber near the end of the fight.

Amir and Tareq carried no identification. Their bodies were given a proper funeral and buried in unmarked graves just outside the city of Bahir Dar. Tareq's friend in Bahir Dar could not be found. Both men are credited with saving the lives of five of the aid workers and the one local resident, Ibrahim Chenzira. Other than Ms. Govender, whose recollection of the events is unclear, there are no other witnesses to the actual gun battle. Aba Govender wrote an account of her ordeal as best as she could recall. She was hailed as a hero in her native country of South Africa.

✳✳✳

One week after the incident in Ethiopia, two government officials paid Lidia Gunderson a visit. They informed her that her husband, Joseph Gunderson, was dead.

"But on the web, I saw someone with a white beard wearing his baseball cap. He can't be dead. You must be mistaken."

She was informed that her husband had given the cap to a local man who had sheltered the refugee aid group. They apologized for the confusion and the delay in identifying his body. It would be another three weeks before Joey's body would be returned to the United States. Lidia was devastated by the news. Her children and their families mourned his death and tried their best to comfort their grieving mother. All of Joey's personal belongings were returned, including his wedding band, but no cross was found on his body.

The network news only briefly mentioned the initial account, which reported all twelve hostages were rescued unharmed. The news was dominated by other, more important events that week. No further updates were ever given by the US news after the initial report that all hostages were safe.

***

Joseph Gunderson had specified in his last will and testament that he wished to be cremated and his ashes buried on a small sand bar near the edge of the Stanislaus River, where he and his friend Big Ed used to fish. The small patch of earth only appeared in late summer, as the water level of the river receded. Joey used to wade out to the small mound and fish. It was his favorite spot along the acre of land his family owned. That little patch of ground would only be visible for less than two months, before the water level again rose up with the winter rains. Since it was late October when Gunner's body was returned to his family, it would be at least ten months before he would be laid to rest along the Stanislaus River.

***

Adam Montgomery's enlistment ended in June. He decided not to reenlist. Instead, he planned to move and work with a friend and former navy frogman who now operated a wilderness training school in Southern California. The wilderness and survival guide job was located just outside of Sequoia National Park. Part of his duties would be to write a monthly newsletter about wilderness living and how to live off the grid for all who trained with the Sequoia wilderness team.

After arriving in California, Adam unpacked his bag and pulled out the old vest and shemagh he had worn while on covert assignment in Libya. They were among the few items of clothing that had not been cut off of him before the initial surgery on his legs. Both the vest and shemagh had been dusted and folded but had not been washed. Adam decided he would wash them later. As he laid the vest down, he noticed a wrinkle in the top right portion of the garment. As he ran his hand across the material to flatten it out, he realized something was tucked in the inside pocket. He pulled out a broken chain with a cross hanging from its end.

What the hell, he thought. *Where'd this damn thing come from?* Adam fixed the chain and began to think back. Then it hit him. He vaguely remembered the old man who had given it to him on the rutted road in Ethiopia. He remembered what the old man had told him. *Maybe this trinket will help my memory return,* he thought, but unfortunately, the only thing he remembered was the old man kneeling, what he had said, and then the hand with the grenade. After that, everything was blank. Adam put the cross and chain back into the pocket of the vest.

The next day, Adam phoned his former commanding officer and asked to speak with his covert case handler. He reported he had found an item belonging to an American who died overseas. A week later he received a call advising him to discard the item.

Adam almost put the cross in the trash that week but took it out. He couldn't destroy what that old man had given him to keep. Adam placed the cross back into the inside pocket of the vest and left it there.

***

Adam Montgomery wanted his memory back, and he wanted to know more about the man who had given him the cross. He had read a news article written by Aba Govender while he was rehabbing in Germany, and he knew something wasn't right. The old man had still been alive right up to the end of the fight. He didn't die in the beginning, as Aba's story indicated. The old man didn't have a weapon when Adam crawled up to him. Adam had the weapon, so maybe the part about him and Tareq fighting off the Levant soldiers was true, but there was still something missing. He didn't know what, and it haunted him.

Adam was able to obtain the address of Lidia Gunderson. He felt compelled to meet with her and learn what her late husband was like. He also knew he could not talk about his time in Ethiopia. After all, he had never been in that country, at least not on record.

On his first weekend off in early August, he devised a plan. He called Mrs. Gunderson and asked to speak with her about an article he was writing about her late husband and his work in Ethiopia. She agreed to meet with him that weekend. Adam drove the three hours north to Lidia Gunderson's home. His goal was to understand who Joseph Gunderson was. He believed it might help him remember what had truly happened that day.

He would tell Mrs. Gunderson that he believed that there was more to the story about her late husband than what she had been told. He wanted to write about the forgotten American, Joseph Gunderson.

Lidia Gunderson answered the door and welcomed Adam into her home. She mentioned that her family was just finishing a discussion about Joey's final arrangements. He was welcome to stay, and they would talk afterward. Sandwiches and snacks were on the table for all to share after the meeting. Before he could say another word, a tall, older-looking man introduced himself as Ed Davis. Ed then introduced Adam to all of Gunner's children. Lastly, he introduced Adam to his youngest daughter, Adelynn.

"Haven't we met?" Big Ed asked Adam. "I never forget a name or a face. I know I have seen you somewhere before."

"I don't believe we have. I grew up in Virginia and did a couple tours of duty in Afghanistan. I've never been this far west before," Adam replied.

"Have a seat. We're about to finalize the plans for my friend Gunner's funeral. After we're done, me, you, and Liddy can talk while we have lunch."

***

The discussion was pretty straightforward. Big Ed would ensure chairs and shade structures and food were in place for the funeral and for socializing afterward. A marine color guard would present the flag. People would then be invited to talk about Gunner. Gunner had requested that just one song be sung at his funeral. His son and daughter volunteered to sing it. Then his ashes would be laid to rest. Everything would be done in the order Gunner had specified in his will.

While this discussion was going on, Adam kept glancing over at the beautiful Adelynn Davis. He was looking for a ring on her finger. She didn't wear any rings. Adelynn caught him looking at her. She smiled back at him.

Big Ed always brought his dog Rex along wherever he went. Rex the Wonder Dog was the smartest dog he had ever seen, except for maybe Odie, who had lived a total of seventeen years. Gunner and Liddy had buried Odie on top of the Mori's Point bluff, overlooking the *Nordic Prince* rock. Rex walked over to Adam and lay down at his feet.

"Looks like my dog likes you," Big Ed commented.

***

The family meeting ended, and soon Big Ed walked Adam over to Lidia. Lidia asked Adam if he knew her husband.

Adam lied and said no, that he just felt compelled to write a story about her late husband. He needed to know more about him. Adam looked at Ed and could tell that he was still trying to figure out where he had seen Adam before. Adam watched as the big man reached into his pocket and rolled Valhalla into his palm.

"Have you ever seen anything like this marble before?"

"No…not that I can recall," Adam lied again because he now realized that the big man was one of the men he had met at the airport when he was just a kid. The other man with him must have been Joseph Gunderson, the one with the shiny coin.

As Ed was showing Valhalla to Adam, Lidia got up and went to her room. She returned with a small flash drive. Lidia told Adam that Joey, as she always called him, spent the last year summarizing the notes in his journal on his laptop. He had planned to rewrite his memories in the form of a book. Joey wanted his family and friends to know about his life and times, and about the lives and times of those he knew. She handed the small memory drive to Adam.

"This is an extra copy. I've deleted a few very personal journal entries, which will remain between me and Joey. If you want to know about my husband, take this and read it. He wanted to rewrite it as a book before he died. I've asked Big Ed to help me finish his work, but with Bethie's death months ago, we just haven't been able to even begin to think about it. I wanted the book to be a surprise for all my children and our friends. I suppose now I'll need to ask my oldest son to help me write his father's story."

"I'll finish it if you let me. Maybe I could meet periodically with you and Mr. Davis, and together we can finish what your husband started," Adam offered.

"Tell me, Adam. How did you find out about my husband, and why are you so eager to help us?"

"I was in the military overseas when I heard about the kidnapped aid workers. Only one of them died, an American. So little is known about that day, and I became obsessed with finding answers. I believe there is more to the story than what we've been told. I never actually met your late husband, nor was I ever in Ethiopia. I just feel there is more to Joseph Gunderson than just a footnote in a newspaper."

"We will have his funeral the second Saturday in September, when the Stanislaus River is at its lowest. You are welcome to attend. Be sure to read his journal entries, and let me know if your offer still stands. I'll talk with you again then. Big Ed will give you the details," Lidia responded.

They ate lunch, and Adam talked with other members of Joe's family. He also spent some time in conversation with the beautiful blond woman, Adelynn.

Adam realized that he would have an opportunity to return the stained cross to its rightful owner. At the end of the funeral, he planned to discretely bury the cross near the water's edge by Joseph Gunderson's ashes. Adam was happy that he would finally be relieved of the burden of carrying the old man's cross.

CHAPTER 19

NEVER LET GO

Adam read every entry in Joseph Gunderson's journal. He felt obligated to help finish what he viewed as the journey of not just one man, but the journey of three.

He began to remember bits and pieces of the fight on the rutted road. In his memories, he saw glimpses of the old man fighting the Levant soldiers outside the shanty in the distance and of Aba running for her life. Adam remembered sneaking up to get a better look at what was happening. He had the same thoughts over and over again, but they still weren't complete. But he believed more than ever before that his memory of that day would soon return. It was now clear to him that Gunner fought to protect Aba Govender. After reading the journal, he never again thought of Joe Gunderson as "the old man." To Adam, the old man became "Gunner."

Adam began to write the journey of the three. He prepared a draft of the book's first chapter. He would send Joe's lovely wife, Lidia, the first chapter via the web, in the hope that she would allow him to complete the rest of the story.

***

Early in the morning on the second Saturday in September, Adam met with Big Ed Davis, Adelynn, and Gunner's two sons, Lennard and Abe. Adam didn't own a suit, so he wore his military dress uniform. He caught Adelynn looking at him several times. He smiled at her each time.

Big Ed brought his large vacation trailer. They all helped unload and set up a shade shelter, chairs, table, and a large cooler with refreshments.

Gunner's older son, Lennard, placed a box with his father's ashes on a tree stump where his dad used to sit and relax after a day of fishing. Big Ed leaned a beautifully framed picture of his friend against the box but quickly covered it with a red, blue, and white cloth.

Curious, Lennard removed the cloth and looked at the picture. There before him was a picture of his father when he was young, dressed in his finest military attire. On either side of his picture, embedded in the matting, was a medal—a Purple Heart on one side, and a Bronze Star on the other. Below his picture was a single dog tag bearing Gunner's name. On each side of the dog tag were a series of military service ribbons. Beneath the ribbons was a summary of his citation of valor.

Tears came to Lennard's eyes as he placed the picture frame back down and covered it once again. Gunner had never told his children or his wife about what happened in Vietnam. Big Ed walked over to Lennard and put his arm over his shoulder. They walked away as the older man comforted Gunner's son.

A while later, friends and family began to arrive. Big Ed took a shovel and waded through a small stretch of water to a mound of gravel and dirt that protruded above the surface of the river just a few feet offshore. He cleared rocks from the surface of the mound and then jammed the shovel into the soil. He walked back and sat down on the chair next to his daughter and Adam, who were now sitting together and talking with each other.

Lidia Gunderson, her children, and other family members sat together in front of the covered picture and box that were on the stump.

The minister of her church gave a short sermon, not exceeding five minutes, as her late husband had requested. A military honor guard opened and then folded an American flag. The carefully folded flag was then presented to Lidia. She was thanked for her husband's service, and after that, taps played in the background. Both Big Ed and Adam stood up and saluted. For the first time in months, Liddy could no longer hold back her tears. Thoughts of both Joey and Lenny mixed together with the sound of the bugle.

The honor guard departed, and Gunner's friends and family were invited to speak about the man, Joseph Gunderson. His sons spoke briefly about their father and how he loved to play his guitar but would never sing. His daughter, Madelyn, spoke up and said her father once sang to her when she was very young. One of her brothers chimed in and said she must have been dreaming because he never sang.

Last to speak was Big Ed Davis. He removed the cloth and presented the picture of Gunner to Liddy and her grown children.

"I always called my friend Joe 'Gunner.' That's how I'll always remember him. When Gunner's parents died, I helped him sort out their belongings. In their garage was a footlocker that contained all of their son's military memorabilia. Buried at the bottom of the locker were the items shown in this picture and a page torn out of his journal. To my disbelief, Gunner put them in the pile of things to be discarded. I pulled them back out and asked him why he would dishonor what had been given him? In answer, he told me a story. I had heard part of the story before, but he had never completed it. That day as we sat in his old home, he told me everything. He had ripped the full story out of his journal and substituted a short summary instead. In his revised entry, he mentioned a battle where three of his friends had died and where he had been saved by a man he knew as River Hawk, but he left out a few things. Why? It was because he was ashamed and viewed his actions that day as a failure. He was too scared to shoot straight, he told me. I won't go into the details as to how scared he was, but I'll tell you this much. Lance Corporal Joseph Gunderson, as frightened as he was, charged the enemy firing a pistol that he picked up off the severed leg of his CO. He ran forward, not back to safety as most men would have. He heard his buddies cry out in the darkness from a dirt hole on the ridge of that small hill in Vietnam. When his pistol ran out of ammo, he threw it at the enemy and engaged in hand-to-hand combat…"

Big Ed choked up and had to stop for a moment before continuing. "He picked up any weapon that was on the ground and fired down the hill, slowing the enemy advance. There's a lot more to tell, but I'll end this by saying that he couldn't save his friends that horrible night, and the fear he felt haunted him. He believed he was undeserving of any medals. I told him he had had a choice to turn back, but he didn't. He couldn't run away. It just wasn't in him. I knew that from long ago. We weren't exactly friends during our teenage years, and even so, he and Liddy's brother, Lenny, helped me fight off three men that I feared. It was then that Gunner gave me the agate marble I always carry. No man could have had greater friends than Gunner and Lenny. Gunner never thought himself as a hero, but I know different, and so should you. I present this picture and citation to you and your children, Liddy."

Liddy smiled at Ed. "Joey was always a hero in my eyes, but for other reasons. I could see him as nothing less. He was even brave and loving enough to sing our daughter Maddie to sleep when she was frightened of the dark. One night, I quietly stood outside our daughter's door and listened to him strum his guitar softly and sing for the very first time. Joey sang our daughter the song 'Goodnite, Sweetheart, Goodnite.' I had never heard of the song or the artists before. It was a song by a group called the Spaniels. He changed a few of the words, and it came out so sweet, his rough voice didn't matter at all. I didn't want him to stop. By the time Joey had finished singing, our little daughter was sound asleep. These are the memories I'll always hold in my heart."

Maddie moved to her mother's side, leaned her head on her shoulder, and wept.

***

Lidia looked at Big Ed, and he knew it was time. Gunner's son Lennard carried the box containing his father's ashes to the mound above the water. Gunner's younger son picked up his guitar, and he and his sister moved to a point above the river and waited.

Gunner's son Lennard opened the box as Big Ed dug down into the dirt. He dug down deep and a bit of water began to seep into the hole. Lennard took a handful of his father's ashes and let them fall from his hands into his father's final resting place. Big Ed took the rest of the contents, poured them out, and immediately covered the hole with dirt and gravel. As the men stood there, a guitar sounded, and Gunner's other son and daughter began to sing the song their father had requested.

Maddie introduced the song as her brother strummed his guitar softly in the background. "This is a song my father once heard that he never forgot. It was sung by an Englishman by the name of Matt Redman. It's titled 'You Never Let Go.'"

They both began to sing the song with great feeling, with passion in their voices. They had practiced it many times before. Maddie was sure she could get through it without crying. Her voice cracked a bit in the middle of the song, but she quickly recovered.

Adam began to sweat as he heard the words. He loosened the top button of his uniform. Beads of sweat appeared on his forehead and upper lip. He could hardly breathe. Adelynn asked if he was all right and then pulled a bottle of water out of the cooler for him to drink.

Every time Adam heard the verse—"Oh no, you never let go"—a flood of memories of the rutted road returned. Before the song ended, he remembered everything.

Gunner wasn't asking him to hold his hand because he was afraid. He was just reciting the song as a prayer before he died. Adam looked at the river and knew then that he could not bury the cross.

***

Just after the song ended, there was a loud crack down by the river. Big Ed had taken the shovel and jammed it deep into the ground. He held the top of the wooden handle with one hand and stomped on the lower inside of shovel near its blade, breaking the wood at its base. He took the handle and threw it in the river. He left the shovel blade buried deep in the dirt. Big Ed stood and watched as the handle floated down the stream.

It was a feat of strength that Adam had never seen before, especially from an older man such as Ed.

"That shovel will never bury another person," Adam heard someone say.

After the funeral, Gunner's friends and family mingled and socialized as a luncheon was prepared just outside of Big Ed's trailer. Adam took the opportunity to speak with Lidia. He asked her to sit down. He wanted to give her something.

"A man who was with your husband before he died gave me this, and I believe it belongs to you."

Adam placed the still-stained cross and chain into her hand. She looked at the cross before folding her fingers around it and holding it to her breast. "What did my husband say to you when he gave you this cross?"

Adam was taken aback by her words. How could she know that the man he was talking about was himself?

"I'm sorry, but this was given to another man."

"And what did my husband say when he handed over his cross?" she repeated.

Adam thought for a moment and decided to tell her exactly what Gunner had said. "He told the man, 'You are my purpose. Take this. I give it to you freely.' He asked that it not be cleaned until its time. The man didn't know what that meant."

Lidia opened her hand and asked Adam to open his hand. When Adam opened his hand, she placed the cross into it and closed Adam's fingers around it.

"This was a gift from my husband, given for a purpose. It cannot be returned. You shall keep it. I know it was given to you. I'm not asking you to wear the cross, only to keep it safe. Write my Joey's book, and tell the whole story—the good, the bad, the happy, and the sad. That's the way he would write it. Big Ed and I will help you along the way."

Adam could see she saw right through him. It was as if she already knew who he really was. He placed the cross back into his pocket. He would no longer hide who he was and what had really happened to her husband. They talked some more, and then she called Ed over and asked him to help in writing the story.

Ed agreed but only if Adam would drive up to fish on the Stanislaus River or off the Sharp Park pier. Adam agreed that every other month, he would spend a weekend visiting with Big Ed Davis and Lidia Gunderson.

"I don't own a fishing rod. I do have a small stick with fishing line and a hook that I use in my survival training class, but that's about all."

"Don't worry about it. I'll provide all the equipment you'll need. Just bring a sleeping bag," Ed replied.

***

The first trip up to Northern California was one month later. They met at Lidia Gunderson's home. Big Ed, Adelynn, and Lennard, were there waiting for him.

They spent two days camping on Big Ed's land by the river, just north of where Gunner's ashes had been buried.

Big Ed gave Adam an old, green, metal tackle box and handed him a fishing rod and reel.

"This gear belonged to Gunner. He always caught fish with it. Let's see if you can do the same."

They walked down to the river, and Adam opened the tackle box. In it was an old Bible with the tiniest of print.

"Oh, by the way, before we fished, Gunner always read a verse or two. Please do us the honor," Big Ed asked Adam.

"I'm really not sure. Perhaps it would be better if Lennard or you read a verse."

"Oh…come on. Just read a verse so we can start fishing."

As Adam opened the book, its old withered cover fell off. Adam laughed and joked, "See? This is a sign."

Big Ed just looked at him and waited. Adam opened the book and randomly picked something to read. He read verses from a section called Ecclesiastes.

To everything there is a season, and a time to every purpose under the heaven:

A time to be born, and a time to die; a time to plant, a time to pluck up that which is planted;

A time to kill, and a time to heal; a time to break down, and a time to build up;

A time to weep, and a time to laugh; a time to mourn, and a time to dance;

A time to cast away stones, and a time to gather stones together; a time to embrace, and a time to refrain from embracing;

A time to get, and a time to lose; a time to keep, and a time to cast away;

A time to rend, and a time to sew; a time to keep silence, and a time to speak;

A time to love, and a time to hate; a time of war, and a time of peace.

Adam closed the book, and placed it back into the tackle box.

Big Ed spoke up. "Good! You just read some of the lyrics from the old song, 'Turn, Turn, Turn,' by the Byrds. Now it's time to fish. The one with the lowest weight of no more than three fishes cleans and guts all the fish caught today."

"A song by the Byrds?" Adam questioned, but no one explained. All were now too busy casting their lines into the river.

Adelynn sat next to Adam. She handed him a beer, and they talked more than they fished. By the end of the day, Adam lost the challenge. Adelynn helped Adam scale and clean the fish. She enjoyed helping him.

Big Ed talked with Adam about his time growing up with Gunner. Adam carried a voice recorder, and they talked until it was time to bed down. They all slept in Big Ed's travel trailer.

From that day on, Adelynn talked with Adam nearly every week via webcam.

***

Two months later, Adam was invited to Big Ed's beach home in Pacifica. Ed Davis and Adam walked to the pier. Adelynn was nowhere in sight. Adam was disappointed.

"Look down there on the beach, just by the end of the paved trail. That's where the Leaf and Gunner found Valhalla. Someday, you and I should take the long walk to Mori's Point. At the edge of the golf course is where we used to play marbles. We called it Ringer Rock." Ed pointed to the bluff in the distance. "See the first large rock off the point? That's what we call the *Nordic Prince*."

"The names are familiar. I've read about them in Gunner's journal. It's nice to finally see them."

They each carried a fishing rod and reel. Ed carried the old green tackle box. Adam carried a cooler filled with ice and a few bottles of water.

Big Ed opened the green metal box and pulled out the Bible, the cover now held on with duct tape.

"Why not just buy a new one?" Adam asked.

"This one belonged to Gunner, and it's still good enough to read."

Big Ed read a couple of verses, put the Good Book back into the tackle box, and dropped his line into the surf below.

"Ed, do you believe we each have a higher purpose in life? I mean, I used to think that we're just here by random chance. Now, I'm not so sure."

"We all should make our purpose in life to do good to others. That's what Gunner used to say. But if you're asking me if we are given a higher purpose than just to live out our days, then yes, I believe everyone is given a purpose to fulfill. For some, it is a small thing. For others, it is much more. I don't believe most people even recognize when that special purpose is fulfilled."

"I remember Gunner's words about his purpose, that his purpose was me. It was as if he knew that I would live through the hell of the rutted road. When I was rehabbing my legs, I did a lot of reading and began to change how I viewed my life and life in general. I still have a lot of questions."

"Shoot away," Big Ed responded.

"Maybe some other time. Let's fish and then talk later about the life and times of you, Gunner, and Lenny. I'm making good headway on the book, but I still need more information from you and Lidia."

Adam stopped talking when he saw a beautiful woman in tight black running shorts and a skin-hugging tank top running along the beach trail. Her blond hair was in a ponytail that bounced as she ran. She had a dog on a leash, which ran slightly in front of her. *Wow,* he thought. He knew instantly it was Adelynn, but he had never seen her dressed like that before. The day was always much better when she was around.

***

Adam was invited up to Big Ed's home in Pacifica three months later. Adam arrived late on a Friday evening and spent the night in the beach house's guest room. Big Ed went to bed early, but Adelynn and Adam watched TV and ate popcorn late into the night.

The next day was foggy and cold. Ed got up and went into his garage and returned with the old green tackle box. After looking outside and seeing how foggy and cold it looked, he decided it would be better to stay in and just talk about Adam's progress on Gunner's book. Adelynn was scheduled to work a half-day at the clinic, and she had already left for work.

Big Ed sat in his favorite lounge chair, and his dog Rex laid down on the rug next to him.

Ed looked out the large plate-glass window. "Even when it's foggy, it's still a great view."

"I'm troubled by something, Ed. Maybe you can explain to me something that I just don't understand."

"Fire away. If I can't answer it, maybe Rex here can," Ed joked.

"I read in Gunner's tackle-box book that in ancient times, the soldiers of Israel were ordered to kill every man, woman, and child of a particular enemy nation. It was God who ordered them to do this, according to his book. Why?"

Ed stopped rocking and reached down to pet his dog. "Rex, do you know the answer to that question?"

Ed got up and walked over to the coffee table and opened the old green tackle box. Gunner's beat-up old Bible was missing. He asked Adam if he had seen it.

"I borrowed it. The cover really needed fixing. I'll return it when I'm back up here again."

"Hmm…to your question, it's funny you should ask. I made the mistake of asking Gunner the very same question many years ago when he read those verses as we fished along the Stanislaus. I kept asking him questions and didn't focus on my fishing. He ended up getting the biggest catch of the day."

Ed ran his fingers through his white hair and thought for a moment. "Here's what Gunner told me. What you're reading is not one book. It is many different writings that in some cases were written many hundreds of years, even a thousand years apart. They are simply a collection of the historical records of a people that became the nation of Israel and of their relationship to the eternal Father—and in later years, the story of a promised savior.

In many cases, it gives eyewitness accounts of man's relationship, both good and bad, with our creator, and eyewitness accounts of the messiah. The authors wrote what they saw, heard, and believed. Was what they said from God directly? I really can't say, but it's what they believed. We can believe it as direct testimony or not, but it is what they wrote, and I believe them."

"You haven't answered my question. Why order the soldiers to kill the children, the babies of their enemies? That just doesn't sound like a very forgiving God."

Big Ed responded by saying, "The ancient writings don't always paint a very pretty picture. I suppose in a way it makes the story truer. I like to think that all people can be redeemed, but sadly, I know there are those in the world today that are totally evil and beyond redemption. It has been that way in the past, and unfortunately, evil will remain until the end.

"As for the nation of Israel, I do know that whatever the enemies of Israel did to them, they in turn would do to their enemies. If their enemies did such things to them, they would sometimes pay back in kind, other times they would show mercy. We have done similar things in our time."

"The hell we have," Adam replied.

"Just after I was born, our nation dropped two atomic bombs on cities in Japan. They were dropped to save the lives of hundreds of thousands of soldiers who would have otherwise died while invading the Japanese homeland. Innocent men, women, and children died by those atom bombs. The United States did it to stop the war. It was, in a way, the nuclear option, as we would say today. In other words, it was viewed as a way to end the war quickly and to prevent future catastrophic wars. Perhaps, for the nation of Israel, the utter destruction of its enemies was the nuclear option of their day," Big Ed calmly replied. "By the way, don't change the Bible cover. The duct tape was all it needed. That's the way Gunner would have kept it. Return it just the way it was."

Adam pondered all the things Big Ed had said, but doubt still remained about what he truly believed.

***

Adam met with Ed Davis and Lidia Gunderson quarterly. He was almost finished with the book. Adam never asked Ed more questions about the Bible, but Big Ed still followed the tradition of reading a verse or two whenever they went camping.

One afternoon, as they drank coffee, Adam said to Ed, "I read why you carry the marble you call Valhalla. You believe it has a power. Your friend Gunner wasn't quite so sure, was he?"

"You know it has power, Adam. You held it once yourself, didn't you? You were the young boy in the airport who picked it up and didn't want to give it back. I believe your mom called you Amir. You couldn't hold it for too long back then. Let's see how you do now."

Big Ed handed Valhalla to Adam. *What a memory the man has,* Adam thought. The marble at first felt cool, but it was heavier than it looked. It was a hot day, and the sun reflected off the polished gemstone, causing Adam to blink and drop the marble. He picked it back up, but now Valhalla was warm, and it was getting warmer. Adam tossed the marble from one hand to the other, just as he had done as a kid.

Ed reached out, caught Valhalla in midflight, and placed it back into the silk pouch.

"It's a beautiful gemstone. It reflects the sun and warms very quickly. I think I understand why it's special to you. It is because Gunner gave it to you more than for any other reason."

"You are learning, Adam, but you're only half right. Now if you could only learn how to be a better fisherman. You still have a long way to go, my friend."

***

Adam traveled to Northern California four times a year. Adam knew he was very much in love with Big Ed's daughter, Adelynn. In all that time, he hadn't even kissed her, let alone tell her he was in love with her. He decided that on his next trip to Northern California, he would not talk about the book, fish, or let anything else deter him from having a true date alone with Adelynn. Adam contacted Adelynn via webcam and officially asked her out.

"God, I thought you would never ask. Of course I'll go out with you. Just let me make all the arrangements. I know this area very well. My father will be so happy. I haven't dated in over two years. I can't wait to see you again, Adam."

They talked more, and they set a date for one month later. When that day finally came, Adelynn and Adam had a great night of dining and dancing. He drove her home, kissed her on her front door step, and then started walking back to his car.

"Where are you going?" Adelynn asked. "You are staying here for the night, aren't you? My dad wants to spend some time with you tomorrow."

She walked down to where Adam stood, took his hand, and led him back into her home. Big Ed was sitting in his favorite lounge chair, rocking ever so slightly. His dog, Rex, was by his side. Ed just smiled at them and announced he was going to bed.

As soon as her father was out of sight, Adelynn and Adam embraced again. Adelynn finally pushed herself away. Her face was flush, and her eyes were wild with desire. She kissed Adam one more time and ran upstairs to her bedroom.

CHAPTER 20

FINAL HONOR

Three months later, Adam asked to go camping along the river where Gunner's ashes had been placed. Lidia's family was also invited. They would make it a party to celebrate what Adam said was the finished book. Big Ed and Adelynn brought the travel trailer, food, and drinks.

Everyone had arrived. Big Ed wanted to fish. He hadn't been feeling well and thought relaxing by the river would perk him up.

Adam just sat on the tree stump just above the river and watched as Big Ed wandered by with two poles in hand.

"Let's go, Adam. What are you waiting for? I can hear the fish jumping out there. They're hungry. Now's the time," Big Ed exclaimed.

"That's not why I asked you here, Ed. I want you to do me a favor."

"And what favor would that be?"

"I want you to baptize me, Ed."

"Don't joke with me that way, my friend. It's not funny." Ed gave Adam a very serious look.

Adelynn stood there in shock at what she had just heard.

"No, I'm serious. I've been doing a lot of thinking about Gunner, who he was, and what he believed, and what you and I have talked about. It caused me to search for answers."

Adam told Big Ed and Adelynn what he now believed. He confessed his misdeeds and had asked God for forgiveness. He had killed men in battle, and for the first time, he felt sorrow about those he killed. It was the same feeling Gunner expressed years ago when they were together on the rutted road.

"This isn't a church, and I'm not a preacher," Big Ed protested.

"This here is my church, and you are the only one I'll let pour water over my head. The time is now, and you have been asked." Adam got up and walked into the river. The cold water came up well past his waist when he knelt down. He pulled a now clean shiny cross out from under his shirt and said, "I'm ready."

Lidia took notice of the clean cross he wore and was pleased. Ed looked at Adelynn. She nodded her head in approval, and Big Ed did something he had never done before. He baptized Adam Amir Montgomery in the waters of the Stanislaus River.

Adam was soaking wet and cold when he came out of the water. Still wet, he approached Lidia, and removed the cross from his neck, and gently placed it around hers. The purpose has been fulfilled, and I return the cross to where it belongs. Lidia smiled and cried as the words "thank you" flowed from her lips. Adelynn rushed a towel to Adam and began to dry his face and hair. She kissed him on the cheek for what he had just done, and they sat and talked the rest of the day. Adam announced that the book was finished, with the exception of the epilogue. He would see that each family member received a copy.

Adam informed Ed and Adelynn he would be gone most of the following month on a survival excursion, and afterward, he'd visit with his love, Adelynn.

***

Adam hadn't talked to Big Ed or Adelynn in over a week. He was working in the field with his partner, as they planned their annual survival-training excursion. It was late August of 2013 when Adam took a group of seven people on a twenty-one-day survival training in the woods just outside of Sequoia National Park. The group had no phones, no high-tech gear of any sort. Each person was given just one day's worth of food and water, nothing more. They had all been taught how to survive, and now they were going to be put to the test. Adam would assess how they were doing and assist, but only if absolutely necessary. The only communication available was his partner's satellite phone, and it was only to be used in case of an emergency.

Once the survival training was over, he planned to drive directly to Big Ed's beach home in Pacifica.

***

Big Ed asked Adelynn to walk with him and Rex to the pier. Ed was moving much more slowly than normal.

"Oh, before I forget, please be sure Adam gets this envelope the next time he is here. I believe he mentioned he'd return in a little over three weeks." Big Ed told Adelynn. "Better yet, put it on the mantel, so we remember to give it to him."

"What's in it, Dad?" Adelynn inquired.

"It's something for him to do in a few months. When he opens it, he'll understand."

Big Ed Davis put on a large black overcoat, called his dog, Rex, and leashed him. Rex escorted them to the pier. Adelynn asked her dad why he was moving so slowly. Big Ed simply replied that he was feeling a bit tired and wanted some fresh air to wake him up. He walked just past a small coffee shop at the front of the pier and stopped. He leaned on the concrete rail and pointed down the beach. It was cold, and Adelynn pulled herself close to her father. Big Ed took an orange marker out of his coat pocket and drew an arrow pointing south on the top of the rail.

"Dad, what are you doing? You shouldn't mark up the pier like that. I'll get some cleaner from home and wipe it off."

"No…it's important that you leave it here, at least until Adam returns."

Big Ed put the marker back and pulled out his small silk pouch containing Valhalla. Adelynn watched him as he rolled the marble into his palm.

"It's time…" Big Ed said as he looked at Adelynn.

"What do you mean, Dad?"

"Valhalla is heavy in my hand, and even though it's cold and foggy, I feel its heat."

Adelynn watched as her father held his arm over the edge of the pier and let Valhalla roll off the tips of his fingers and fall into the roaring surf below. Adelynn attempted to reach out and pull his arm back, but she was too late. She watched as the marble hit the water and disappeared.

"Why…"

"Big Ed put his finger to his daughter's lips and replied, "It was time to return it to where it came from. Perhaps one day another person will find it and recognize its beauty. It will find its rightful place. When Adam comes to visit, I want you to bring my fishing pole and tell Adam to drop his line right where this orange arrow is. Promise me, Adelynn."

"Let's go home, Daddy. You need to rest. Don't worry, Daddy. I promise."

Adelynn walked her father home. He sat in his favorite lounger and gazed out the window. Rex lay down on the rug next to Ed's lounger.

"Rex, you are the best." Ed reached over and stroked the dog's head. He leaned back, closed his eyes, and rocked himself to sleep.

Adelynn received a call from her aunt Coleen. She checked on her father, and he was snoring as he slept in the lounger.

"Dad's asleep. If he wakes up soon, you can talk with him." Adelynn told Coleen what her father had done. She planned to make a doctor's appointment for him first thing Monday morning. He just was so tired looking. When Adelynn and Coleen finished talking, she went to check on her father once again, but he was still asleep. He looked so peaceful.

Rex had moved from the side of the lounger to directly in front of it.

Rex never sits in front of the lounger. Adelynn became concerned. She walked closer to her father, and a cold chill went through her body. He was not breathing. She dialed 911 and asked for help. Try as she might, she could not revive her father. Big Ed Davis, her loving father, had drifted off into the deepest of sleeps, one from which he would never awaken.

Two weeks later, the big, badass Edward Davis was laid to rest next to his wife, Beth Ann, at a memorial park in the hills above the coastal town of Half Moon Bay.

Adelynn was unable to get in contact with Adam. She called, texted, and put notices out on social media, but she never received a call back from him. He was still in the wilderness and would be there six more days.

***

Adam drove his car directly from the survival training camp to Big Ed's home. He couldn't wait to see his love, Adelynn.

He ran up to the door and knocked just as he had done so many times before. Adelynn opened the door. All of her sisters were there with her.

"I tried my best to reach you, Adam."

Adam could see the sadness in her eyes. He looked around for his friend, Big Ed. "What's happened? Where's the big man?"

"My father died in his sleep three weeks ago."

Adam sat down in disbelief. He held Adelynn close and told her that he wanted to visit her father's resting place the next day. He saw all her relatives and said he'd get a room at one of the hotels in Rockaway Beach, but she told him no. She wanted him to stay with her. They'd sleep together on the living-room rug. She did not want to let Adam go.

The next day all of Adelynn's siblings visited the grave of their mother and father. Adam stood next to Adelynn as she said a final prayer and placed flowers on her parents' brass marker. Her sisters and their families left later that day. Adam stayed with Adelynn, and they sat down on her sofa. Adelynn got up and retrieved the envelope that was on the mantel.

"I almost forgot. My dad wanted you to have this."

She handed the envelope to Adam. He opened it, but it did not contain a letter. Inside was a eucalyptus leaf, nothing more.

"He said you would know what to do with it."

"I know exactly what he wants done."

Adelynn asked Adam to walk with her to the pier. She told him her father had asked one more thing of Adam. She grabbed her father's fishing pole from the garage, and they walked to the Sharp Park pier.

It was there that Adelynn told Adam what her father had done.

"He dropped Valhalla into the water from right here," she said as she placed her finger on the orange coloring on the top rail. "Drop your line into the water here."

"Why? We're too close to the shore to catch any fish from this spot. I don't feel much like fishing anyway."

"I promised my father."

As soon as Adelynn said she had promised her father, Adam dropped his fishing line down into the shallow water below.

"Hey…you didn't put any bait on your line, and you're much too close to the shore. Move down the pier if you want to catch anything," an old bearded fisherman called out. The old man was leaning against the pier's coffee shop and motioned for them to move farther down the pier.

Adam ignored the bearded man and continued to talk with Adelynn. Suddenly, Adam's fishing line took off, and Ed's old fishing pole bent.

"Damn…what the hell! He's got a big one on the line," shouted the old fisherman.

Other people ran over and watched as Adam skillfully worked the rod and reel. It took a while, but he reeled in a striped bass. Adam removed the hook and dropped the fish back into the ocean.

"You just let go the biggest fish of the day, young man." The old fisherman shook his head and walked away.

"How did my father know?" Adelynn questioned.

"Can it be a coincidence, or was it the power of Valhalla? I guess we'll never really know for sure," Adam replied.

Adelynn looked at Adam, the man she loved. She kissed him and said, "Valhalla."

***

Less than a year later, Adelynn moved away to start a new life in Southern California. No vestige of the Leibowitz, Gunderson, or Davis families remained in their seaside hometown. Even the town's name of Salada was all but forgotten.

***

The Final Trip to the Wall

On the eighth of November 2014, Adam and Adelynn placed a leaf below Lennard Leibowitz's name at the Vietnam Memorial.

Adam placed his fingers on Lenny's name. "Lennard, this leaf is in remembrance of you. It was your friend Ed Davis's last request. I know Gunner is here too. I can almost feel their presence. It is my honor to act in their stead."

Adam walked the wall and ran his fingers across each of the names Gunner had run his fingers across years before. He stepped back and saluted. Each name had a story, but so many would never be told.

Lennard's story and those of his friends, Gunner and Big Ed, together with the mysterious agate orb, would however, live on in *The Journey of Three*.

EPILOGUE

The man on the high berm stood up and continued on his way to the Mori's Point bluff. He had never ventured that far before. He and his friend Big Ed Davis had tended to stay mostly near the pier, where they'd talk and fish together.

As he approached the point, he could see that a good portion of the bluff had fallen into the sea. The Mori's Point Inn had long since disappeared. Up ahead were a series of steps. He followed them to the top of the bluff and looked down at the *Nordic Prince* rock. *Amazing,* he thought, as he remembered that Lenny the Leaf once sailed that rock ship.

He held the voice recorder and spoke. "My name is Adam Montgomery. The journey of these three friends is now complete. They will not be forgotten. One saved the life of a fellow soldier. The second one saved me. And the third, the one I knew the best, well…he helped save my very soul. Unlike the untold stories of so many other heroes, their story will be told over and over again."

Adam paused his voice recorder to gather his thoughts before continuing. "I changed some names, including my own, as well as dates, locations, and certain events. I also classified the manuscript as fiction so as not to betray any obligation of secrecy regarding my past covert mission. The families of the three understand and know the truth. I pray that I have done them proud. It was an honor." Adam turned off his voice recorder.

Adam had already hired a trusted author, one who once lived in the Manor, to publish the work. This writer was the perfect choice for he had known the three—Lenny the Leaf, Big Ed Davis, and Gunner—personally. Everything was now complete.

Adam began his walk back down onto Salada Beach. He walked barefoot along the gray sand, looking for a glint of light. In his pocket was a red silk pouch waiting for its occupant to return.

He could hear music playing on Sharp Park's Palmetto Avenue. It was September and time for the annual festival of the fog. Up ahead on the pier was his lovely wife, Adelynn with their dog, Rex. She waved as he walked closer.

Every year during the fog festival, the two returned to rekindle memories of long ago, and Adam walked the sands again, searching for Valhalla.

End

www.ingramcontent.com/pod-product-compliance
Lightning Source LLC
Chambersburg PA
CBHW050353260626
47156CB00003B/713